British by birth, Colin Peel has spent the greater part of his life outside his native England. With his wife Julie, he now lives on the coast of a remote peninsula in New Zealand — an environment that allows him to pursue his interest in dogs, wildlife and archery.

COGAN'S FALCONS

In one of the world's largest swamps, it is easy to follow trails that are not what they seem to be. For air accident analyst Jim Cogan the trails lead him into an unmanageable and obsessive relationship with a young woman for whom the swamp has become a refuge. Determined to unravel the mystery of her past, Cogan takes her to a desolate region of Iraq. There, the development of a frightening new weapon system is threatening to destabilize the whole of the Middle East. Against a backdrop of terror and betrayal, Cogan and the woman find themselves fighting simply to survive . . .

Books by Colin D. Peel
Published by The House of Ulverscroft:

FLAMEOUT
BLOOD OF YOUR SISTERS
CHERRY RED AND DANGEROUS
ADAPTED TO STRESS
HELL SEED
NIGHTDIVE
GLIMPSE OF FOREVER
FIRESTORM
COLD ROUTE TO FREEDOM
BITTER AUTUMN
WHITE DESERT

COLIN D. PEEL

COGAN'S FALCONS

Complete and Unabridged

ULVERSCROFT
Leicester

First published in Great Britain in 1999 by
Robert Hale Limited
London

First Large Print Edition
published 2003
by arrangement with
Robert Hale Limited
London

British Library CIP Data

Peel, Colin D. (Colin Dudley), *1936 –*
Cogan's falcons.—Large print ed.—
Ulverscroft large print series: adventure & suspense
1. Aircraft accidents—Investigation—Fiction
2. Suspense fiction 3. Large type books
I. Title
823.9′14 [F]

ISBN 0–7089–4805–7

Published by
F. A. Thorpe (Publishing)
Anstey, Leicestershire

Set by Words & Graphics Ltd.
Anstey, Leicestershire
Printed and bound in Great Britain by
T. J. International Ltd., Padstow, Cornwall

This book is printed on acid-free paper

'From what I've seen, the airborne laser could be in the same league as the invention of Stealth, the development of GPS, and the Manhattan Project.'

Sheila Widnall
Secretary of the
US Government Air Force

Prologue

There had been mornings like this when she'd been young, frozen mornings so still and so cold that the ring of axes from five miles downstream could be heard distinctly at the cabin.

She listened for the sound now, searching for echoes of her childhood, for a reminder of those weekends when, as a little girl, she had stood here on the cabin steps pretending she was alone in this white Alaskan wilderness.

Today there was no need to pretend. And, as though she had always known today would be the day, ever since Peter had left she had been waiting — waiting for an end to the listening, the watching and the fear that had brought her here to this last, quiet place where her memories were uncomplicated and unspoiled.

She made herself recall each precious winter, remembering every snowfall, every beaver, every deer and every bear she had ever seen; feeling herself falling through the candle-ice on the Tatalina river, smelling the smoke on the night the cabin chimney had collapsed and remembering the first year she

1

had won the annual race against her brother on the snow-shoes they made from the light, evergreen boughs cut from trees behind the cabin.

Before her, imprinted in the overnight blanket of fresh snow, were the tracks of his departure, as clear now as they had been an hour ago when he'd made them. They led away in a long curve to the north, tell-tale evidence for someone else who had been waiting. She wondered who it was and how easy it had been for them to trace her this far north when she had tried so hard to be careful.

Lifting the rifle to her shoulder, she used the telescopic sight to scan the boulders along the river-bank. There was nothing to see, but the snowcat was closer than it had been when she'd first heard it. Six or seven miles away, she thought, moving quickly, the driver following her brother's tracks as a means of avoiding hidden rocks and fallen trees.

That it was coming here she had no doubt. But, for the first time in three months, her fear had gone.

Leaving the door of the cabin open, she set off through the snow, rifle in hand, heading for the high ground on the northeast ridge where the lodgepole pines would make it difficult for anyone to find her and where, perhaps for a while, there would be more time for her to remember.

She was halfway there when the wrong set of memories began to surface — images of Sara, the desert, the minefield and of the missile exploding on its gantry in the quarry. And with these memories came the familiar feeling of detachment. She let it come, using it to deaden her senses and to muffle the sound of the approaching snowcat.

Shortly before she reached the nearest pine she heard the engine stop. It had stopped suddenly, either because the driver had arrived at the cabin and intended to check it out, or because he was wary of following her tracks in case of a trap.

With sweat running cold against her skin inside her parka, she turned to see the figure of a man standing motionless on the cabin steps. He was looking at her through binoculars, too far away to attempt a shot, but close enough for her to pick out the rifle in his hand.

As if to acknowledge her presence or to signal his intentions, he waved to her before returning to his snowcat and restarting it.

Knowing she had already been identified, rather than carrying on to the other pines, she remained where she was, chambering a round and flicking off the safety-catch while she estimated the range to the boulders where she guessed he would take cover before beginning his hunt on foot. She was still detached and very calm, endeavouring to remember the lessons she'd been taught, waiting now for the driver to gun his engine.

It took her a second to understand that the snowcat had always been a decoy, and another second for her to slowly lower her rifle.

There was no regret, no sense of having failed. Instead, her thoughts were elsewhere. She was with her brother again, skating on the river ice on another cold, clear morning with the wind in her hair, travelling so fast that she could imagine going on forever.

The bullet came from behind, catching her between the shoulders to drive her first to her knees and then face-down into the snow. But the snow was soft and welcoming, and there was no pain — nothing except a spreading warmth, a glimpse of her mother smiling at her and the salty taste of blood pumping steadily up into her throat.

1

Yesterday evening, after his long drive from Atlanta, Cogan had started to question what he was doing. At breakfast this morning, before Brady had arrived to collect him from the motel, he'd decided that the exercise could easily turn out to be a waste of time, and by now he was almost certain it would be.

He braced himself, gripping the door handle as Brady slid the car around more potholes and lined up the wheels for the next corner. The road was atrocious, winding through a mixture of cypress trees and tangled vegetation that was blocking out the sunlight and reinforcing Cogan's conviction that he should be somewhere else. He was also uncomfortably hot and sticky.

Brady made another attempt to light the charred stub of his cigar. He was a ranger with the US Fish and Wildlife Service, a large, solidly built man with close-cropped hair, strong hands and a tendency to speak his mind. 'So what else do you know about this girl?' he asked.

'Nothing,' Cogan said.

'We don't get faxes and phone calls from Washington asking us to help people who don't know anything. The way I see it, you haven't come all the way from London to check out her legs.'

Cogan smiled. 'I need to talk to her, that's all. The whole thing's a long shot.'

'Bet on it. Even if she's up here somewhere in the swamp, she won't talk to you — not unless someone twists her arm. You don't understand the kind of people who work in a place like this.'

'What kind of people?'

'I'll tell you.' Brady slowed the car and pulled off the road onto a pad of soggy gravel. 'You want to take a leak?'

Cogan shook his head, waiting while the ranger set fire to his cigar and kicked open the door to let the smoke out.

'It's real simple,' Brady said. 'For a start, the only reason anyone works for a cowboy outfit like South Carolina Logging is because they can't get a job anyplace else. That means half of them are in the country illegally. They come from all over — you name it, we've got them — wetbacks and gooks mostly. The rest'll be drifters or crackheads who can't remember where they came from. You don't spend ten hours a day up to your balls in snakes and alligators

6

unless you're trying to keep out of sight.'

'I don't know why she's working here.' Cogan could smell the swamp, a musky, pungent odour that was stronger than the smell of the cigar smoke.

'What did SCL say when you called them?' Brady asked.

'That she'd been driving for them in South Carolina last year, but moved down into Georgia after Christmas on a logging contract in the Okefenokee basin.'

'She won't be driving through the swamp — not unless she's got something with tracks on.' Brady pointed. 'Ten feet off this road and you're in deep shit. You can stand on the peat, but you sure as hell can't drive on it. Do you know what Okefenokee means?'

'No.'

'It's Indian for land of the trembling earth. We've got four hundred thousand acres of it in Georgia — three-quarters Wildlife Refuge and the rest a National Wilderness Area. The only logging you'll come across is up along the headwaters where the tupelogum stands are being thinned out.'

'Is that where SCL's working?' Cogan said.

'Right. They're supposed to have three gangs operating somewhere near the north entrance. The guy I called said to look for

7

signposts with T3 written on them. That's where your girlfriend might be.'

'If we can find her,' Cogan said.

'I can find her for you.' Brady spat out what remained of his cigar. 'Maybe this is where you get to tell me why I should. So far you haven't told me a hell of a lot.'

'OK.' Cogan got out of the car and leaned against the door. He was not altogether surprised that Brady was seeking more information. On the drive from Brunswick, the ranger had tried hard to contain his curiosity, but once they had left Highway 82 and entered the outskirts of the swamp, it had become obvious that he wanted to know more about the girl and what had brought Cogan here to see her.

'You work for the Federal Aviation Administration, right?' Brady joined Cogan outside the car. 'They've flown you over from England because you're some kind of expert on plane crashes?'

Cogan shook his head. 'I'm a metallurgist. I work for myself, but people hire me if they think I can help them figure out why a plane has gone down somewhere.'

'People like the FAA?'

'Sometimes. I've got a couple of contacts in the US National Transportation Safety Board, and there's someone in the FAA who

8

owes me a favour. He's the guy who phoned you.'

Brady made no comment, waiting for Cogan to go on.

'I've been in Atlanta all week,' Cogan said, 'at a conference on air safety. So I thought I'd see if I could find this girl Shannon while I was here.'

'She's going to tell you why some plane buried itself in the Okefenokee swamp?'

Cogan grinned at him. 'Not unless there's been a crash I haven't heard about. Look, I know how this sounds, but I'm not sure why I need to talk to her. I've no idea who she is, or why she's working for SCL. All I know is that a couple of months ago I got a letter from someone who said I should ask her about TWA 800 and the A-10 Thunderbolt that disappeared over Colorado in 1997. That's it. End of story.'

Brady looked sceptical. 'Was TWA 800 the 747 that exploded over Long Island?' he said. 'That real bad bastard?'

'Yes. I worked on the project in New York for a while.' Cogan knew the explanation sounded thin. He also knew he'd already said too much.

'So I'm playing tour guide while you're on a half-assed, wild-goose chase for yourself.'

'Depends what the girl has to say.'

'I've told you: she won't even say hello. You've got as much chance of getting information out of her as I have of getting laid tonight.'

Up to now, Cogan hadn't been sure whether he liked Brady or not. But on balance he thought he did. Being able to talk to someone who meant what they said was fairly refreshing after five days at the conference, and apart from the ranger's pessimism about the girl, he was cheerful enough and better company than Cogan had expected him to be.

'What do you say we get on with it, then?' Brady climbed back into the car. 'It's going to get hot pretty soon and I don't want to spend the whole goddam day up here.'

Over the next twenty minutes there were occasions when Cogan thought they might be spending several days in the swamp. The road was continuing to deteriorate, and in some places where logging trucks had cut axle-deep ruts in the surface, only Brady's determined driving was keeping the car moving. But the scenery and the wildlife were extraordinary. Cogan had never seen anything quite like it. Nor had he ever imagined that a swamp could be so vast.

Between towering stands of cypress he could see prairies of burned-out vegetation, huge areas of marsh and numerous lakes and islands, all surrounded by the tea-coloured, slow-moving waters of the wetland. There were waterlilies and sweet-bay flowers, herons, egrets and ibis. And everywhere, filling the car and saturating the air, was the same oppressive, all-pervading smell.

The first T3 signpost appeared at an intersection a mile from the northern entrance to the Refuge Area. All of the subsequent signs were redundant. Travelling in ruts so deep that even if Brady had wanted to turn off the road it would have been impossible, the car was lurching from one bottomless puddle to another, spraying mud and gravel over the windows until it became difficult for Cogan to see anything at all.

He continued hanging on, only releasing his grip on the door handle when the road widened out into a clearing where Brady finally brought the car to a standstill.

At the entrance to a water trail on the east side of the clearing, a rusty, half-loaded logging truck was parked near a dump of forty-gallon drums. Closer to the trees, beside a portable wooden shed, stood an even more dilapidated vehicle. Slatted sides gave it the appearance of a cattle-truck, but Cogan guessed it was used to transport workers to and from the site.

He opened the door and went to stand with Brady in the sunshine. Although for late June the weather was not particularly warm, because of the humidity, Cogan felt as though he had stepped into a sauna.

'How do you fancy being a swamp logger?' Brady grinned. 'Smells good, doesn't it?'

Cogan didn't answer. He was listening to the noise of distant chainsaws and to what sounded like the growl of a heavy diesel under load.

A man came out of the shed and walked towards them. He was black, unshaven and shirtless. In his hand he carried a small, two-way radio.

Because Brady was in uniform, the ranger made no effort to introduce himself. He didn't introduce Cogan either. Instead, after adjusting his hat to shield his eyes from the sun, he squinted at the logging truck. 'That yours?' he asked. 'Or are you the supervisor around here?'

'You won't find no undersize logs. And there ain't nuthin' wrong with the rig.'

'Good.' Brady redirected his attention. 'I'm looking for a couple of rednecks,' he said. 'They've been shooting wild pigs up here somewhere. A guy from Waycross called to say he'd seen their pick-up heading this way on 177.'

The man was relieved. 'They'd have to be pretty dumb to come down this far,' he said. 'Where they gonna hide a vehicle?'

'No place around here, I guess.' Brady listened to the noise of the diesel. 'Is this the outfit that's got a chippy working for them?'

The attempt to put the man at ease had been only partially successful. His expression changed, but he was too slow.

Before he could move, Brady had him by the wrist, and the radio was lying in the mud.

'You weren't going to press any little red button, were you?' Brady smiled pleasantly at him. 'How long before she's due back?'

'I don't know. Five minutes maybe.'

'What's her name?'

'Shannon. Jesus — ' The driver winced from the pressure of the ranger's thumb on the inside of his wrist. 'Everyone calls her Shannon.'

'OK.' Brady released his grip. 'Now you listen to me. While my partner and I stretch our legs and wait for your friend to show, you're going to have a nice sleep in your truck over there.'

'She ain't my friend.' The driver tried to bring back some circulation into his hand. 'I'm just supposed to buzz her if anyone comes around.'

'Doesn't look like you'll be doing that now,

does it?' Brady said. 'And you won't be waving hello to her when she arrives either. Try that and I'll have you off the road for a year. Understand?'

'I get shafted by the company if I lose the radio.'

Brady picked it up, removed the batteries and gave it back to the driver who wisely decided not to say anything before he trudged off through the mud.

Cogan was keeping a straight face, as much amused as he was impressed.

'I'll move the car over behind the shed,' Brady grunted. 'What's so funny?'

'Nothing.' Cogan headed for the building on foot, wondering if the ranger would treat the girl with the same efficiency, and whether she'd turn out to be as uncooperative as the driver of the truck had been.

The answers were not long coming. By the time the car had been positioned out of sight, the roar of the diesel was a good deal louder. The noise was coming from the north, not far from the truck and the loading area where vehicles had churned the water trail into a soup of shredded tree roots and mud.

'That's got to be one big bastard of a bulldozer,' Brady said.

Cogan thought so too. But he was wrong.

Emerging from a canopy of vines like some

yellow monster from the swamp was not a tracked machine, but an enormous six-wheeled skidder. It was towing several tons of logs at the end of a steel hawser and riding on heavily ribbed, balloon tyres, each one over eight feet in diameter. Unlike the trucks in the clearing, the skidder was nearly new with a bright-red SCL logo painted on its side.

As soon as it stopped, Cogan focused his attention on the cab, looking for evidence to confirm that the driver was who he hoped she'd be.

'Well, what do you know?' Brady pointed.

Climbing down the ladder from the cab was the unmistakable figure of a young woman. Although she was wearing knee-length boots, jeans and a denim jacket, her hair gave her away. Cogan could see she had it tied back in a pony-tail. He could see the sweat-band round her forehead as well.

'OK.' Brady removed a rifle from the trunk of the car. 'Let's go and say hello.'

Because she had left the engine of the skidder idling and was busy at the controls of a hydraulic hoist, their appearance caught her by surprise.

She swung round, her face filled with alarm.

'Your name Shannon?' Brady asked. He studied her carefully, waiting for an answer that was not forthcoming.

When there was no reply after Brady asked her again, Cogan decided to try. 'I'm sorry if we made you jump,' he said. 'My name's Jim Cogan. This is Ranger Brady. He's driven me over from Brunswick. I'm looking for someone called Shannon. Is that you?'

She shook her head.

'Smarten up,' Brady said. 'You don't want to do this the hard way.'

'All right.' She compressed her lips. 'But I'm not wasting fuel for you; I'll have to cut the engine.' She put a foot on the first rung of the ladder, then twisted away and suddenly was gone, sprinting for the vegetation at the edge of the wetland.

If Brady was concerned he showed no sign of it. Unhurriedly, holding his rifle in one hand, he fired a shot in the air before levelling the barrel to fire again.

Cogan saw water fountain up ahead of the girl who almost lost her balance before she stumbled to a halt. She remained where she was, sixty feet away, ankle-deep in peat with her back to them.

'What did I tell you?' Brady lowered the rifle. 'If you want to turn that engine off, I'll go and fetch her. I'll meet you at the car.'

Cogan hadn't expected the girl to run. Nor had he expected Brady to use the gun. It was a lesson, he thought, proof of what the ranger had been trying to tell him — that the US was not the UK, and that even if the Deep South was less deep than it used to be, the Okefenokee swamp was still nothing like the rest of Georgia.

At the top of the ladder, after he'd reached into the skidder's cab to switch off the ignition, he took a moment to see if the girl had left anything behind. Except for a snake-bite kit clipped to the instrument panel beside another two-way radio and a vacuum flask of coffee, there was little else, and nothing which would provide a clue to her identity. The smell, though, was overpowering — a mixture of hot oil, diesel fumes and mud.

Leaving the key in the ignition, Cogan returned to the ground and made his way over to the car where Brady was in the process of handcuffing the girl's wrists behind her back. She was out of breath and clearly scared.

'You don't have to put those on her,' Cogan said. 'She hasn't done anything.'

'How do you know?' Brady squinted at him. 'What about that 747 in New York? I thought you wanted to find out if she's part of some hairy-assed terrorist group. Or has this got kind of hard for you all of a sudden?'

17

Cogan thought it might have done. 'Has she said anything?' he asked.

'Sure. She called me a dick, and when I told her who you are, she said if I believe that I had to be brain-dead.' Brady grinned. 'She's real pretty though, don't you think?'

Cogan hadn't noticed. He tried without success to meet her eyes. 'Look,' he said. 'I only want to ask you some questions. I'm not trying to get you into trouble.'

She raised her head, but before he could speak to her again she spat at him.

'OK.' Brady pulled her away. 'That does it. We either leave her here in the swamp where she belongs, or she comes back to town with us.' He looked at Cogan. 'What do you want to do? If you want to try talking to her tomorrow, I can get the Police Department to hold her overnight. After that I'll have to let her go — unless you can get someone to run a check on her.'

Cogan was recalling the morning he'd received the letter in London, remembering how often he'd re-read it and how easily he'd made the decision to follow up the information. Too easily, he realized — because he'd never thought it through, and because he'd never expected to end up in a waterlogged swamp confronted by a girl who wanted to spit at him. Instinct was telling him to forget the whole thing, the same feeling he'd experienced on the project in Africa last year when he'd been right to walk away. And if he chose to walk away from this one, the girl's behaviour was a good enough excuse.

He glanced at her again, wondering whether mentioning the letter would make any difference.

This time she spoke. 'You've screwed up,' she said. 'You should've come by yourself.'

'What's she talking about?' Brady asked.

'I don't know.' Cogan made up his mind. 'Is it OK for you to take her into town?'

'Sure it is. She's hauling logs in a protected wildlife area. Until I see a permit, that's illegal.' Brady opened the rear door of the car and pushed the girl inside. 'We'll see if she unwinds a bit once we get her away from here.'

Cogan doubted it. He took a last look around the clearing before getting into the car, aware that he was probably making a mistake by prolonging his trip, but wanting to believe he could still learn something to justify the effort. It would be several hours before the extent of his mistake became obvious, and by then he would have started to understand why walking away had never been the option he'd thought it was.

Cogan drained his glass, positioning it carefully on the bar-top in front of him. Because the bourbon wasn't working, today's visit to the swamp was still fresh in his mind and he had not yet given up trying to make sense out of what had happened there.

Hardest to forget was the expression on the girl's face when he'd last seen her. For the entire duration of the journey back to Brunswick she had sat silently in the car, unresponsive, not even answering when Cogan had offered to buy her a soft drink at a truck-stop. Mostly it was her eyes that he'd found disturbing, he decided, the look of hostility and distrust in them when Brady had dropped him off at his motel and driven her away.

Cogan endeavoured to think of something else, knowing it wasn't worth trying with so many of his questions still unanswered. Why was she scared? Who was she? And why the hell should he care one way or another?

Earlier this evening when he'd set off to sample Brunswick's night life and started drinking here at the little bar in Reynolds Street, the need for explanations had seemed less pressing. By now, though, he was conscious of a growing unease. It was his fault she was in trouble, Cogan thought. He was responsible for what had happened to her. And while he was sitting here drinking in the comfort of an air-conditioned bar, she was locked up alone in a cell somewhere.

After another unsuccessful double bourbon, Cogan paid his bill and walked out into the night air to clear his head. But the night was too warm, his thoughts still confused and the short-skirted young woman who followed him to his car was too obvious.

'No thanks.' He smiled at her. 'You'll do better with someone else.'

'Are you sure?'

'Yeah, I'm sure.' He unlocked the car, seeing her return his smile before she tripped away on her high-heels.

Brief though the exchange had been, its effect on Cogan was longer lasting. He drove back slowly to his motel, unable to prevent himself from comparing one young woman with another. They were nothing like each other, two strangers living out their lives as best they could in the environments they knew best — but somehow, in some inexplicable way, to Cogan they were the same. Except that for one of them everything had been changed, he thought, because he had come along and changed it for her.

Before he reached the motel he was almost

certain of what to do, and by the time he'd parked the car and let himself into his room, most of his reservations had gone. In case they hadn't, and to guard against any further indecision, he picked up the phone at once, dialling the number Brady had given him, speaking confidently as soon as the ranger answered.

★   ★   ★

It was nearly 8.30 when a knock on the door told him his visitors had arrived. The girl entered the room first, still tight-lipped, handcuffed again and with the faint smell of the swamp still on her clothes and on her skin.

Behind her, out of uniform apart from his ranger's badge and his hat, Brady stood blocking the doorway.

'You're crazy,' he said.

'I know.' Cogan stood aside while he came in. 'Look, I'm sorry I called you at home. I just got to thinking.'

'And you want me to leave her here?'

'If that's OK?'

Brady shrugged. ' 'Long as you don't mind if she takes off. Is there a window in the other room?'

'No. Why?'

22

'Hang on a minute.' Propelling the girl towards the bedroom, Brady removed her handcuffs, pushed her inside and closed the door. 'I called that guy at SCL again,' he said. 'The same guy you spoke to. He says her name's Shannon Lockhart. She's a loner, no family except for an uncle, no boyfriends and, as far as he knows, she hasn't been in any kind of trouble before.'

'She isn't in any kind of trouble now,' Cogan said.

'Try telling her that. Ask her why she carries a knife in her boot.' Brady paused. 'Listen. I figured I'd be doing you a favour by giving you a big build-up — you know, explaining who you are and what you do for a living. But I picked it wrong. You've got a problem.'

'Like what?'

'She was fine when I went to collect her, but the minute I get her in the car and say where we're going, she starts trying to kick holes in the door. That's why I need to see your passport.'

Cogan was unable to follow the logic, but he went to his briefcase, found his passport and handed it over.

'I figured she'd have it wrong.' Brady flicked through the pages. 'She said you wouldn't be English.'

'What else did she say?'

'Not a lot — except that she's pretty sure you're going to kill her.'

'What?' Cogan was taken aback. 'Why?'

'Who knows?' Brady dropped the passport onto the table. 'She won't tell me. Maybe she'll tell you. One thing, though: if she winds up in a ditch someplace, the State Police will be looking for you first. That'd be fair, don't you think?'

'Yes,' Cogan nodded. 'That'd be fair.'

'OK.' Brady grinned. 'Have a nice evening. Don't call me if she disappears five minutes after I've gone.' He walked to the door. 'If you want to buy me breakfast in the morning I'll come by to see how things turned out — just so long as you don't ask me to drive you back out to the swamp.'

'I won't.' Cogan smiled. 'Thanks.'

'My pleasure.' Brady let himself out, making sure the door was securely latched behind him.

When Cogan turned round, the girl was already coming from the bedroom. She went to stand by the table, her eyes on the passport.

'There's a photo,' he said. 'Take a look.'

She made no attempt to do so. Nor did she say anything.

'OK.' Cogan remained by the door. 'Now

before you start screaming rape and throwing stuff around, just listen for a minute. All I want to do is talk about a letter I got from someone called Peter Kennedy. He's an American pilot and he had a sister called Catherine who was killed six months ago in Alaska. Do their names mean anything to you?'

'I need to use your bathroom.' She looked at him.

'Along there.' Cogan pointed. 'Did you know Catherine Kennedy?'

'Yes, I knew her.' She turned to walk away. 'Hadn't you better come and watch me pee in case there's a window?'

Cogan ignored the remark. Despite her attitude she was less apprehensive and there were signs of a thaw. As a result he could see that his initial impression of her had been incorrect. She was quite small, no taller than five foot three, but rather attractive, or in Brady's words, real pretty. Her hair was nearly black, she had large dark eyes and her skin colour was unusual — not that of a European but a light, sunbleached brown. Her features were not entirely European either, making Cogan wonder if she was from somewhere in South America.

'You don't have to keep guarding the door.' She re-entered the room and went to sit down on the sofa. 'The ranger says you're an air accident investigator. Is that what you really are?'

'Have you ever heard of metallurgy?'

'Well, Lordy me, Mr Cogan.' She put on an exaggerated Southern accent. 'What in the world could that be now?'

Before he could say anything her eyes were flashing.

'Maybe you should start again,' she said. 'Or shall I carry on pretending I'm the little swamp chippy you and Brady think I am?'

His impression hadn't just been wrong, Cogan realized. He seemed to have misjudged her altogether. To recover lost ground he selected some reports and photographs from his briefcase and gave them to her. 'Peter Kennedy wrote to me after he read an article of mine in a magazine called *International Aviation*. It was about aircraft wreckage analysis and the study of penetration punctures from things like cannon shells and warhead shrapnel.'

She inspected one of the reports. 'Why should your clever magazine article have anything to do with me?'

'Peter Kennedy thinks his sister was murdered because she was one of two people in North America who might be able to shed light on some unexplained air accidents around the world. He said the other person was you.'

She frowned. 'I don't believe you. He couldn't have told you that any more than he could've told you I was working in the Okefenokee swamp. I've never met him.'

'Kennedy didn't know your last name, but he knew his sister used to write to someone called Shannon, and that the letters were addressed care of a company called South Carolina Logging in Charleston. I took it from there.'

'How long ago was this?' She crossed her legs and leaned back in the sofa.

'Back in February somctime.'

'It hasn't taken you since then to find me, has it?'

'No.' Cogan smiled. 'For a start I wasn't sure the letter was worth following up, and I've been sort of busy on other things. But last month I was up in Canada on business, so while I was there I hopped on a flight to Alaska and went looking for Peter Kennedy to see what else he could tell me.'

'About Catherine?'

'And about you.' He looked directly at her. 'You didn't know she was dead, did you — not until I told you?'

'No.'

'But you're not surprised?'

'Should I be?'

'You can ease up on the act,' Cogan said. 'I've already got the message.'

'What did Kennedy say when you saw him?'

'He wasn't there. He's working in Africa — flying supplies into Angola for an international aid organization.'

'Did you speak to anyone else in Alaska?' She hesitated. 'About Catherine, I mean.'

'Yeah.' Cogan nodded. 'You see, once I started asking questions, the whole thing got more interesting. There's a guy in Fairbanks who covered Catherine's death for his local newspaper. He'd already done some work trying to figure out why anyone would've wanted to shoot her. He rented a float plane and flew me forty miles up north to the cabin on the Tatalina river where she'd been staying with her brother. I spoke to the police as well. They gave me the Kennedys' family history.' Cogan stopped talking, aware that he could be mistaking conversation for progress.

'You're trying too hard,' she said. 'And you're only telling me what you think I want to hear. Why come all the way to Georgia to find me?'

'Because when I got back to London I made some overseas phone calls to see if I could learn a bit more about Catherine.

That's how I found out what she'd been doing in the Middle East, and what you might've been doing there with her. Does that explain things?'

Cogan had chosen his words carelessly, but he could not have found a better way to break through her façade. One of her hands had started shaking and her expression had slipped.

'You didn't phone anyone in Iraq, did you?' She stood up. 'Not anywhere in the northern no-fly zone?'

'The US State Department gave me a couple of numbers there to try. Why?'

She took a deep breath. 'Brady said you'd been at a conference in Atlanta. How many people knew you'd be there?'

'How would I know? It was an international conference. I had to present one of the papers.' Cogan could see she was struggling to conceal her concern. 'Listen,' he said, 'I've no idea what it is you're scared of, but you don't have to be frightened of me. You don't have to handle the problem by yourself either. If I've made things worse, why not give me the chance to help you sort it out?'

Instead of answering she walked over to a window and stood there with her back to him. When she turned round, some of her composure had returned. 'I've been really rude, haven't I?' she said. 'But I'm not going to apologize. You've cost me a day's pay and my weekly bonus.' She attempted a smile. 'I think that means you owe me a cup of coffee.'

This was the time to capitalize on what seemed to be a change in her attitude, Cogan decided, right now — before everything turned sour again. 'I can do better than coffee,' he said. 'Suppose I take you out to dinner?'

'Without a shower? Dressed like this? I don't think so. I might not be able to smell the swamp on me, but I know you can. Coffee's fine.'

'OK.' Cogan went into the kitchenette to fill the percolator. 'How about this for an idea?' he said. 'I'll drive you home to wherever you live to clean up and change, then we'll find somewhere nice to eat so you can tell me what Peter Kennedy thought you could tell me, and so I can figure out how to fix what's scaring you half to death.'

'All right.' She spoke quietly from the other room. 'But I don't think you can fix it. If anyone could, Catherine would still be alive. You don't understand.'

Cogan knew he didn't understand, but he felt more confident and cautiously optimistic about his progress.

Not until he returned to the lounge to find

his dinner-date and his car keys gone did he realize how misplaced his optimism had been and how very thoroughly he'd been deceived.

Other than the half-open front door there was no sign she had ever been here. Which was exactly what Brady had predicted would happen, Cogan thought; confirmation of what he should've known all along.

Too annoyed with himself to bother checking whether she'd stolen his rental car or not, he slammed the door shut, took a bottle of Scotch from the fridge and went to lie down on the bed. But like the bourbon earlier in the evening, the alcohol proved ineffective, and after half an hour Cogan was still wide awake. Much of his anger had gone, though, and he felt less frustrated, half-inclined to believe his offer of help might persuade her to return.

Shortly after ten o'clock a gentle tap on the door told him that she had.

He was mistaken.

No sooner had he unfastened the safety-chain than the door burst open into his face, throwing him backwards hard against the table.

Before he could regain his balance two men entered the room. They were in their early thirties, well dressed, and both carrying small-calibre automatics.

One of the men closed the door. He was European or American, tall, with a pale complexion and blue eyes. 'Mr Cogan,' he said. 'Good evening. My apologies for calling on you so late. I'm afraid it took us rather a long time to get here from Atlanta. Allow me to introduce myself. I'm Walther Van Reenan.'

Too shaken to reply, Cogan was struggling to assess the situation. The break-in had occurred so suddenly that he was off-guard, uncertain of how to handle the intruders.

'My colleague's name is Massoud Khadim.' Van Reenan nodded at his companion, a shorter, dark-skinned man who pushed past Cogan on his way to check the other rooms.

'I assume she's not here.' Van Reenan pocketed his gun. 'What a shame. Perhaps you could tell us where she is.'

'Perhaps you should tell me what the hell you're doing in my motel room.' Cogan's brain was beginning to function at last.

'Certainly.' Van Reenan produced a sheet of paper. 'If this information is correct, you're the metallurgist who gave a lecture on aircraft accident analysis in Atlanta on Monday.'

'So what?' Cogan said.

'So presumably you're the same person who, some months ago, was enquiring into the whereabouts of two young women in the Middle East. As I'm sure you discovered, they were at one time based at a place called Erbil in northern Iraq as members of the US-backed faction of the Patriotic Union of Kurdistan.'

'I wasn't enquiring about anyone,' Cogan said. 'I was getting data on a Cayuse helicopter that went down on the Turkish border.'

'I see.' Van Reenan inspected the sheet of paper again. 'Earlier today, the receptionist at the Peach Tree Plaza Hotel in Atlanta assured me you were travelling to Brunswick on business. I expect you remember her. She was the lady who arranged for your rental car and made this motel booking for you.'

Cogan could guess what was coming next. He kept his mouth shut, unable for the moment to comprehend why anyone would have wanted to trace his movements.

'The motel manager has been equally helpful,' Van Reenan said. 'He doesn't believe you're here on business at all — not since he saw a young woman in handcuffs being delivered to your room this evening.'

Cogan's answer was interrupted by the return of the man whom Van Reenan had introduced as Khadim.

'Anything?' Van Reenan asked him.

'No. The Englishman will tell us where we shall find her, I think.'

'I don't know,' Cogan said. Truthful though his statement was, he knew a lie would have been a better choice. His misgivings were increasing, made worse by the knowledge that he was rapidly getting out of his depth.

'Where did she go?' Van Reenan asked.

'She walked out on me. I don't know where she's gone any more than you do.' Before he'd finished speaking, Cogan saw how seriously he'd misjudged his position.

The automatic was in Van Reenan's hand again, and he was clearly preparing to bring the interview to a close. 'Mr Cogan,' he said, 'despite what you may think, I take no pleasure from this. Understand that I'm simply doing my job.'

Cogan's mouth was dry. Keeping his eyes on the muzzle of the automatic, he slid away from the table.

He was in time to catch a glimpse of Khadim's knife, but too slow to avoid it. Like a white-hot iron the blade swept sideways, cutting through his shirt to open up a gash across his chest.

The pain was sudden but short-lived, overriden by Cogan's instinct for self-preservation. Ready to defend himself, he retreated, dripping blood, walking backwards until he reached the wall beside the kitchenette.

'There is nowhere for you to go,' Van Reenan said. 'Answer my question, and do not test my patience with another lie.'

Answering with a lie was no more of an option for Cogan than making a rush for the door. He knew it, just as he knew there had never been the slightest chance of talking his way out of this. These were men who had come to kill — men who, for one reason only, had made not the slightest effort to conceal who they were or what they wanted.

Ignoring the pool of blood at his feet, Cogan started estimating the distance to the nearest chair, wondering if he could swing it at the man with the knife before Van Reenan could use his gun.

The wail of a siren made him reconsider. Although the vehicle was several blocks away and it was impossible to tell in which direction it was travelling, the noise was close enough to interrupt the proceedings.

'Bring the car round.' Van Reenan tossed a set of keys to Khadim. 'Wait for me outside.'

Cogan knew what he had to do. Teeth clenched he waited for Khadim to leave the room, then, at the instant Van Reenan began to raise the gun, Cogan made his dive to overturn the table.

Luck and agility saved him from the first shot, but in shoes that were slippery with blood he was at a disadvantage. Before he could use the table as a shield there was a second muzzle-flash and a bullet grazed his shoulder.

A third shot drove wood splinters into his face as he scrambled away, only to slip again and crash back helplessly against the wall.

For a second he thought Van Reenan was reluctant to finish the job. But, like all the other times today when Cogan had been mistaken, on this occasion too he saw that he was wrong.

2

Three years ago at an accident site in Afghanistan, Cogan had narrowly escaped execution at the hands of Taliban rebels. Now, in the same way that time had stood still for him then, it was standing still again.

Holding his breath, he waited for Van Reenan's finger to tighten on the trigger.

Where the bullet went, Cogan never knew. He was conscious only of an earsplitting crash as a section of the room exploded inwards.

The impact had been centred on the door, smashing it to pieces along with the frame and part of the front wall. From the wreckage protruded the crumpled rear end of a car.

Through the dust and the mess of broken timber and shattered plasterboard, Cogan could see it was his car. But he couldn't see Van Reenan.

'They're gone.' The girl clambered over the debris. 'The tall one got out the window.' She looked at his bloodstained shirt. 'How bad are you hurt?'

'It's a cut.' Cogan got to his feet, listening

to the approaching siren. 'Did you order some help?'

'I made a 911 call. Now you know why you shouldn't have tried to find me, don't you?' She turned to leave.

'Hold on.' He grabbed her arm. 'Where the hell are you going?'

She wrenched herself away and picked up a long sliver of glass. 'Try to stop me and I swear I'll kill you.'

As well as the siren being closer, doors were slamming all along the motel, and people were shouting, making it difficult for Cogan to think.

He made a quick assessment of the damage to the car, assuming she would attempt to drive it away. But she had no intention of doing so.

Instead, she dropped the piece of glass, climbed onto a chair and was halfway out the window before he decided to stop her.

Seizing her first by the belt, then by her pony-tail, he hauled her back inside.

She fought him, trying to gouge out his eyes until he began to shake her at arm's length, using all his strength in an effort to wear her out. When she finally stopped kicking, he let her go.

'You've got twenty seconds to get in the damn car,' Cogan said. 'One more stunt like that and I'll throw you in on your head. I've had enough of you.'

Eyes flashing, she stared back at him in defiance.

'Now,' Cogan said. 'You're leaving with me right now — otherwise I stay to talk to the police.'

More shouting and the sound of squealing tyres brought her to her senses. Leaving him to collect his jacket and retrieve his passport from the floor she scrambled over the litter and reached the car before him.

'I'll drive.' She slipped behind the wheel. 'You don't know where to go.'

There was no time to argue. Yanking open the door, he pulled himself into the passenger seat and waited while she used up precious seconds fumbling with the key.

The instant the engine came to life she rammed the selector into drive and put her foot down hard.

There was the sound of splintering wood, a lurch, then suddenly the car was free. Tyres smoking, it shot forwards, dragging part of the door-frame out into the car park where people began scattering in all directions.

Cogan caught a glimpse of the motel manager and of a woman who only just avoided being run down by a police car coming the other way.

'Ease up.' He was looking through the remains of the rear window. 'They're not following us.'

'They can radio for backup.' She put the car into a slide at the first intersection. 'Once they see the blood in your room, they probably will. You should've let me go. All you've done is made things worse.'

'It's your fault not mine,' Cogan said. 'How the hell was I supposed to know there are other people looking for you?'

'You've hurt my arm,' she said.

'Good.' Cogan didn't care. 'Slow down,' he said. 'One of the rear wheels is scraping on something. I can smell rubber.'

'We can't slow down — not yet. Not until we're clear of town.' She was concentrating on her driving, handling the damaged Mazda with considerable skill. 'I'll check your cut as soon as I can.'

'It's OK,' Cogan said.

'No one loses that much blood from a cut that's OK.' She braked for a red light then accelerated again, heading west on a road that Cogan thought he recognized.

'Stop at a phone box,' he said.

'Why?'

'Just do it. We need to contact Brady. He might be able to call off a chase.'

'If he knows you're in one piece, you mean?'

'He'll be more interested in hearing that you're all right.' Cogan pointed ahead. 'Over there by that drug store. Don't argue.'

She seemed uncertain, but did as he said, parking in the shadow of a billboard on the far side of the street.

Cogan got out first and waited for her to accompany him to the phone box.

'I don't want to speak to Brady.' She was on edge, watching each approaching car as though she was expecting something else to go wrong.

Cogan was being careful too, keeping an eye on the traffic while he put in some money and pushed what he hoped were the right buttons.

Brady answered on the second ring, interrupting before Cogan could begin to explain.

'Listen,' Cogan said. 'I'm only calling to say you were right. She said she'd talk to me if I took her out to dinner, but the minute I had her in the car she grabbed the shift lever and things sort of went wrong.'

'I've had four phone calls in ten minutes,' Brady said. 'You want me to believe you backed your car into a wall by accident? Is that the story?'

'It's not a story. It's what happened. If anyone finds some blood around, tell them not to worry. I cut my finger.'

'The police are more worried about your pretty friend,' Brady grunted. 'They say a woman at the motel thinks she saw a girl behind the wheel when you took off, but she's not sure.'

'Everything's OK,' Cogan said.

'Are you telling me? Or do I get to hear from the chippy?'

Quickly Cogan handed over the receiver.

She hesitated before beginning to speak in the voice she'd used in the swamp this morning. 'I've already told Mr Cogan I'm sorry about his car,' she said. 'He'll pay for the damage to the motel wall, but I'm taking him to get his finger fixed first — you know, because it was kind of my fault.' She listened for a second before hanging up.

'Well?' Cogan enquired.

'Brady says I'm no better at lying than you are. But it was a neat idea to call him. I suppose I ought to thank you.'

'For what?' Cogan was suspicious.

'For trying to make sure no one finds out what those men wanted.' She started walking back to the car.

'Hey.' Cogan caught her up. 'I didn't do it for you.'

'I know. But you still think I might answer your questions now, don't you?'

'Will you?'

'No.' She paused. 'I'll take you somewhere safe, though, so I can disinfect and dress your cut, and I'll fix you something to eat. I know you don't like me, but that doesn't mean I'm the sort of person you think I am.'

'You've already tried that line,' Cogan said. 'Enlighten me. Why did you come back to the motel?'

'So you wouldn't report me for stealing your car. I can't afford any more problems. I drove around for a while, then when I was sitting in it back at the car-park, I saw those men break into your room.'

'And you guessed what they were after?'

She nodded. 'That's why I called 911. But when I heard the siren and saw one of them come out again I decided I'd better do something.' She endeavoured to smile. 'I don't usually drive into things.'

'I don't usually pull people around by their hair.'

'But you don't often meet people like me, do you Mr Cogan?' She climbed back in the car. 'If you didn't find out my real name when you made those phone calls to Iraq, it's Sara Hamaid. You can call me Sara if you want.'

'OK.'

'Shall I carry on driving?'

Cogan didn't mind one way or the other. Nor did he mind when she refused to restart the car until she had torn a sleeve from her jacket in order to fabricate a bandage for him. It was all part of a varied and eventful day, he thought, a day in which a girl who had spat at him in the swamp this morning, had, by tonight, not only saved his life, but turned into someone else altogether.

* * *

Water droplets were dripping onto the roof. Cogan was counting them, trying to predict when the next one would splatter against the corrugated iron so he didn't have to think about anything more complicated. When he reached fifty he gave up and went to stand outside on the open section of the platform.

Like the walls of the tiny cabin it supported, the platform was made of plywood nailed to a crude framework of blackgum logs. But in every other respect the construction was an engineering marvel. Anchored at one edge to the trunk of a massive cypress tree, the platform was cantilevered out over the swamp floor, hanging in free space from ropes descending

44

from branches high above.

Because Cogan couldn't imagine how she had ever built it, he was beginning to appreciate that behind her offhandedness and apparent independence there was a good deal more to Sara Hamaid than either he or Brady had first thought.

Last night in the moonlight, after she'd concealed the car in bushes on the north-west boundary of the swamp and guided him to the creek where her canoe was hidden, she'd offered little in the way of an explanation, saying only that the swamp would guarantee their safety.

If he hadn't been sure whether to believe her then, he did now. It had taken her the best part of an hour to navigate the narrow creek in the dark, using her paddle to feel her way whenever clouds or the canopy of vegetation obscured the moon and, by the time they'd reached the little cabin, Cogan had the impression of being lost in a shadow-filled wilderness of water trails, islands and soggy wetland.

Since dawn, though, with sunshine filtering through the leaves and with birds singing everywhere, the swamp was a different place. That no one would track them here seemed to be beyond question. But his feeling of being lost had gone, and with it had gone his surprise at the transformation of Shannon Lockhart into someone called Sara Hamaid.

Wondering whether she'd caught any fish yet, Cogan went back inside to see if there was enough hot water left in the saucepan for another cup of coffee.

Conditions in the cabin were cramped. Boxes of canned food and bottles of mineral water were piled against each wall to form work-tops on which stood a primus stove, several flashlights and the first-aid kit she'd used last night. Above the work-tops, hanging from the rafters alongside a mosquito-net were a .22 calibre Remington rifle, fishing rods, plastic bags containing toilet rolls and clothes, and a cake tin which served as a makeshift bookcase. The only thing missing was a mirror, making it difficult for Cogan to inspect the cut across his chest.

He removed the bandage then ran his fingertips over the wound to feel the stitches she'd put in. There were twelve of them, neat sutures of fine, nylon fishing-line that she'd sterilized in boiling water before starting work on him with her needle. For the whole time she had said nothing, sitting cross-legged on the floor beside him as though stitching up a knife wound was something she did every day. Another skill, Cogan thought, another example of how easily she seemed to accept

46

situations that other people would have found bizarre.

He'd finished making himself more coffee and was standing outside again when the rhythmic swish of a paddle announced her return.

She brought the canoe round the bend in the creek too fast, colliding with a tree root and almost overshooting the steps to the platform.

'What's the hurry?' Cogan took the bow rope from her.

'I wasn't thinking.' Ignoring the hand he offered, she extricated herself from the canoe and climbed onto the platform without his assistance. 'Why have you taken off your bandage?'

'Just checking. Did you catch anything?'

'A bream and a perch, but the perch is a bit tiny. We can have it for breakfast if you want. It'll be better than eating canned food again.'

Cogan wasn't listening. Instead, because she was wearing shorts and a T-shirt, he was looking at the variable colour of her skin. Her calves, and to a lesser extent her forearms, were much darker as though she'd been rubbing shoe polish on herself.

'Don't stare at me like that.' She was angry. 'It's tannin stain. You get it from working in the swamp. Or are you trying to decide

47

whether I have a nice figure or not?'

There was no need for Cogan to try. She had a taut, athletic body and her figure was faultless.

'Shall I gut the fish?' she asked. 'Or do you want me to check your stitches for you?'

'Look,' Cogan said. 'Stop being so damn prickly. You don't have to play at being a hunter-gatherer and nurse at the same time.'

'I'm not playing at being anything.' She compressed her lips. 'You need a clean dressing. Cuts don't heal up when it's as humid as this.'

Cogan sat down while she applied a fresh gauze pad and rewound the bandage around his chest. 'Is this your place?' he asked.

'No. Well, bits of it are. I paid for the plywood, the roofing, the nails and all the rope. It belongs to a friend of mine — Jeremiah. He's a Seminole Indian, or part Seminole. His great-grandfather was Scottish or something. We built this together. It was only finished three weeks ago. I didn't expect to need it so soon.'

'Do you usually live somewhere else?'

She smiled. 'I've got an apartment in town with running water, a proper toilet, doors and windows and all the toys rich people like you have in their apartments. You don't think much of me, do you?'

'I don't know the first damn thing about you,' Cogan said.

'But after what happened last night you're going to find out, aren't you? I can tell. You'll start digging around until you've learned all you can about me, about who I am, where I've been and what I've done.'

'What do you expect?' Cogan wanted her to look at him. 'It'd be fairly hard to pretend none of this ever happened, don't you think?'

'I suppose so.' She swung her legs over the edge of the platform. 'It doesn't matter anyway. I've already decided. That's why I went fishing this morning — so I could decide.'

'Decide what?'

'If I don't explain, you'll just make everything more difficult for me — more dangerous.'

'Look,' Cogan said, 'if you give me half a chance maybe I can make things better. I know a lot of people in a lot of places.'

'That's nice for you. Aren't you going to tell me how important you are as well?'

'No.' Cogan was careful not to bite. 'If you've decided to explain, why don't you just start?'

'I'm not sure how to.'

'Catherine Kennedy,' Cogan said. 'Start with her.'

'All right.' She took a deep breath. 'Catherine was born in Alaska — she grew up there and went to school in Fairbanks with her brother. I think her parents were fairly wealthy. They had a big home, a boat and they owned that cabin off the Elliot Highway on the Tatalina river — the place you said you went to. Catherine never stopped talking about it — you know, the cold, the snow and skating and stuff.'

'Were her parents American?' Cogan asked.

'As far as I know. Her father was an engineer for an international oil company. Catherine said he used to travel all over the place — mostly to the Middle East. He was there when the Gulf War broke out, but he never made it home. To begin with the family couldn't find out what had happened to him. They didn't even know he was dead until the military flew the body back to Alaska, but no one was allowed to see it. That's why Catherine decided she had to learn the truth. She'd been very close to her father, and it was really important to her to find out how he died.'

'How did he?'

'Iraqi Republican Guards hammered nails into his eyes. They thought he was spying for the US Government.'

'Jesus.' Cogan frowned. 'Where did the

information come from?'

'An army sergeant recovered the body in Kuwait City. He wasn't supposed to say anything, but Catherine flew all the way to Arizona to visit him so I guess he thought he had to tell her.'

'She'd have been better off not knowing,' Cogan said. 'How did she handle it?'

'She didn't. She started having the most awful nightmares while she was still at school. By the time I met her she'd developed the nearest thing to hate I've ever seen in anyone. She wasn't a very well-adjusted person and I think her father's death tipped her over the edge — maybe because it happened when she was quite young. The first thing she did after leaving college was join an organization called the Iraqi National Congress. It was partly funded by the CIA and based in northern Iraq above the 36th parallel where the US maintain the no-fly zone. Catherine's job was to recruit Iraqi dissidents and transmit anti-Saddam Hussein radio and TV propaganda into the rest of Iraq, but she did other kinds of work for them too. All she cared about was avenging her father's murder. It was an obsession with her — that's the word she used.'

'So you met her in Iraq?'

'Not right away. She'd only been there

three months when the INC was infiltrated and overrun by the Mukhabarat — they're the Iraqi Secret Police. A lot of people were killed but Catherine got away. After that she lived in a Kurdish village for a while, then became involved with a rebel army called the Patriotic Union of Kurdistan. They're as dedicated to overthrowing the Baghdad Government as the INC were, but the PUK doesn't bother with propaganda. They're a proper army with proper equipment. Most of the people in it hate Saddam and the Republican Guards as much as Catherine did. She sort of felt she was among friends, I think.'

Cogan looked at her. 'You were in the PUK too,' he said. 'The tall guy with the gun said you were.'

'There are over a hundred and fifty women in the PUK, but Catherine and I were the only two Americans. It wouldn't be hard to trace us. You did.'

'Except I didn't know your name then,' Cogan said.

'You don't use it now you do.'

He smiled at her. 'Why would a nice American girl called Sara want to go halfway across the world to join up with the Patriotic Union of Kurdistan?'

'Because I'm not American: I was born in

Iraq.' She stood up and went to stand at the edge of the platform. 'In 1980, three years after the start of the war between Iraq and Iran, my parents decided there were going to be terrible problems. So, when I was six years old, I was put on a plane and sent to live with my uncle Abu in South Carolina. He runs a heavy machinery business in Charleston.'

'Is that where you grew up?'

She nodded. 'My parents used to write to me all the time, but I turned into a little American girl — pigtails, bobby-socks, the whole bit. I went to school in Charleston, went to my first dance and had my first date in Charleston. I worked there too. Then I ran away.'

'Why?'

'It's not important. I don't see why I should give you my whole life history.'

'If you think I'm going to dig it up anyway, you might as well,' Cogan said. 'So far I've heard more about Catherine Kennedy than I have about you.'

'Catherine wasn't like me. All I ever wanted was to be a biologist. I always wanted to be one, but my uncle wouldn't pay for me to go to college.' She paused.

'Go on,' Cogan said.

'When I was seventeen everything started falling apart. First of all my parents suddenly stopped writing. They just disappeared. I tried to contact them through organizations in the Middle East, but it was as though they'd never existed. Then, one night after Christmas, my uncle tried to rape me. I think he'd decided my parents were dead so he could do whatever he wanted. We had a terrible row and I went to stay with a girlfriend for a while. But then he came up with what he used to call our arrangement. He offered to put me through college if I'd undress in front of him once a week. He said that watching me would be cheaper than buying videos and that I owed him for all the money he'd spent raising me.'

Cogan wished he hadn't asked. 'I'm sorry,' he said.

'People like you aren't sorry for all the rotten things that happen to people like me. I'm only telling you so you'll understand why I went to Iraq. My uncle never touched me again; he just watched.'

'But you didn't finish your degree?'

'No. In the first semester of my second year the cheques stopped coming. After being a bachelor all his life my uncle decided to get married — to some awful woman from Miami. At the time it didn't seem so bad. I'd felt dirty and disgusted with myself for months and I figured I could stay at college by working nights as a waitress. But I couldn't even earn enough to pay for my board. That's when I realized what a mess my life was and that I needed to go searching for my parents. I know it sounds stupid, but I was really unhappy. I was lonely too.'

'Did you have other relations in Iraq?' Cogan asked.

'No, but there was an Iraqi student at college called Tareq — his family were gassed to death when Saddam Hussein tried to clean out the Kurds from the north of the country. Tareq said he had friends who could help me at a place called Mosul in the no-fly zone. So I borrowed some money and off I went on my big overseas adventure. A month later I met Catherine Kennedy.'

'And she persuaded you to join the PUK?'

'It seemed like a good idea. I suppose I was looking for excitement or for something that would make me feel worthwhile — and I needed time to get some leads on where my parents might be.'

'Were there any leads?'

'I never got that far. I enjoyed being in the PUK, though. Because I'd always been around heavy machinery in my uncle's yard when I was growing up, it was easy to learn how to drive trucks and tanks. The PUK taught me other things as well. I can shoot straight, I know how to survive in hard country and I could probably break your neck if you tried to shake me again like you did at the motel.'

'Or you could fix breakfast,' Cogan said.

'Not unless I get some answers from you.' She jumped down off the platform to collect the fish from the canoe. 'It's your turn. I need to know more about who you are.'

The question was not unreasonable, Cogan thought. Except that he had no real idea what she wanted to hear.

'Well?' Carrying a fish in each hand, she brushed past him on her way into the cabin.

'What do you want to know?'

'Why you get uncomfortable when I dress your cut. Why you're pretending not to look at me. Why you're a metallurgist. Why you work on air accidents. Why you had Brady take me to your motel last night.'

To shut her up Cogan ignored her first two questions and instead began to summarize his jobs in London and Chicago, skipping as much detail as he could before going on to describe the breakthrough that had seen him assigned to his first go-team on the TWA 800 investigation.

'I read about it,' she interrupted. 'People thought the crash was caused by a missile, but it was because of an explosion in one of the fuel tanks. Did you figure that out?'

Cogan grinned at her. 'There were a couple of hundred other guys on the job besides me. But it's where I got my experience. You don't become a wreckage analyst unless you've been involved with a major crash somewhere.'

'Do you have to get to an accident before anyone else?' she asked. 'While all the bodies are still there?'

'It helps. If you're lucky, once in a while you can figure out what went wrong by having a look at how and when the passengers died — even if it's only by seeing when their watches stopped. Mostly you need to photograph the impact impressions and wreckage pattern. There's not much point in studying bits of metal under a microscope unless you have a fair idea of what caused the crash.'

'But that's not all you do, is it, Mr Cogan?' She finished gutting the perch and laid it in a frying-pan on top of the primus. 'The report you showed me wasn't about fuel tank explosions or bird-strikes or pilot error. You're too smart to work on ordinary crashes any more. People call you in when they suspect an aircraft has been deliberately shot down or blown up, because you can tell them if it was caused by a missile or a shell or a bomb, can't you?'

'Sometimes.'

'How about lasers?'

By endeavouring to overlook her sarcasm, Cogan had let his concentration slip. Now he was paying more attention.

'Here.' She handed him two enamel plates. 'They're dirty from last night. If you go and rinse them in the creek we can use them again. Breakfast'll be ready any minute.'

'Lasers,' Cogan said.

'Wait until we've eaten. I want to show you something, too. I can guess what Brady said about the swamp, but I'd like you to see it for yourself.'

Although the offer had sounded sincere, Cogan had already learned the rules. She was buying time, hoping for an opportunity to correct his impression not so much of the swamp, but of her.

It wasn't a bad attempt, he thought, but unnecessary because his opinion was nothing like the one she imagined he had of her.

★   ★   ★

Sara had gone ahead, leaving him standing on what seemed to be dangerously unstable ground.

'Ready?' she called.

'What for?'

58

'This.' She started jumping up and down. 'Can you feel it?'

He didn't have to feel it. He could see it. She was at least twenty feet away, but all around him the trees and bushes were trembling as though the whole area was being swept by an earthquake.

'The peat's really thick in places,' she said. 'The Indians say that if you dig down you can't find the bottom because there isn't one. Jeremiah showed me once.'

'Why did you help him build the cabin?' Cogan squelched his way over to her.

'He needed somewhere to stay when he comes trapping. It's illegal but he doesn't take young animals and he's fairly careful. I met Jeremiah because SCL were using him as a guide when they started on the logging contract.'

'That doesn't explain why you put up the money for the cabin.'

'It's my insurance.'

'From Van Reenan and Khadim?'

'I didn't realize you knew their names.' She looked at him. 'Could Van Reenan be South African?'

Cogan remembered the peculiar accent. 'Maybe. Does it matter?'

'No. Come on. We're nearly at the prairie.' Sara began picking her way between the more sodden patches of the marshland, heading for a group of trees where the sunlight was brighter.

Cogan followed in the heat, less conscious of his sweat-soaked bandage than he had been when they'd started out. He'd become more accustomed to the smell of the swamp as well, he realized. And if he didn't yet quite share her fascination with the place, he could at least appreciate its uniqueness and how remarkably silent and unspoiled it was. Wildlife was everywhere — more than he'd encountered on his trip to Africa, but only visible in glimpses here and there through the vegetation.

In the short space of half an hour he'd seen herons, sandhill cranes, wild turkeys and what Sara had said was a female ibis. She'd also made him listen to the sounds of newly hatched alligators clucking to their mother on the sloping bank of a water trail, and she'd showed him orchids and an insect-eating plant whose name she couldn't remember.

Now, through the trees, Cogan had his first sight of the prairie. It was huge, a flat ocean of grassland stretching away to nowhere in a haze of shimmering sunshine.

'Recognize it?' Sara asked. 'You know where you are now, don't you?'

'Sure. Somewhere in the Okefenokee

swamp.' Cogan smiled. 'Will that do?'

'You've seen part of this prairie before — yesterday, when Brady brought you to the logging site.' She pointed. 'It's over there.'

He listened for the sound of chainsaws, but could hear nothing except for a trickle of water coming from somewhere nearby. 'How far away is it?'

'I don't know. People who live or work in the swamp don't measure distance in miles. At this time of year you could probably walk it in an hour. In the winter you'd have to go by boat on one of the water trails.' She sat down on a fallen tree. 'You didn't finish telling me about yourself.'

'Yes I did.'

'Is there a Mrs Cogan?'

'Not any more. She's living in the Caribbean with someone else.'

'How long were you married?'

'Fourteen months and three days. Not long enough to bother about. I want to hear what happened to you and Catherine in Iraq.'

'I know you do.' She sat in silence for a moment before she spoke again. 'After the Gulf War, the US and its allies drew an imaginary line across the north of Iraq and told Saddam not to cross it. The idea was to protect the Kurds who live there.'

'What you call the no-fly zone,' Cogan said.

'Above the 36th parallel.'

She nodded. 'It halfway works when the Kurdish tribes aren't fighting amongst themselves, but it's not much of a base for the PUK. They haven't been able to stop Iraq buying new military equipment. It comes in from all over the world — tanks from Russia, missiles from Bulgaria and electronics from everywhere — all paid for by oil. There's a UN Security Council resolution that's supposed to stop Iraq from selling oil, but Saddam found a legal loophole.'

'Surprise,' Cogan said. 'Who buys the stuff?'

'Turkey mostly. Iraq claims that pipelines running across the Turkish border are being corroded away by stagnant oil, so the UN has given Baghdad permission to flush out the pipes and to refill them. It's done about once every two months. Guess how much each flush is worth to Iraq.'

'No idea.'

'About twelve million barrels. That's around three hundred and fifty million US dollars' worth a year. Iraq is only supposed to receive humanitarian aid for the oil, but the US doesn't ever check because they don't want to upset the Turkish Government.' She paused. 'So the PUK decided to do something about it.'

'While you and Catherine were in Iraq?'

'Mm. We were part of an explosives team that was sent to blow up a section of the pipeline. The plan was to detonate charges well south of the 36th parallel so the Iraqis would suspect Iranian terrorists instead of the PUK. But everything went terribly wrong. Out of the fourteen of us who went on the mission only Catherine and I got back.'

'Did you blow up the pipeline?' Cogan asked.

'No. We never even found it. Somewhere north of a village called Ba'iji we ran into a minefield and got lost. Then, after we'd started following a road that wasn't on our maps, we were captured by Republican Guards. They trucked us to what we thought was a quarry, but it wasn't a quarry at all.' She leaned forward to pick a stalk of grass. 'It was a military installation.'

'For lasers?' Cogan was doubtful.

'I'm not a hundred per cent sure.'

'But that's what you think?'

She nodded. 'I didn't at the time, of course, but the Iraqi guards who interrogated us weren't awfully bright. They were so convinced we'd been sent to attack the place that they assumed we knew all about it. They kept asking us what we knew about things like infrared adaptive optics and high-speed oxygen pumps. We saw a test in the quarry too.'

'What kind of test?'

'Eight of us were locked up in a little room. There was a window with bars across it looking out over part of the quarry. I wouldn't be alive if it hadn't been for that window. In the afternoon the building was so hot we couldn't touch the walls with our hands.' She glanced at Cogan. 'You can't imagine how bad it was.'

'The test,' he said quietly.

'I'll have to tell you about the place first. The road isn't just a road. It's used as an airstrip. What's supposed to be a rock-crushing plant is really an aircraft hangar, and the Iraqis have tunnelled into the east wall of the quarry to make living-quarters and workshops. It's an underground complex, but no one would ever know. Satellite pictures wouldn't show anything unless they were taken at exactly the right time and you knew exactly what to look for. But we were there on the ground, every day and every night for over a week.'

Despite his impatience, Cogan was reluctant to press her for information. She was ill at ease, stabbing at her leg with the piece of grass and speaking in a flat voice.

'We couldn't see much from the window,'

she said, 'but on one of the nights Catherine was taken for questioning she saw a Scud missile being assembled on a steel gantry that had been concreted into the wall of the quarry. The Iraqis had teams of people working on it all night long. The next morning, a big transport aircraft took off. It was a Russian Antonov 32 with some kind of pod fitted to the side of its fuselage. Half an hour after it had gone, the Iraqis ignited the booster rocket on the missile. Because the missile couldn't go anywhere you can guess what that was like. There were flames and a tremendous amount of noise.'

'How long did it last?' Cogan's doubts were beginning to disappear.

'Not long. Three of us were watching from the window. About thirty seconds after the booster fired, a section of the missile began to glow white hot — just a circular patch on the side of it. Then the whole thing exploded. The technicians were really pleased. They were all laughing and shouting and picking up pieces of the missile afterwards.'

'So you believe it was targeted by an airborne laser in the aircraft?'

'I do now. When Catherine and I got back home we went to a library in New York — just to see if we could make sense of things. We identified the aircraft and found a picture of a Scud missile. And we read a book on military lasers.' She took a breath. 'I can't prove it was a new form of airborne laser we saw being tested; all I know is that the military in the US and other countries are trying to create incredibly powerful beams of infrared light from the chemical reactions of things like iodine and oxygen. It's not classified information.'

'Unless you've got a development programme running in a quarry somewhere in Iraq,' Cogan said. 'You'd be pretty interested in keeping that secret.'

She threw the piece of grass away. 'Why else would Catherine have been murdered? Why do you think those men want to find me?'

'I don't know. If the Iraqis are trying to keep their project under wraps, why did they let you go?'

'They didn't; they didn't let any of us go. We lost six people in the minefield and the rest of the men were executed while we were in prison. The Republican Guards shot them one at a time after they'd been questioned. Catherine and I were saved until the end.'

'Because you were Americans?'

'Because we were women. The Iraqis have a thing about American women, and Catherine was pretty. She was a blond, too. One of the guards told us we were going to be gang raped before we were executed, so Catherine promised we'd be extra nice to him if he'd make sure none of the other men touched us.' She stopped talking abruptly.

'Finish it,' Cogan said.

'No.'

'How did you escape?'

'Catherine. Escaping was her idea.'

'How?' Cogan was searching for the right approach, aware of her unwillingness to continue, but anxious to hear the end of her story.

'You don't have to keep on prompting me. If you have to know — if you think it's so damn important — I'll tell you — I'll tell you exactly what happened. Then perhaps you'll stop asking me questions because you'll have some idea of what it was like for us. A Kurdish woman had taught Catherine how to bend a piece of steel wire into something the Kurds call a *tala meashk* — that means mousetrap. It's shaped like a heart with the two ends of the wire facing towards the centre, but held apart where they touch in the vee at the top. Catherine made one for herself from a bedspring. You hide it between your thighs, right high up so that once a man is inside you and he pushes hard the two ends of the wire slip off each other and spring inwards. It's only any use if you know you're going to be raped ahead of time — but both of us did know.'

Disconcerted by her ability to describe the most appalling circumstances in a matter-of-fact manner, not for the first time Cogan found himself at a loss for words.

'It was dreadful,' she said. 'I was supposed to strangle the guard with his belt, but he was screaming so much that Catherine had to do it. We used his key to unlock the door — then we just ran. If it hadn't been dark we'd never have made it. They even sent helicopters after us — three of them with halogen search-lights.'

'How long did it take you to get back to your base?'

'Nearly three weeks. We only travelled after dark and we had to spend half of each night searching for water and things to eat. By the time we reached the camp we were both sick and Catherine was hallucinating. I can remember thinking we had to be the luckiest two people in the whole world.'

'Until you arrived home in the States,' Cogan said. 'And realized your luck wasn't holding.'

'We didn't realize — not at first. Cath and I rented an apartment together in New York. We were all screwed up and needed to get back to normal somehow. We never dreamed we'd be followed all the way from the Middle East. But we were wrong, of course. In August last year someone tried to drive us off the side of a bridge by shooting out the tyres of my car. Then, about two weeks afterwards, Catherine was knifed on her way home one night. She was OK, though. The cut was nothing like the one you've got.'

'The whole thing's crazy,' Cogan said. 'The Iraqis are either out of their minds or they're paranoid. You're no threat to them. You didn't see enough.'

'It's not what we saw; it's because they believe we know where the quarry is. They've already stopped Catherine from ever telling anyone. Now they're trying to stop me. That's why the whole thing's crazy — because she never did know. And I don't either. We were lost, trying to stay alive after people had been blown up all around us in the minefield.'

'Have you had a look at a decent map?' Cogan asked.

'There aren't any good ones of that part of Iraq. If there were the PUK would have them. The road doesn't exist on any map. Nor does the quarry. There's just desert, mountains and rocks. You wouldn't ask if you knew what it's like.'

Cogan had a better idea than she thought

he did, but instead of telling her so he changed the subject. 'When did Catherine go to Alaska?' he asked.

'Last October — a month before I became Shannon Lockhart and started working for SCL. I should've been more careful, shouldn't I?'

'About what?'

'I should have guessed Catherine would tell her brother. If I'd thought, I could've told her not to.' She paused. 'I suppose it wouldn't have made any difference; sooner or later those men are going to find me.'

'Not in the middle of this swamp, they're not,' Cogan said.

She smiled. 'There was no work in South Carolina so I asked my uncle to get me a job driving for SCL. He sells them some of their equipment. That means anyone who talks to my uncle can trace me to SCL.'

'Look,' Cogan said, 'there's a way to stop this. I can introduce you to some people who'd be pretty interested to hear what you saw in Iraq.'

'I've only explained what happened to me to stop you making any more stupid phone calls. I don't want your help.'

'What if Peter Kennedy is right? What if Iraq is using a high-powered, airborne laser as a terrorist weapon?'

'What if they are? It's nothing to do with me. I just want to be left alone.'

'How about this?' Cogan said. 'I'll do some groundwork then I'll speak to someone in the US Defense Department — at least let me do that. You can't live here forever.'

'Yes I can.' Stepping out into the waist-high grass of the prairie, she began to walk away, not stopping until all he could see of her was the distant white smudge of her T-shirt.

She stayed there for nearly ten minutes before returning to stand in front of him. 'Two weeks ago there was a bald eagle here,' she said. 'I watched it circle and climb until I couldn't follow it any more because my eyes were watering. I've never seen one before. It was wonderful.'

Cogan remained silent.

'Now I've told you what you wanted to know, will you promise me something?' she asked.

'Sure.'

'Promise you'll forget about me.'

'I won't tell anyone what you've told me. Will that do?'

'All right.' She met his eyes. 'You haven't asked why I was scared you might be South African.'

'I haven't asked you a lot of things. What's

the big deal about me not being South African?'

'Eight days after Catherine went off to Alaska, a man came to fix the heating system in the apartment we had in New York. The radiators had stopped working and it was a cold afternoon. I shouldn't have let him in, but I did. He was South African. He was really nice until I went to the kitchen to make him coffee, then he came at me with one of those thin steel wires with handles on the end. I've still got a mark from it round my neck.' She tipped back her head. 'See?'

Cogan was watching her face, conscious of the awkward way she was speaking.

'Don't you want to know what happened?' she asked.

'As long as you want to tell me.' He saw her discomfort become more acute.

'I stabbed him in the arm with a breadknife and managed to turn myself around, but he wouldn't let go of the wire. He just kept on twisting it tighter and tighter.'

'It's OK,' Cogan said quietly.

'No it's not. Don't you understand? I killed him. I cut his throat and I killed him.' Her voice tailed off.

Cogan stood up, intending to put an arm round her.

'Don't.' She pushed him away. 'Don't you dare touch me.'

He could see her eyes had clouded over, but she was clearly no more willing to acknowledge her distress than she was to accept his assistance. Which complicated things, he thought, not so much because her toughness had proved to be contrived, but because it was now just about impossible for him to decide what the hell he was going to do with her.

3

The swamp was having an effect on Cogan. He'd been aware of it since his second night here, a growing sense of being cut off from reality that was not altogether unpleasant as long as Sara was nearby. But there were other conflicting feelings as well, either brought about by the environment or because of her.

This evening, at the beginning of his fifth night at the cabin, Cogan was searching for another means of broaching the subject of tomorrow. Having tried twice already, and after backing off on both occasions for reasons that had more to do with himself than with Sara, he was no longer sure of how to approach the matter.

He wasn't sure of his options either. Until recently, he'd been reluctant to consider returning to London and leaving her here to fend for herself. But with the swamp distorting his judgement, and the relationship between them deteriorating almost by the hour, Cogan was beginning to realize how limited the alternatives were. As a consequence, the hole he'd dug for himself seemed to be getting progressively deeper.

To avoid having to talk to her, he jumped down off the platform and began walking along the creek bank, insensitive to the chorus of frogs and insects as he tried to find a solution to his problem.

On his first day here she'd continued to be co-operative, describing how she'd burned the passport of the man who had tried to kill her in New York before she'd driven all the way out to the Heckscher State Park on Long Island to dispose of the body in the sea. But her willingness to talk had soon evaporated, and with each successive day she had become more introverted, apparently as uninterested in Cogan as she was in his offer to help her out of the mess she was in.

Except that it wasn't just her mess, he thought: it was his as well. And unless one of them sorted it out fast, things were going to get more confused than they were already.

There were too many unresolved questions — too many loose ends. Had she really witnessed a test of an airborne laser? And if so, why had the target been a stationary missile under full thrust from its engine? And what on earth could link the Iraqi Government to the South Africans who had been sent to take the lives of Catherine Kennedy and Sara Hamaid?

The answers remained elusive, no closer

than they had been yesterday or the day before. Worse still, since last night, Cogan had been forced to confront his increasing preoccupation with Sara herself. To begin with he'd been able to pretend that any attraction was more imagined than real, the result, perhaps, of sharing the tiny cabin with her for too long, or because he was sorry for the lousy hand that life had dealt her. But he knew it wasn't either of those things. They were excuses — a cover-up for something he could no longer deny. Despite her resentment of him, he had gradually become aware of everything about her — the touch of her hands when she changed his dressing, the shape of her mouth, the sleepiness in her eyes when she awoke in the morning, the half-smile on her lips whenever she was caught off-guard and, more than anything, her unconsciously provocative self-sufficiency. There was the smell of her too, the sweet, musky smell of her skin that never went away and that seemed to follow him wherever he went.

The swamp was to blame, he decided, a place where solitude and silence combined to produce an atmosphere in which it was too easy to fantasize.

He pushed his thoughts aside and retraced his steps, arriving back at the cabin a few minutes before nine o'clock.

On top of the primus stove, a candle burning in a jamjar was throwing shadows across the floor, making it difficult for him to see her face. She was nearly asleep, curled up inside the mosquito net on a pile of clothes, using a plastic bag for a pillow.

'Where have you been?' she asked.

'Nowhere. I needed to figure out something.'

'About when you're leaving? Do you want me to take you to the car tomorrow?'

'I didn't say I was going tomorrow.' Cogan sat down and leaned back against a cardboard box. 'Why not come to London with me? That'd be better than you hanging around here. I've got friends you could stay with.'

'You're doing it again,' she said. 'I thought we agreed not to talk about it any more. You do what you like, and I'll do what I like. If you're so anxious to get home I don't see why you've stayed this long.'

'It was your idea,' Cogan said, 'remember? Something about making sure we understood each other — about you needing time to trust me.'

'I didn't ask you to stay. All I said was that you didn't have to leave unless you wanted to. There's a difference.'

Cogan abandoned his efforts to be reasonable. She was using the same tactics she'd used before, being deliberately abrasive to end the conversation as quickly as she could.

'I'll take off in the morning,' he said. 'Go back to sleep.'

'I wasn't asleep. Don't you want a corner of the mosquito net?'

'Keep your mosquito net. By this time tomorrow you'll have your whole damn cabin to yourself again. Then you won't have to share anything with anyone. Won't that be nice?' He stood up to blow out the candle. 'I'll be outside. If you have to go to the toilet, don't trip over me like you did last night.'

'I didn't trip over you. You only thought I did.'

Cogan turned his back on her and went to sit on the platform in the moonlight. The mosquitos weren't too bad, but as a precaution he used the stick of repellent she'd given him, smearing his hands and face with the stuff so he'd only have the whining to contend with. But he was not yet sleepy and still unaccustomed to the night sounds of the swamp — the splash of frogs, the scratching of insects and the occasional cry of some unfortunate animal that had become dinner for an alligator or a snake. He listened to them all, wondering how long it would take him to forget that he'd ever been here and trying to decide what her reaction would be if he offered to send her money once he got back to London.

He managed to make himself more comfortable by wedging his shoulders between two of the platform support ropes, and was on the point of dozing off when he heard a muffled cough followed by the rustle of the mosquito net being rearranged.

It took him several seconds to realize he'd misinterpreted the sounds. Sara was crying, using a crumpled ball of netting to stifle her sobs. He could just see her in the moonlight, hunched up in a corner, her whole body shaking with the effort of trying to keep quiet.

Knowing what her reaction would be if he went anywhere near her, Cogan stayed where he was. When he failed to reply after she called out to him, she spoke his name.

'I'm outside.' He stood up. 'Did you have a nightmare?'

'No.' She rose unsteadily to her feet. 'It's always the same, isn't it? You don't even try to understand.'

'You tell me that every damn day,' he said. 'Now you're telling me in the middle of the night. What is it this time?'

Making no attempt to answer, she

approached him slowly with her eyes lowered, then stood on tiptoe and kissed him gently on the lips. 'I'm not very good at this sort of thing.' She wiped her face with her hand. 'But I don't know what else to do.'

Cogan was unsettled, not yet certain he was reading the signals correctly.

'Oh God.' Flushed with embarrassment she turned away. 'I've got it wrong, haven't I?'

In case the swamp was playing tricks with his imagination he grabbed her by her pony-tail, half expecting her to vanish in a puff of smoke before he could spin her round to face him again. 'You haven't got anything wrong,' he said.

She was still embarrassed. 'Is that all you're going to say?'

He was searching for an answer when she stood on tiptoe again, this time kissing him open-mouthed, pressing herself against him so hard that she nearly tipped him off the platform.

The taste of her tears was as compelling as the scent of her skin, and now she was in his arms, he knew that she had wanted this as much as he had. Her kisses were intense, each one more searching and more lingering than the one before, her tongue alive inside his mouth while she pushed her breasts against his chest.

Wriggling away from him she stripped off her T-shirt and tried to unfasten her belt, wide-eyed, fumbling nervously with the buckle.

Cogan could barely look. Even in the moonlight he could see enough of her to make him catch his breath, but it was the expression of anticipation on her face that made her so impossibly desirable. If he had thought she was provocative before, now, as she finished undressing, he saw why it had been so easy to fantasize about her.

She was beautiful — her figure, the slenderness of her waist, the tantalizing swell between her thighs — all exaggerated and made more irresistible by her invitation for him to respond.

She stood quite still when he went to her, opening her mouth again, but this time offering more, allowing him to kiss her breasts before she made him slip his hands down over her stomach to caress her between her thighs.

For Cogan, after being warned to never touch her, the experience of doing so was exquisite. She was like satin, the warmth and the texture of her skin arousing him so fully that when she was finally able to remove his clothes to take what she wanted, she had almost become too eager, holding and

81

stroking him with trembling hands while she spread her legs to let him enjoy her more thoroughly.

Soon she began to gasp, drawing her palms and her fingertips over him with increasing urgency until she could wait no longer.

'Cogan,' she whispered. 'Please.'

For a second he considered carrying her into the cabin so they could lie down, but, as if she had guessed what he was thinking, she leaned back against the wall and quickly guided him inside her.

She relaxed at once, closing her eyes while she accepted him, whispering his name until he could penetrate her no further. Only then did she start to move, pleading with him to hurry, using her contractions to drive him on.

Cogan was lost, drowning in the pleasure she was giving him, no more able to hear her whispered demands than he was able to control the beginning of her climax or his own heart-slamming release.

He held her through her shudders, supporting her, waiting for himself to start breathing again before he told her to open her eyes.

She shook her head. 'I don't want to. You might drop me.'

'What do you mean?'

She stifled a giggle, then began to laugh. 'You're holding my feet off the ground.'

'Jesus, I'm sorry.' Cogan lowered her cautiously. She was still giggling, and where ten minutes ago her face had been wet with tears now her expression was entirely different.

She prevented him from withdrawing. 'Don't spoil it,' she whispered. 'I wasn't expecting this to happen, but now it has I don't want it to stop.'

'I don't know how it happened at all,' he said.

'I told you: because you don't understand. You've spent the last three days not looking at me and I've spent the last three days trying to make you. There wasn't any other way I could think of to stop you leaving.'

'So this is a trap?'

'It's your fault,' she said. 'You shouldn't have made me cry.'

'I didn't.'

'Yes, you did. It was such relief to tell someone about Iraq and all the other things, but you just kept on asking me questions about lasers. You listened as though I didn't matter — as though I was nobody. Then you started ignoring me. Don't you see what a let-down that was?'

'You're inventing this as you go along,'

Cogan said. 'You planned the whole damn thing.'

'I had to. I've got an immune system that rejects men. I frighten them off. I had to do something to make you like me.'

'There's not enough of you to like,' he said. 'You're only half the size of anyone else.'

'Oh.' She frowned, then fastened her mouth onto his and kissed him until she ran out of breath. 'Take me inside,' she said.

Picking her up in his arms, he carried her into the cabin, kicking the pile of clothes into the semblance of a bed before he laid her down.

She curled up against him, rubbing her nose along the row of stitches in his chest. 'Now you can talk to me,' she said. 'I don't want to fall asleep.'

'I'll still be here in the morning,' Cogan said.

'Talk to me anyway — otherwise I won't know how well my trap worked, will I?'

Her choice of words confirmed what he had suspected all along. He imagined she'd intended to sound possessive, but her directness showed that she too was under the influence of the swamp — that it had cast its spell on her as well as on him.

The idea was irrational, he thought, an incomprehensible notion that should have either gone away by morning, or at least be easier to disprove in the light of day.

★ ★ ★

There was no opportunity to prove or disprove anything in the light of day. Instead, Cogan woke shortly after dawn with the knowledge that the swamp was not as it should be. The pine warblers had stopped singing, and all around the cabin, red-headed woodpeckers were deserting the trees — driven away by the faint but unmistakable sound of an outboard motor.

Quickly untangling himself from the mosquito net, he shook Sara to wake her and started pulling on his clothes.

'Hi.' She smiled sleepily at him.

'We've got visitors.' Cogan found her T-shirt and shorts and gave them to her. 'Better put those on.'

She listened for a second without saying anything, then began scrambling to get dressed while Cogan went outside.

The sound of the motor was steady, coming from some distance away, but its direction told him his fears were correct. Whoever was using the creek as a waterway was coming here.

Sara brought his shoes out to him. She was

uneasy, but endeavouring not to show it.

'Get what we need from inside,' Cogan said. 'My things are in that plastic bag on top of the cake tin. Bring the rifle too.'

She hesitated. 'We don't know who it is. Suppose it's just someone out hunting?'

'Who do you think they might be hunting for?'

'You don't have to be smart when I've only just woken up. Where are we going?'

'I don't know yet. We'll take the canoe.'

She bit her lip. 'I knew something would go wrong.'

'Nothing's gone wrong yet.' Cogan started off down the steps. 'Fetch the stuff — go on, hurry.'

By the time she joined him on the bank, he'd made a rough estimate of how long it would take the approaching boat to reach the cabin. It was travelling slowly, probably because the creek was too narrow and too overgrown for any reasonable sized craft, but it would still be here in less than ten minutes.

Taking the rifle from Sara, he held the canoe while she climbed in and stowed their belongings at her feet. 'Upstream,' he said. 'Don't stir up too much mud. Once we're clear of the bend, carry on for a couple of hundred yards then find somewhere for us to stop.'

'Why not keep going?' Paddle ready, she waited for Cogan to slip into the cockpit behind her.

'We need to see who it is. You might be right; for all we know it's some guy out fishing for his breakfast.'

'But you don't believe that, do you?' She pushed off and began to thread the canoe through some vines, using her hands to keep the bow away from the bank until she was in more open water.

Cogan wasn't sure what to believe. Nor did he have a strategy in mind if the visitors turned out to be as unfriendly as he thought they might be.

In front of him, Sara was working harder now, driving the canoe forwards with increasing speed. He could hear the intake of her breath as she ended each sweep of the paddle, and was close enough to her to be conscious of the sheen to her skin — an observation that was as untimely as it was inappropriate.

'Will this do?' She changed course, angling the bow towards the bank. 'We can hide the canoe in the weed over there.'

'OK.' Cogan made himself concentrate on what he was doing, consulting his watch to see how long it would be before the owners of the outboard arrived at the cabin. 'Never mind the weed,' he said. 'We're cutting things too fine — just tie up. We've only got four minutes to find somewhere that gives us a decent view.'

'I know where.' She let the bow drift into the bank, throwing the rope to Cogan as soon as he disembarked.

'Bring some spare clips of ammunition,' he said. 'You never know.'

'There aren't any spare clips. I forgot.' She climbed out of the canoe without looking at him. 'You shouldn't have made me rush.' She brushed past. 'There's a patch of scrub by that dead pine tree I showed you the other day — where I said the ospreys were nesting in the spring. We'll be able to see the cabin from there.'

Although the scrub turned out to be sparser than Cogan would have liked it to be, by the standards of the swamp it was on high ground, growing on an elevated pad of dry peat. There was enough of the foliage to conceal them both and, except for a bush and one or two clumps of undergrowth, their line of sight to the cabin was unobscured.

'How much longer?' Sara lay down beside him.

'I don't know.' He had given up trying to judge how far away the boat was. 'It's harder to tell from here. Maybe they've got tangled up in something.'

'No they haven't.'

Eighty yards away, rounding the bend in the creek was a narrow, flat-bottomed punt. In the stern at the controls of a light-weight motor, Khadim was sitting behind the taller figure of Van Reenan, while crouched uncomfortably in the bow was a young woman with shoulder-length dark hair. She had her head lowered, apparently uninterested in her surroundings.

'Oh my God.' Sara gripped Cogan's arm. 'It's Jeremiah.'

Not a young woman in the bow, Cogan saw now, but a young man — her Indian friend, the only other person who knew the location of the cabin. 'Looks like that nice uncle of yours told someone you've been working for SCL,' he said.

She frowned. 'Even if that's how they found Jeremiah, why would he bring them here?'

'He didn't have a choice.' Cogan pointed.

Holding what looked like a Kalashnikov assault rifle, Van Reenan was standing on the creek bank now, surveying the swamp as Khadim forced the Indian up the cabin steps, prodding him roughly in the back with the muzzle of a machine-pistol.

The Kalashnikov alone confirmed what Cogan had already guessed. On this occasion, Van Reenan was taking no chances, equipping himself with a guide and enough firepower to guarantee success.

'We have to do something,' Sara whispered.

Unwilling to risk a shot with an unfamiliar rifle against two armed men with a hostage, Cogan was considering his options.

'Use the gun,' she said.

'We need to see what they do first.'

'I can tell you what they'll do. Once they're sure we've been at the cabin, they'll try to make Jeremiah track us. But he won't be able to because we took the canoe.'

She had barely finished speaking when, without warning, Khadim pushed the Indian bodily off the platform and began shouting something at him.

At the same time, Cogan realized this was no prelude to any tracking exercise. He watched in horror as Jeremiah started backing away, his hands raised ineffectually to protect himself from what he knew was coming.

Cogan already had the rifle to his shoulder, but before he could flick off the safety, Khadim opened fire, raking the Indian from throat to abdomen, killing him instantly.

So swift and so cold-blooded had the execution been that Cogan had frozen with his finger on the trigger. Sara, too, was numb, staring disbelievingly at the crumpled body.

'Jesus,' Cogan muttered. 'Who in God's name are these people?'

'Give me that.' She reached for the gun. 'If you won't do it, I will.'

'No.' He pushed her away. 'Listen to me: Jeremiah's dead, you can't help him.'

'I don't care.' She managed to seize the rifle barrel. 'They shot Catherine, they tried to kill me, and now they've murdered Jeremiah — just because he was no more use to them. I won't let this go on. I have to stop it.'

'You can't — not while we're out in the open.'

'We're not in the open.' She maintained her grip on the barrel.

'You don't go up against a machine-pistol and an AK47 with a bolt-action twenty-two. You know that as well as I do.' He looked at her. 'This is your territory — you're our ticket out of here.'

They were going to require more than a ticket. Either because of sunlight glinting off the rifle or because Van Reenan had focused his attention on the scrub, Cogan suddenly knew they were in danger.

Sara escaped the first burst of fire by the slimmest of margins, the bullets slamming into the peat only inches from her face. A second, more prolonged burst was more accurate, but by then Cogan had rolled on top of her and pulled her to safety behind the pine. She was shaken, white-faced and smothered in dirt.

'Canoe,' Cogan said. 'Now.'

To his relief she didn't hesitate, running ahead of him, risking high ground whenever there was sufficient vegetation to cover them, taking a shorter but more exposed route back to the creek.

But their lead was never going to be enough, and no sooner had she slid down the bank than there were more shots.

Cogan had no idea where they had come from, nor was there time to find out. 'Leave the canoe,' he shouted. 'It'll be too slow.'

Throwing him the plastic bag, she took his outstretched hand and let him drag her back over the mud on her stomach.

'There.' She pointed quickly. 'In the vines. I saw something.'

Cogan wiped the sweat out of his eyes, scanning downstream for any sign of movement.

It was Khadim — hidden in the shadows, slightly more than a hundred yards away.

Cogan had begun to raise the Remington when Sara stopped him. 'He's not being careful enough,' she whispered. 'He must know we can see him.'

'Decoy?'

She nodded. 'It's the other man who's dangerous — the tall one.'

Cogan knew she was right. At this range, Khadim's machine-pistol was far less of a threat than the high-powered AK47. But of Van Reenan there was no sign. No birds were leaving the trees and there was no other kind of disturbance that Cogan could detect.

He made his decision. 'There'll be people at the logging site,' he said. 'It's our best chance.'

'That means we have to cross the creek.'

'OK. I'll cover you.' He wondered where the hell Van Reenan was and how rapid Khadim's response would be.

'You don't have to cover me. We'll go together.' She allowed herself to slither back down the bank, towing Cogan behind her until she was neck deep in weed. 'Come on.'

Although the creek was no more than fifteen feet wide, the mud on the bottom was slippery and softer in some places than others, making it difficult for them to keep their footing. As a result Cogan was unprepared for the sudden appearance of the punt.

Van Reenan was using a branch as a pole,

standing in the stern with his Kalashnikov on the seat in front of him.

Sara shouted a warning then launched herself forwards, swimming the last few feet to the bank so she could hold out her hand for the rifle.

There was no time for Cogan to give it to her. Squinting into the sun, he levelled the barrel and squeezed off two rounds, the first ricocheting off the water to the left of the punt, the second forcing Van Reenan to duck his head.

Neither of the shots had been well aimed, but they bought the four or five seconds Sara needed.

Before the awful sound of the AK47 hammered out again along the creek she had melted into the trees and taken Cogan with her.

And so began their run through the marshlands of the Okefenokee, an energy-sapping game of cat and mouse across terrain that could vary in the space of a few yards from sodden peat to matted tree roots to ankle-wrenching mud.

Making it worse was Cogan's concern about the extent of their lead and the impossibility of disguising their footprints on patches of silt along the water trails.

Twice he made Sara go ahead while he

waited gun in hand for an opportunity to slow down their trackers, and twice he caught her up simply by following the imprint of her shoes.

The men behind them were quick to learn the lesson, gaining nearly fifty yards at one point when Sara elected to skirt the boundary of the prairie instead of venturing out into the open. But gradually, as the swamp became more treacherous, so Van Reenan and Khadim lost the advantage, outmanoeuvred by her local knowledge and her speed.

For much of the journey it was Sara who set the pace, navigating her way through the forest sure-footedly enough, but misjudging her staying power so that when she finally slowed to a walk, Cogan could see how close to the limit of her endurance she was.

He was in no better shape, filthy and drenched in sweat, conscious of the concern on her face. Something besides exhaustion was worrying her — disturbing her more with each step she took.

'It's too quiet.' She glanced at him. 'Why can't we hear the saws working?'

'Where's the site?'

'The clearing's just over there.' She nodded towards a stand of tupelogums. 'I know we're in the right place. You can see the slash.'

The litter and the stumps were clearly visible, but Cogan was far from sure that the clearing was nearby. He was trying to listen when she stopped walking altogether.

'What day is it?' she asked.

Before he could figure it out, she answered her own question.

'It's Sunday,' she said slowly. 'We never thought. No one's here.'

How he could have been so stupid, Cogan couldn't imagine. The mistake was fundamental, a blunder that had brought them all this way for nothing. 'How far are we from the road?' he said.

'It won't help us. We'll be better targets on the road than we are here.' She took a deep breath. 'How many cartridges have we got left?'

'Why?'

His reply was interrupted by a shout and the stutter of a machine-pistol.

This time, without the protection of a pine tree or a creek-bank, the danger was much greater. Bullets were zipping past them, shredding bark from branches above their heads.

'This way.' Sara began to run again, drawing on reserves that Cogan didn't think she had. Forcing his legs to work, he ran with her, weaving between what trees there were until they suddenly found themselves on the outskirts of the clearing.

'Shed,' she panted. 'We're nearly there.'

It took them over a minute to cross the gravelled turn-around area, a long, heart-stopping minute with nowhere to go if Khadim tried again. Even after they reached the building, Cogan remained wary, knowing the protection it offered was largely artificial.

Taking the rifle from him, she placed the muzzle against the padlock on the door, firing shot after shot to empty the magazine.

Not until she wrenched the door open, darted inside and emerged with a key in her hand did Cogan realize what she had in mind.

Giving him a tight smile she started off towards the water trail on the east edge of the clearing, trying to hurry, but running out of steam and stumbling to a halt before she was anywhere near the skidder.

Cogan helped her, locking his arm round her waist while they staggered the last fifty yards together.

'Other side,' she gasped.

Only the skidder saved them from another barrage of shots, and it was only the skidder that saved them from the next one.

Sheltering from a hail of bullets ricocheting off the bodywork, he pushed Sara up the ladder and threaded her into the cab ahead of him.

She started the diesel easily, her eyes on the instrument panel, waiting for full hydraulic pressure before she released the brakes.

From the cab, Cogan had a bird's-eye view of the clearing now. He could see Khadim at the shed loading a fresh clip of ammunition and, as the skidder at last began to move, he could pick out the figure of Van Reenan coming from the trees. He was limping badly, supporting himself on the mud-caked stock of his assault rifle, but endeavouring to make up lost ground.

Although Cogan was anticipating trouble from Khadim, he was not prepared for Van Reenan's uncompromising sense of purpose.

At a range of well over 200 yards, the South African had dropped to one knee, assuming the position of someone who was about to open fire.

'Look out,' Cogan yelled.

There was just time for Sara to duck her head before the frightening noise of lead spattering against steel drowned out the roar of the engine, and every window in the cab exploded.

But Van Reenan had underestimated the strength of a machine that had been built to handle the rigours of swamp logging. Travelling backwards, its occupants unharmed and with only minor damage to its paintwork, the skidder gathered speed.

Lying sideways on the seat, covered in broken glass, Sara was using the rear-view mirror as a periscope, her expression one of cold determination.

Cogan guessed her intentions. 'Don't be bloody silly,' he shouted. 'They'll shoot our tyres out.'

'We've got six of them and they're all filled with plastic foam.' She opened the throttle wide, holding the skidder in reverse to protect the cab from another attack. 'You'd better hold on.'

Instead of taking her advice, Cogan risked a look, sticking his head out of the cab in time to see Khadim abandoning his position behind the shed.

A second later, on board the skidder, a slight lurch was accompanied by the sound of splintering timber.

Like Khadim, Van Reenan too had decided to cut his losses. He was on his feet again, retreating, his gun held loosely by his side, evidently unwilling to take on twelve tons of heavy machinery that was bearing down on him.

'That'll do,' Cogan yelled at her. 'Back off.'

'No. This is for Catherine and Jeremiah.' She sat up, putting the skidder into a long, bouncing turn before she changed into a higher gear and began accelerating again in a forward direction.

'You can't run the bastards down,' Cogan shouted. 'They're already in the trees.'

'I can push trees over. Watch.'

To prevent her from attempting the impossible, and because she was vulnerable to a lucky shot from somewhere in the forest, he grabbed the steering wheel.

She had not the strength left to fight him, and at the last minute she lost her nerve, letting go of the wheel completely so he could swing the nose of the vehicle round.

'You damn near got us both killed,' he said, 'You're crazy.'

Her reaction was the one he was becoming used to. She refused to look at him, driving slowly back across the clearing, detouring only to avoid the pile of matchwood which once had been the shed.

Cogan was still angry. 'Where the hell are you going now?' he asked.

'I don't know.' Bringing the skidder to a standstill, she slumped against the wheel with her face in her hands.

'We're not out of this yet. We're still in range.' He cleared some glass off the seat.

'Brady was talking about a place called Waycross north of here. Can you get us that far?'

'I have to go back. I can't just leave Jeremiah where he is — because of the alligators.'

'You're not going back anywhere,' Cogan said. 'Do you want me to drive?'

'No.' Making herself sit upright, she put the skidder into gear and began driving towards the north exit of the clearing. 'What happens when we get to Waycross?'

'We dump this thing somewhere before we get there and walk the rest of the way into town. Then we either rent a car or hitch a ride so we can dig my Mazda out of the bushes where we left it.'

'I don't think anyone'll talk to us. You haven't shaved for five days, we're both covered in mud, and your cut's bleeding again.'

'I've got money and credit cards.' Cogan paused. 'Look, from here on you're going to do exactly what I tell you to do.'

'What does that mean?'

'It means I'm going to sort out this bloody mess once and for all. Trying to ram Van Reenan into a tree isn't the answer. I'm going to stir up so much trouble in Washington that the Iraqis will wish they'd never even heard of

101

you or Catherine Kennedy. Once I've done that, and someone wakes up the State Department and the CIA, instead of Baghdad having a nice underground laser development complex in the desert, they'll be left with a lot of dead Republican Guards and a quarryful of the rocks they started out with. If you don't like the idea, hard luck. That's how it's going to be.'

'You said you wouldn't tell anyone. You promised me.'

'For Christ's sake,' Cogan said. 'Catherine's dead and Jeremiah's dead. Do you want to go on wondering how long it'll be before it's your turn?'

'You've forgotten something: I killed that man in New York. Cogan, I won't spend the rest of my life locked up just because you feel sorry for me.'

'I didn't say I felt sorry for you. No one's going to lock you up — you haven't done anything you didn't have to do.'

'But I can't prove it, can I?' She slowed the skidder for a bend in the road. 'You're sticking bits and pieces of my life together to make a picture of who you think I am so you can play at being a white knight. But I won't let you do that. It's my life not yours.'

'You don't have a choice,' Cogan said. 'You never did have. And I don't want to hear any more crap about you being able to look after yourself. Have you got that?'

To his surprise, instead of continuing to argue, she clamped her mouth shut and for the moment seemed prepared to accept what he'd said. Another twist, Cogan thought, another illustration of how unpredictable she could be and why, after last night, irrespective of how many bits and pieces of herself she chose to give him, any picture of her would always be somehow incomplete.

4

Earlier this morning when Cogan had headed out of Savannah the sky had been overcast and threatening. It had remained dull for most of his journey, but in the last ten minutes the sun had broken through, and now, as he got his first sight of the Altamaha river, the last of the clouds were disappearing.

He slowed the car, looking for the place Brady had described on the phone. It was on the other side of the highway overlooking the river, a small, elevated lay-by already occupied by a mini-bus and half-a-dozen other vehicles.

Cogan parked behind the bus, locked up the car and went to see what the view was like. Though the river itself was unimpressive, the water was particularly clean and clear, swirling around some rocks at the foot of an overbridge where a young Japanese girl was taking photographs. Normally the clarity of the water would not have attracted his attention, but with the memories of the swamp still vivid in his mind, it was impossible to avoid comparing the bustle of the river with the slow-moving, brown stillness of the creek.

It was eight days since they'd made their way to safety, but he was continuing to make comparisons, he realized, as conscious as ever of the contrast between what Sara called the outside world and the suffocating unreality of the Okefenokee.

For her, the outside world did not exist. She passed through it without ever touching the sides, functioning perfectly well, but somehow never appearing to be part of it. He'd become aware of the illusion during their first few days in Savannah when they'd gone shopping together or eaten out at a restaurant somewhere, only slowly coming to appreciate that the impression she'd given him in the swamp was no different to the impression other people had of her in the city. She was like a pixie, drawing men's eyes to her wherever she went — not simply because of her figure, but because she clearly belonged somewhere else and seemed to be perpetually about to vanish.

He'd got used to it, but not to the point where he'd been happy to leave her behind this morning in case she had disappeared by the time he got back — part of the reason that he'd come here today, and why they'd had the argument before he left.

'Thinking of jumping?' Brady had arrived

unannounced. He was chewing on a cold cigar and seemed more interested in the Japanese girl than he was in Cogan.

'I didn't see your car.' Cogan shook hands with him.

'I'm parked on the shoulder. I wasn't sure you'd be here. You sounded kind of scratchy on the phone.'

'I've been scratchy ever since you drove me out to the swamp. That's why I need to talk to you — why I need a favour.'

'I don't know you from a pile of horseshit. Why would I want to do you a favour?'

'Why don't you wait until you've heard what it is? I couldn't say much on the phone. It's about Shannon Lockhart.'

'Surprise. Where is she?'

'She's OK,' Cogan said.

'Did she ever have anything to say about those air accidents you're interested in?'

'It's a long story. Do you want to hear it?'

'Sure. I'm a sucker for a good story. Why else would I drive fifty miles?' Brady paused. 'Are you going to tell me why we had to meet here?'

'I didn't want to show up in Brunswick again.'

'Because of that car you wrecked? Or did you straighten things out with the rental people?'

106

'I went to see them,' Cogan said. 'They took five hundred bucks off me and rented me another one. I called on the guy who runs the motel too. He says his insurance company are paying for a rebuild of the unit.'

'So you've got all that cleared away, but I still need to do you a favour?'

'Right. Not much of one though.'

'OK.' Brady lit his cigar. 'Next time you see the girl, tell her she hasn't got a job anymore. Some jerk took that machine of hers for a joy-ride last weekend. One of my guys found it up on the logging road with its windows shot out. He said it looked like someone had used it for target practice.'

'She won't be going back to work for SCL.' Cogan stopped Brady from interrupting. 'She's not going anywhere because if she does there's a good chance she'll wind up dead. And if you think that's bullshit, you're wrong. There are people after her. They tried to kill her twice in New York and they've tried twice since she's been living in Georgia. She came here to hide, but then you and I dragged her out of the swamp and started putting up signposts with her name on them.'

'Who the hell's after her?'

'One's a South African; the other guy's an Arab.'

'What did she ever do to them?'

107

'A year ago she got mixed up with a separatist army in the Middle East — an outfit called the Patriotic Union of Kurdistan. These guys are in the States to make sure she doesn't tell anyone what she saw when she was on an assignment in Iraq.'

'So what did she see?'

'I'm not too sure yet,' Cogan said. 'I've made some phone calls and I'm due in Washington tomorrow.'

'We're still talking about international air accidents, right?'

'I'll know more in a day or two. The main thing is that nothing happens to her while I'm away.'

'Hose her down and take her with you,' Brady said. 'She might even come across if you treat her nice.'

'I don't want her hanging around air terminals. She'll be fine as long as there's someone she can get hold of in case of trouble.'

'You've got the wrong guy. I'm a wildlife ranger — remember? Try the State Police or the FBI.'

'I can't.' Cogan looked at him. 'You don't need to know why.'

'If you want a favour out of me, I do.'

'OK. But this is between us — nobody else.' Cogan had used his drive from

Savannah to rehearse what he was going to say. He began talking, providing enough detail to support his request for Brady's help, touching only briefly on what had happened to Sara in New York and by-passing the events that had taken place in the swamp. Although it took him nearly a quarter of an hour and another five minutes to answer questions, by the end of the exercise he'd begun to realize that it had served another purpose. Talking to someone else had clarified some of the muddle, and as well as feeling more confident about his decision to arrange a safety-net for Sara, he was finding it easier to plan his approach for tomorrow when his audience would be rather different to the one he'd had today.

He accompanied Brady to his car, said goodbye and returned to the lay-by, staying there for a while watching the river before he started out on his sixty mile drive back to Savannah where he hoped Sara would be waiting.

★ ★ ★

She met him at the door of their motel unit, shoeless, wearing a white blouse, a knee-length yellow skirt and black stockings.

'I went out and spent some more of your

money.' She twirled round. 'What do you think?'

Cogan knew the question was a red herring, a way for her to avoid asking him about his trip. 'Great,' he said. 'Not the sort of thing you'd want to wear in the swamp, though.'

She wrinkled her nose at him. 'I bought the stockings because I've seen how people stare at me — you know, because of the tannin stains.'

She believed it, he realized. She honestly believed it was the stains. 'Don't you want to hear how I got on?' he asked.

'I suppose. Shall I fix you a sandwich or something?'

'No. I'm OK.' He followed her inside. 'Brady was pretty good — well, he was, after I'd told him I wouldn't be away more than a couple of days. He says all you have to do is phone him day or night. There's a Mrs Brady too, so don't be surprised if she answers if you have to call.'

'I won't be calling anyone.'

'Fine.' Cogan was in no mood to argue. 'Now, look, I don't want you going out by yourself while I'm gone,' he said.

'Van Reenan and Khadim won't be anywhere around here. Why should they be?'

'Just stay in the motel until I get back, OK?

With any luck, it might only take a day.'

'I haven't decided whether to stop you going yet.' She sat down on the edge of the bed and swung her legs. 'What if these people you've faxed want to talk to me?'

'They won't. All I'm going to do is push some buttons. Once the US gets decent satellite coverage, everyone'll forget about you.'

'The quarry won't show anything in satellite photos. I've already told you that. If the complex could be seen from the air the US or the United Nations would already know about it. They'd have bombed it in 1998, wouldn't they?'

'No one's been looking for a laser base,' Cogan said. 'There hasn't been any reason to — not until now.'

'You're assuming they'll believe you.' She paused. 'Do you really think Iraq could be using an airborne laser as some kind of terrorist weapon?'

'Who knows? A friend of mine in London is faxing a whole bunch of stuff through to my hotel in Washington, and if I can get on the FAA computer for a couple of hours I'll have a better idea. I need to put myself through a quick course on laser technology so I can figure out what high-output oxygen pumps are used for and why anyone would target a laser on a stationary missile.'

'What are you going to say about Van Reenan?'

'Nothing.'

'If you don't mention him or the man who tried to throttle me in New York, why should anyone believe that Iraqi Intelligence have people from South Africa working for them?'

'I don't much care what Washington believes as long as they get the bastards off your back.'

'The whole idea's crazy,' she said. 'The US aren't going to launch another air strike against a quarry in Iraq just because you want them to. All the while the West's trying to destroy Iraq's chemical and biological weapons, they're not likely to bother much about lasers, are they?'

'Depends whether Saddam's been using one like Peter Kennedy thought. Don't forget it's a hell of a lot easier to take out a quarry than a biological plant. You don't scatter thousands of litres of anthrax spores in the air by destroying a quarry. Anyway that's not the point. All we need is for the US to find the place. Once Iraq knows their security's blown, they'll lose interest in you right away.'

'Perhaps you'll lose interest in me too.' She put her hands behind her head. 'When I was a little girl I used to think that if anything good ever happened, something bad would come along to cancel it out. Since I've met you I've started thinking the same way again.'

'And?' Cogan said.

'Well, if I begin with my parents sending me to live with my uncle, I get no good things and lots of bad ones — you know, having to drop out of college, Iraq, Catherine and what happened when I got back. If I start with Peter Kennedy writing to you, it's a bit better. When we were at the cabin together I even thought I might be winning for a change, but that was before Jeremiah was killed. I knew something would go wrong. It always does. People say you have to make your own luck, but it doesn't work for me.' She hesitated for a moment. 'You think I've gone all cold, don't you? But I haven't. It's just that as soon as I start feeling happy I get screwed up inside.'

'Because you're frightened of being happy?' Cogan spoke quietly.

She nodded. 'And I'm not sure we'd have made love if I hadn't asked you. I don't even know what you really want from me.'

'Why do you think I'm going to Washington?'

'How about because you've got yourself so interested in what Catherine and I tripped over in Iraq?'

'All right.' Cogan had guessed where this

113

was leading. 'What do you want me to say?'

'You could try being nice. I bought the blouse and skirt for you.'

'I'll tell you what,' Cogan said. 'Seeing as you have to take me to the airport bright and early in the morning, suppose we spend the rest of today building up some credit for you?'

'I don't understand what you mean.'

'Your backlog of bad things. You need to cancel out as many as you can, don't you think?'

'Oh.' She raised her eyebrows and adopted her southern accent. 'I do believe you have me at a disadvantage, sir. Whatever can you have in mind?'

To make his intentions clear, he pushed her back onto the bed and slowly slid a hand under her skirt.

She pretended to resist, holding her legs together, turning her face away when he tried to kiss her and refusing to let him unbutton her blouse. But in the end she was betrayed by her own desire.

Unable to maintain the pretence, she surrendered suddenly, returning his kisses while she drew up her legs and helped him slip off her blouse.

For Cogan this was less of a beginning than a continuation of the night when they had last

114

made love. She was as willing as before, but this time, like him, eager to prolong their enjoyment of each other, wriggling away if he became too demanding, rewarding him with her mouth and her body only when he slowed down or gave her pleasure in the way she wanted.

Soon she was naked but for the skirt around her waist, pressing her breasts against him, her mouth on his mouth, allowing him to explore her between her thighs while she held him with both hands and arched her back to receive him. Even then there was the same unspoken understanding. Instead of urgency there was a shared invitation to linger, an acknowledgement that the longer they could extend their pleasure, the more intense it would become.

Twice she slipped from beneath him, first to lie on her side and then to sit upright upon him so she could control what he did and how he did it. Eyes closed, her mouth partly open, she waited for him to move before she moved, stopping him gently whenever she began to tremble or felt him responding too quickly to her rhythm.

And so they spent their afternoon together, a few uninterrupted, self-indulgent hours in a motel room in Savannah where the outside world could be forgotten and where, for a while, Cogan could put his doubts aside. But in the days to come, his recollections of this afternoon would all be spoiled, overridden by his memory of her standing forlorn and lonely at the airport, her hand half-raised as she waved goodbye to him.

★ ★ ★

The venue and the early scheduling of the meeting had caught Cogan short on time and ill-prepared. He'd been in the Pentagon on a previous occasion, but not in this wing or on this floor where the decor was more impressive than it was in the parts of the building he'd seen before. The air-conditioning, though, was as he remembered it, producing a stale, stuffy atmosphere which wasn't helping him to think.

The woman at the desk coughed politely. 'Are you certain you wouldn't like some coffee?' she asked.

'I'm fine, thanks.' He was too busy to look at her, thumbing through the papers on his lap to locate the research report on military applications. He had seven reports altogether; three from the Massachusetts Institute of Technology, two from the Centre for Science and International Affairs at Harvard and the rest from Cambridge University — all except one of them dealing with the science of infrared lasers rather than their use as practical long-range weapons. As a consequence, despite having spent the whole morning reading in his hotel, he was still conscious of being vulnerable if someone asked an awkward technical question.

He was less than a third of the way through the report when a buzzer sounded behind the desk.

'Mr Cogan.' The woman smiled at him. 'That's you. Go right on in.'

There were four people in the room, three men and a woman sitting around a glass-topped rosewood table.

One of the men stood up. He was in his late fifties with bushy eyebrows and silver-grey hair. 'Mr Cogan,' he said. 'I'm so pleased you could come. I'm Charles Greenwald from the US Defense Intelligence Agency.'

Cogan shook hands with him, trying to assess how receptive the other people in the room were going to be.

'Now then,' Greenwald said. 'First let me introduce you to Madeline Isaacs. Madeline is an associate administrator at the National Transportation Safety Board with responsibilities for civil aviation security in the Middle East. Terry Reed sitting over there is from the State Department, and this rather sleepy-looking gentleman is Richard Dowell who has kindly agreed to join us, although I'm afraid he can't stay very long. When he's not overseas, Richard hides in one of the upstairs offices of Special Operation Command.'

Because no one else offered to shake hands, Cogan nodded his hello across the table, aware of what he thought was indifference from the woman.

'Please do have a chair, then we can begin.' Greenwald sat down and opened a folder. 'Well, let me see now,' he said. 'As I understand it, you've recently been in Atlanta presenting a paper at a conference on air safety.'

'Right,' Cogan said.

'And you've contacted us through people you know in the NTSB — because you believe the US Administration may be unaware of a weapon development programme that you say is taking place somewhere in Iraq.'

'I explained that in the fax I sent.'

'Yes indeed. I'm sorry if our initial reaction was a little low key. Since half the population of the United States has started being abducted by aliens I'm afraid we've become fairly jaded about the authenticity of reports from the general public. In your case, however, we felt obliged to at least listen to what you have to say. You have in the past, I believe, acted as a consultant to the NTSB for the specialized analysis of aircraft wreckage.'

'I worked on TWA 800 and on a couple of US military aircraft crashes.'

'So I'm told.' Greenwald withdrew a sheet of paper from his folder. 'But we're not here to discuss air accidents, are we? According to this information you've provided, you have evidence that the Iraqi Government is engaged in the development of what you call a high-energy, oxygen-iodine laser for airborne use, and that, in your opinion, such a weapon poses a potential security threat to allied aircraft in the Middle East.'

'Not necessarily just in the Middle East,' Cogan said. 'You can fly an airborne laser to anywhere you like.'

'I think we'd know if Baghdad was operating where they shouldn't be.' Greenwald smiled politely. 'But then you're not suggesting aircraft are actually being shot down by tactical Iraqi oxygen-iodine lasers, are you?'

'I have no idea. What I do know is that for the last six years the US has been working to develop the very same system. The British are trying too — so are the French. But it looks like the Iraqis won the race.'

'Are you familiar with the technical difficulties that have to be overcome?' The man Reed from the State Department asked the question. He was twirling a pen between his fingers and sounded slightly patronizing.

'Some of them.' Cogan looked at him directly. 'There's plenty of unclassified literature around. The worst problem is inaccuracy caused by air turbulence and varying air density in the atmosphere which deflects laser beams over long ranges. To hit a target in the right place with a high-powered infrared beam you have to employ adaptive optics or flexible mirrors to continuously distort the shape of the laser's wave-front. Airborne systems have much better accuracy because air turbulence reduces with altitude, but the systems still have to be enhanced by some means or other. The US do it by illuminating the target with low-powered reference beams first. That provides data on atmospheric conditions so the optics can be adjusted before the main, high-powered laser discharges.'

'I see.' Reed had stopped playing with his pen.

'The US system is supposed to work pretty well,' Cogan said. 'The last test of the Mid-Infrared Advanced Chemical Laser was carried out in the Pacific over a range of three hundred miles at an altitude of nine thousand feet. It generated a beam of more than two million watts for nearly five seconds.'

'Really,' Reed said. 'But, of course, that doesn't explain why anyone would want to evaluate the effectiveness of a high-altitude airborne laser against a ground target, does it? If I interpret my briefing papers correctly, you seem to be claiming that you can produce witnesses who saw an Iraqi laser destroy a missile while it was still on its launch pad.'

'I'm not claiming anything. I just faxed you a summary of the facts. The missile was bolted to a gantry in a quarry. It wasn't supposed to take off. I think there's a perfectly good explanation for that.'

'Perhaps you'd care to share the explanation with us,' Reed said, 'or are you simply offering an opinion?'

'An opinion based on what I've read. I've got a report here describing how hard it is to focus or direct a laser beam onto the body of a missile in flight. Most tracking systems end up locking onto the hot exhaust plume from the rocket motor by mistake. The plume acts as an infrared beacon that can be three or four times longer than the missile itself. So if you want to find out how accurate your laser guidance system is against a solid airframe, you either have to test it against a live target or against one that looks like a live target.'

'Are you suggesting that what these people saw was in fact an experiment using a deliberately restrained missile as a substitute for a free-flight target?'

'Right,' Cogan said. 'A live test, but one that wouldn't attract a lot of attention.'

'I'm afraid it hasn't attracted any at all.' Reed began spreading out photographic prints on the tabletop. 'These are Lacrosse and KH-12 satellite reconnaissance shots of Iraq,' he said. 'They were taken less than a month ago and cover a two hundred mile strip of the country south of the 36th parallel. The oil pipeline you've described is clearly visible. The definition is good enough to identify individual houses in the village of Ba'iji, and I'm told that every stick and stone in the area is precisely where it should be. According to military intelligence, there is no evidence whatever of either an airstrip or an underground weapon development complex.'

Cogan didn't bother to examine the prints. 'The airstrip is a road,' he said. 'And the reason you build something underground is so it can't be photographed from high altitude. Satellite surveillance coverage isn't continuous and, without radar-imaging cameras, most satellites aren't too good in the dark or on cloudy days.'

'But you haven't seen the place yourself, have you?'

'I haven't seen an oxygen-iodine laser either.' Cogan kept his voice level. 'But I'm pretty sure they exist.'

'Yes, of course,' Greenwald interrupted. 'I'm sure Mr Reed is only trying to point out that we can find nothing which confirms the existence of a military installation in the region. I assure you we've been in touch with the UN monitors who are responsible for checking on such things in Iraq, and we've also asked the CIA for information which might substantiate what you've told us. You must understand that we really require more time and more data than you've given us so far.'

'What else do you need?' Cogan asked.

'Who exactly are these people you say were imprisoned at the complex?'

'Two American girls who were part of an explosives team sent in by the PUK to blow up the pipeline. They were the only people who got back alive. One of them was murdered in Alaska six months ago, the other one's still being hunted down because the Iraqis believe she's a threat to them.'

'Mr Cogan.' This time it was Madeline Isaacs who addressed him. 'When you say girls, are we to assume they were sixteen-year-olds? Or were they younger than that?'

Cogan's wariness turned into annoyance. 'They were young women,' he said. 'Does it matter?'

'When the credibility of your story relies on their statements, I think who they are matters a great deal, don't you?' The lady from the NTSB leaned back in her chair. She was straight-faced, ready to embark on a line of questioning that Cogan had hoped to avoid.

'OK,' he said. 'If you want to believe there isn't any underground laser development base . . . that's fine. But someone had better tell me why there's a South African gunman running around right here in the States trying to kill the last survivor of a failed raid on a pipeline in Iraq.'

'I don't think anyone in this room can answer you. I wish we could.' Greenwald busied himself by gathering up the satellite photos. 'Are you certain about the South African?'

'As certain as I can be. It's a pity he didn't come with me to say hello.'

The man from Special Operations left the table. He was amused, grinning at Reed and Greenwald, but ignoring the unsmiling

Madeline Isaacs. 'Well,' he said, 'We sure have made this a worthwhile trip for Mr Cogan, haven't we? First we ask him what he knows as though we're a bunch of weapon system experts, then we tell him he's talking crap because nothing shows up on our pretty pictures. He must be real pleased he took the trouble to let us know what's going on.'

Cogan had been to too many meetings to fall for the ploy. It was a set-up, he realized. Dowell was the good guy; Reed and the woman were supposed to be the doubters, and Greenwald was playing mediator — an orchestrated attempt at realism because the more realistic the meeting appeared to be, the more likely he was to disclose how much he knew and what he was expecting them to do about it.

'You'll have to excuse me.' On his way from the room, Dowell stopped by Cogan's chair. 'Don't get the wrong idea,' he said. 'People who work around here soak up so much information they forget what it's for. We're kind of slow when something like this lands in our laps. But I'll tell you, if Saddam's got his leg over us again, I want to know. Soon as I hear back from our UN monitors I'll be in touch with you. Then, if you're right about this quarry of yours, maybe we can give Baghdad another one of our little surprises.'

Cogan waited until Dowell had gone before he reopened the discussion. 'How many US aircraft have gone missing over the no-fly zone in the last year?' he asked.

'We lost a helicopter there a while ago,' Reed said. 'I haven't seen the report, but I'll make a point of it. If someone's been using a laser, would we be able to pick up evidence of it?'

'If you can find the right pieces and you know what the damage characteristics are like.' Cogan had decided to bring matters to a head. 'Look,' he said, 'I need to know whether you're going to follow up this information, or not.'

'Why do you need to know?' Madeline Isaacs asked.

'I've already told you: there's a young woman with her life at stake over this. All the time the Iraqi Government believe she can pinpoint the location of the quarry, she's in danger. Don't you care about her?'

'Has it occurred to you that we should perhaps be talking to the woman instead of you?'

'She's living in Seattle,' Cogan said. 'And she's scared.'

'All right.' Greenwald placed his palms on the table. 'I think we should assure Mr Cogan that the Defense Agency, the State

126

Department and the National Transportation Safety people will take this matter further by whatever means are necessary and with some degree of urgency as well. It seems to me that no matter how sketchy the data is, we can't afford to overlook any new weapon development by Baghdad — particularly if a tactical airborne laser has the offensive potential we all believe it might have. I'll arrange for more frequent satellite surveillance, radar coverage with a brief to follow up any signatures from Antonov 32 cargo aircraft overflying the region, and, Terry, perhaps you could ask the FBI in Seattle to see what protection they can provide this young woman with in the meantime.'

To safeguard Sara's position and to further conceal her identity, Cogan pre-empted the next question. 'Her name's Virginia Hamilton,' he said. 'All I have is a phone number for her, but I can get an address by calling her tonight.'

'That sounds excellent.' Greenwald was pleased. 'What's the best way for us to contact you? Are you off home to the UK, or will you be here in the States for a few more days yet?'

'There's some business I have to clear up in Atlanta,' Cogan said. 'And there's a guy I need to see in Chicago. I'll let you know where I'll be when I call to give you Virginia Hamilton's address. Is tomorrow OK?'

'Certainly. If I'm not in my office, either leave a message with my secretary, or speak to Madeline or Terry if you'd rather. Now, is there anything else you'd like to ask us before we all get on with what we have to do?'

'I don't think so.' So many questions were swirling around inside Cogan's head that he didn't trust himself to filter out the right ones. The meeting had ended precisely as he had predicted it would end — with a commitment that was as hollow as Greenwald's rhetoric — with a statement to search for something the US Government had no interest in finding because, in the aftermath of the 1998 bombing and in the present political climate, Baghdad was only a shadow of the menace it had once been to the West.

To show his appreciation, before he left he shook hands with Madeline Isaacs and Terry Reed, thanking them for their time and leaving two of his reports on laser technology behind at Greenwald's request for imaginary photocopying and wider distribution.

More irritated than he was disheartened, Cogan caught a taxi back to his hotel, using the journey to wind down, realizing now, that if his cynicism proved to be as well-founded as he thought it was, his problem with Sara had become more complicated.

To discover how obstinate or how co-operative she would be, after paying for the taxi and collecting his key from the hotel desk, he went straight to his room and placed a call to her.

She answered on the third ring, saying hello, but being careful not to give her name.

'It's me,' he said.

'How did it go?'

'OK.'

'Are they going to do something?'

'Yeah.' Cogan paused. 'I'll explain when I see you. I'm confirmed on the first flight out at seven-thirty tomorrow morning. Pick me up at the Savannah terminal about nine. I'll tell you all about it then.'

'I want to know now.'

'I'm pretty sure nothing's going to happen in a hurry, that's all. We're dealing with government departments.'

'If you don't tell me the truth, I'll go out and set fire to your rental car.'

'I am telling you the truth,' he said. 'I just got the feeling I was being given the run-around for some reason.'

'Well, isn't that a surprise? So what do we do now?'

'I haven't figured it out yet,' Cogan said. 'Except we're changing the plan. You're coming to London with me. It's what we should've done to start with. You'll be a whole lot safer there and I'll be able to keep an eye on you.'

'I can't. Have you forgotten I'm Shannon Lockhart? I don't have a social security card any more and I tore up my driver's licence and my passport months ago.'

'I haven't forgotten anything,' he said. 'Leave things to me, will you?'

'Why can't you come back tonight? Have you tried to book on a late flight?'

'I'm going to be busy. I need to phone my office in the UK and see if I can contact a guy I know who might be able to fix you up with a fresh passport in a hurry.'

'Did the people you saw this afternoon ask about me?'

'No,' Cogan said. 'Mostly they were trying to discover what I knew about laser weapon systems and if I could tell them where the quarry is. They had a whole bunch of satellite photos that didn't show anything.'

'But they are going to look harder now, aren't they?'

'A lot harder.' Like the other lies he'd told her, this one hadn't worked either. Her voice had gone flat and she sounded distant as though she was preparing to end the conversation.

'Listen,' he said, 'the longer you stay in the States, the more risk there is.'

'What you mean is that now you've done your big act in Washington you think you'd better do something about me — in case I spoil things for you somehow.'

'This isn't about you or me, it's about us.'

There was a silence of several seconds before she answered. 'You've never said that before.'

'Did I have to?'

'Yes.' She hesitated. 'No — I don't know.'

'OK,' Cogan said. 'I'll buy you breakfast in the morning. We can go to the place where they make those waffles.'

'Well, aren't you one to spoil a girl, Mr Cogan.' Her voice had brightened. 'I'll be sure to put on my best dress.'

'I'll see you tomorrow,' he said. 'Don't leave the unit after dark and lock the door before you go to bed.' He said goodbye to her and carefully replaced the receiver, aware that he'd been lucky to bring about the last-minute change in her mood. It was always the same, he thought; no sooner had she caught him off balance than a chance remark would suddenly turn her round. But this time she seemed to have fallen into her own trap and caught herself off balance.

To avoid worrying about her any further,

he ordered a sandwich from room service then spent the evening on the telephone, waiting until he was in bed before he allowed himself to examine the wisdom of what he was proposing to do. Wisdom wasn't involved, he decided. But if he was playing at being a white knight as she'd suggested, it was her fault for encouraging him, just as it was her fault that lately, whenever he tried to consider the future, it was hard to imagine one without her in it.

★   ★   ★

The terminal was congested with passengers from three commuter flights which had landed within a few minutes of each other. There was also a team of softball players who were milling around in the arrival area. They were throwing empty drink cans at each other and generally making it difficult for Cogan to pick out Sara among the crowd.

Believing he saw her by the door, he pushed his way over to find himself facing a pretty teenaged girl who smiled at him before she joined her mother outside at the kerb.

Sara was not outside the building. Nor, as far as he could determine when he returned inside, had he missed her somewhere between the baggage claim and the exit.

Telling himself she was simply late, he checked once more before going to a ticket counter where he asked if anyone had left a message for him. But no one had, and by now, with the time approaching 9.45, and with more passengers arriving in the terminal, Cogan knew something had gone seriously wrong.

He took the first taxi he could find, trying not to let his concern get out of hand, wasting nearly ten minutes on a fruitless detour to the waffle shop before directing the driver to the motel.

His rental car was still in the car-park, but the door to the unit was locked and there was no response when he called out her name. Instead, a housekeeper appeared at the door of the neighbouring unit where she'd been working — a large black woman wearing an apron and holding an armful of clean linen.

'Are you Mr Cogan?' she asked.

'Why? What's happened?'

'Your wife had to leave.' She took a key from her apron pocket and unlocked the door for him. 'There's a note for you.'

Cogan went in very slowly, refusing to believe the worst.

The room was filled with the scent of her. He could see her everywhere — sitting on the bed, laughing when she burned the toast, frowning at him every time he made fun of her, giving her imitation of the well-bred southern lady she had never wanted to be.

The note lay on the coffee-table, written on a single sheet of paper. He sat down to read it, willing himself to take in each line, but already knowing what it was going to say.

Cogan

I've spent half the night searching for the right words, but I can't find them, so I'm just writing down how I feel, and hope you'll understand why it is I have to go away.

Mostly it's because I won't let myself become a problem for you to solve, and because I'm frightened something terrible might happen to you like it did to Catherine and Jeremiah. I know you keep telling me it won't, but I care about you too much to take the risk, and I can't go on messing up your life the way I have done.

I don't think going to London with you is a good idea — in case things between us don't turn out the way we want them to. Perhaps I'm looking for another bad thing to happen to me — I don't know.

When I was at the PUK camp, Catherine

translated a poem from an old eighteenth-century Iraqi book she found in Erbil somewhere.

Except for this poem, there's nothing else I can give you to keep. It sort of describes how I've felt since I met you. I hope you like it:

When the river of your life you share,
One golden summer with your love,
Of the falcons from your past beware,
For they remain to hunt the dove.

I won't be at the cabin, or at my uncle's, or at my apartment in Brunswick, so please don't go looking. I can't bear the thought of you trying to find me.

I shall always remember how happy you made me, and I shall never forget how much I loved you.

Sara xxx

After Cogan had read the note three times, he read the poem again by itself. Then he went to the fridge, took out a full bottle of bourbon and systematically began to drink.

5

Cogan's London office was one of five on the ground floor of a building in Hammersmith that he shared with other tenants. He also shared the common problem of Bernie Waller. Bernie was the resident computer programmer, an unshaven, shabbily dressed young man with a pale complexion who spent his nights programming and his days talking to anyone who was foolish enough to leave their door open.

This morning he was sitting in Cogan's office with his feet on the desk.

'Go away,' Cogan said.

'Well, look who it is.' Bernie removed his feet, but made no attempt to vacate the chair. 'When did you get back?'

'Yesterday afternoon. Are you going through my mail?'

'This isn't mail. It's more stuff I got for you on lasers. How were those reports I faxed?'

'They were fine — thanks.'

'Did you know oxygen-iodine lasers generate up to two megawatts of power?' Bernie held up a science magazine with a picture of a light beam on the cover. 'That's like concentrating the heat from two million electric fucking fires on one spot. You wouldn't want to warm yourself up in front of one of those babies, would you?'

'No.' On his flight back to London, Cogan had compiled a list of things in which he'd decided to take no further interest. Sara Hamaid was one. Lasers were another.

Unfortunately Bernie hadn't seen the list. 'Why did you need all that information?' he asked.

'I don't want to talk about it.' Cogan began sifting through the envelopes on his desk.

'OK.' Bernie relinquished the chair. 'It says here that you take a whole lot of hydrogen peroxide and mix it with chlorine to produce oxygen atoms which you pump into a cavity the size of a bread-box. Squirt in some iodine at the same time and you've got enough energy to light up half of London. All you do then is bounce the energy off mirrors inside the cavity to get a laser beam that's so powerful it'll burn through a piece of steel three hundred miles away.'

'Amazing,' Cogan grunted. 'Tell me about it another time.'

'We're talking here about oxygen being injected faster than the speed of sound,' Bernie said. 'Real shit-hot technology.'

Cogan's irritation was growing, aggravated

by the discovery of a letter saying his ex-wife was continuing to dispute the terms of the divorce settlement. What appeared to be better news was contained in another letter — this one from the Ministry of Defence. But before he could read it properly, he was interrupted again.

'Did you know why stars twinkle?' Bernie was studying the magazine. 'It's because of air turbulence. That's why lasers can't hit anything at long ranges. The beam gets distorted — so you have to use something called adaptive optics to adjust the shape of the mirrors in the bread-box. If you do that you can steer the beam.'

'Look,' Cogan said, 'I've been away for nearly three weeks, I'm tired, I'm pissed off and if you carry on talking about twinkling stars and bread-boxes, I'm going to ram that magazine down your throat.'

'OK. Let me know if you want me to pick you up some lunch.'

Cogan wasn't listening, too busy with the letter from the ministry to make sure Bernie left the room. The letter was dated yesterday and, at face value, too good to be true, offering him an eighteen-month contract to investigate the failure of unapproved helicopter parts in the UK aviation industry.

After angling for the job for nearly a year

he should have been pleased. Instead, as well as the letter being an anti-climax, Cogan was suspicious. The timing was too much of a coincidence, and the money was too good. Because the UK had joined forces with the US to buy him off? he wondered. Or was he jumping to conclusions? He didn't know, nor in his present frame of mind was he much inclined to care.

Despite the job offer he felt disillusioned and restless, no more willing to readjust to office life than he was to remember the events that had brought him back to London.

The reason for his restlessness was not in doubt: it was Sara. She was the reason he'd gone to Alaska, to Brunswick, to Savannah and to Washington. And, in the end, she was the reason he was back here with nothing except a damn poem to remind him of her, and of what had happened between them.

Taking her note from his pocket he laid it on the desk beside the letter from his solicitor. Then he tore them up, reducing both pieces of paper to tiny scraps before he settled back in his chair to consider his options and to see if he could pretend that the falcons in Sara's poem were no more real than she herself had been.

★ ★ ★

The phone call came late on Friday afternoon at the end of his second day at the office. It was from a woman asking if she could speak to a Mr James Cogan.

'That's me,' he said.

'Oh, good. Mr Cogan, my name's Elizabeth Rawlins. I work for *International Aviation* magazine, and I'd very much like to discuss the possibility of you writing another piece for us.'

'How soon do you want it?' he asked.

'I was wondering if we could talk somewhere?'

'Now, you mean?' He tried to sound enthusiastic. 'Today?'

'Well, yes. There's a restaurant in Kew Gardens. I thought perhaps we could meet there. Would that be all right?'

'OK,' he said. 'How about five-thirty?'

'That's lovely. Thank you — goodbye.'

Because Cogan had no interest whatsoever in writing an article about anything for anyone, if she'd been more pushy he would have turned her down. But she'd sounded reasonable enough, and the diversion would help shorten another evening at home at his flat — or at least provide him with something fresh to think about.

He left at five, putting his head round Bernie's door on the way out.

'Are you busy?' Cogan asked.

'Depends.' Bernie's eyes remained fixed on his computer screen. 'Some outfit in Watford had their invoicing programme turn to shit overnight. I said I'd have it fixed by Monday. What do you need?'

'There's an oil pipeline that runs north out of Iraq into Turkey. It goes past a place called Ba'iji and joins up with the main Dortyol line inside the Turkish border. Could you see what you can dig up on it for me?'

'Has it got something to do with that laser stuff?'

'I'm just wrapping up the project,' Cogan said. 'If you can't find anything it doesn't matter — don't go overboard.' Already he wished he hadn't asked, aware that he was making a mistake.

'Do you want me to call you at home if I get some hits?' Bernie glanced up. 'Or have you got plans for the weekend?'

Since leaving the US, Cogan had adopted a policy of zero planning, but he resisted the temptation to explain, going straight out to his car instead, only to spend the next forty minutes locked in traffic that was barely moving. As a result, by the time he reached the restaurant, if Elizabeth Rawlins had ever been there, she had evidently decided not to wait. It was, Cogan thought, the way things were going lately.

He drove the Volvo slowly back across the bridge, staying on the ring-road for most of his journey home to Hampstead, endeavouring to keep his mind unfocused for as long as possible.

The partly open door to his flat was the first indication that he had a visitor, and a note lying in the hallway confirmed that his visitor was still here. The note was written in black pen:

PLEASE DON'T BE SURPRISED AND
PLEASE DON'T SAY ANYTHING

Cogan picked up the note and took it with him into the lounge to find a young woman standing by the window. She was about thirty with short blond hair, wearing a tailored trouser-suit and flat-heeled shoes.

The moment she saw him she put a finger to her lips, pointing to the table where the telephone receiver was lying on its side in pieces.

She used the tip of a pencil to show him a small, plastic-encapsulated bead that had been taped inside the mouthpiece, then went across to his bookcase and knelt down to point again. The second bug was larger than the one in the phone, nearly half an inch long, attached with adhesive to the underside of the top shelf.

Cogan reached out, intending to remove it, but changed his mind when she shook her head. He was thinking hard now, trying to decide who she might be, what she was doing in his flat and who had been here before her.

As if to answer his questions, she took a notepad from her briefcase and scribbled down another message:

YOU WERE FOLLOWED TO KEW GARDENS. AS LONG AS THERE ISN'T A BLUE ROVER OUTSIDE, CAN WE GO SOMEWHERE TO TALK?

If there was a blue Rover parked in the street, Cogan couldn't see it from the window. Nor could he see anything else that looked out of place or suspicious. He was intrigued, anxious to learn what was going on.

She collected her case and followed him to the door, remaining silent until she was outside walking with him to his car.

'I'm sorry for letting myself into your flat like that,' she said. 'I hope you don't mind.'

'I do mind,' Cogan said. 'Who are you?'

143

'Elizabeth Rawlins.'

'Like hell you are. Magazine editors don't pick locks.'

'I didn't want to use my real name on the phone — in case your office is bugged as well. I'm Judith Safrai.'

Cogan got into the Volvo and waited for her to slip into the passenger seat. 'How do you know someone followed me to the restaurant?' he said.

'I saw them. That's why I didn't stay. I thought it'd be safer to go to your flat.'

'So you could check the place over?' He pushed the car out into the traffic, heading for nowhere in particular while he collected his thoughts. Whoever she was, he knew she wasn't English. She spoke with a slight but discernible American accent mixed with something else he couldn't recognize.

'Where do you want to go?' he asked.

'I have a place in Richmond. We could go there if that's all right. I just need somewhere to explain.'

'About what?'

'Perhaps this will help.' She handed him a wallet containing a small plastic card.

On one side of the card, beneath the embossed insignia of the Israeli Government, were her photograph, her name and a number. The reverse side identified her as a member of MOSSAD, Israel's military intelligence agency.

Surprised though he was, Cogan's reaction was one of caution, knowing that the puzzle had acquired a new dimension, but equally aware that the need for him to solve it had disappeared several days ago.

He gave the wallet back to her, waiting until he'd stopped for a red light before he studied her more carefully. She was quite attractive, with light-brown eyes, unusually high cheek-bones and a mouth not unlike Sara's, but spoilt by the high-gloss lipstick she was wearing.

'You're a long way from home,' he said. 'What's this about?'

'My government has a problem we'd like to discuss with you.'

'I've got enough problems of my own, thanks.'

She smiled politely. 'Can you find your way to Richmond? I can't explain properly until you've made sure I am who I say I am. It's procedure.'

Cogan didn't reply, swinging the car south, telling himself he'd better hear what she had to say if only to learn what the hell she wanted. He concentrated on his driving, containing his curiosity until they reached the house in Richmond where she adopted the unconvincing role of hostess.

The house was one of several at the end of a cul-de-sac on the east side of the park, an expensive home that was clearly not her own. She was unfamiliar with it, giving him the wrong directions for the toilet and having to apologize when she discovered there was nothing but American beer in the fridge.

'It's OK,' he said. 'It's fine.'

'The house belongs to the embassy and I only got here the day before yesterday. I wasn't expecting anybody round.' She passed him the phone book. 'If we could get this bit over with we can talk in the garden.'

'The procedure bit?'

'Yes. You're supposed to look up the number of the embassy yourself, then call them, give your name and ask for a class-two identification for Judith Safrai.'

'Tell me why I should bother.' Cogan looked at her. 'Maybe we're wasting each other's time.'

'Lasers,' she said. 'And someone called Virginia Hamilton.'

Against his better judgement, Cogan found the number, placed the call and spent the next few minutes speaking to a pleasant-sounding gentleman who reeled off a list of characteristics that could have applied to any young woman with short blond hair.

She waited for Cogan to hang up before she went to find a glass for his beer. 'What did they say?' she asked.

'Not a lot.' He left the glass, taking the can from her. 'Who told you about Virginia Hamilton?'

'The garden's through there.' She led him out onto a patio where there were table and chairs. 'It's best if I start somewhere else. Please sit down.'

Cogan didn't want to sit down. He leaned back against the wall of the house, drinking his beer, thinking of another evening — of another place far away where, in place of row upon row of houses and the incessant noise of traffic, there had been nothing but a tiny plywood cabin and the reassuring croak of frogs.

'Four days ago I was on holiday in Israel,' she said, 'visiting my family in Tel Aviv. I'm a field agent so I hardly ever get home. It was the first time I'd seen my mother and father for over a year.'

'You can skip the introduction,' Cogan said. 'What do you want?'

'I'm here to see if you'd be kind enough to put me in touch with Miss Hamilton. My government believes an introduction would be of benefit to her as well as us, and I've been asked to say that we'd be very grateful

147

for any help you can give us.'

'Did anyone tell you how much I charge an hour?'

'Oh.' Her expression changed. 'No. I can get authorization, though. Well, it depends. How much . . . ?' Her voice tailed off.

Cogan had intended to slow her down, but he hadn't meant to be rude. 'I'm not interested in your money,' he said. 'How did you get my name?'

'I have to explain some things first. Do you know anything about the international agreement between Turkey and Israel?'

'No.'

'It was drawn up two years ago to help the economies and the security of both countries by increasing trade and military co-operation. Since it was signed, Israel's been given a contract to refit fifty-four American-made F4 Phantom jets for the Turkish Air Force, and the annual trade between Turkey and Israel is running at over a billion US dollars.'

'Are you sure I need to know all this?' Cogan said.

'Yes, I am. You have to understand that the main strategic advantage to Israel comes from the permission we have to overfly Turkish airspace. Israel has hardly any airspace of its own, and with countries like Syria and Jordan right on our doorstep, airborne military intelligence is really crucial. Turkey is the only Arab country we can do business with.'

'While they're busy buying oil from Iraq,' Cogan said. 'When the Iraqis flush out their pipelines.'

'This has nothing to do with oil. It's about terrorism — about an Israeli Kfir combat jet that was shot down on a training mission in Turkey sixteen months ago — well, that's when the problem began. There were no other aircraft in the area, Turkish radar didn't pick up any foreign echoes, and the pilot didn't see anything either.'

'Did he eject?'

She nodded. 'He said he could've been hit by ground fire, or suffered some kind of catastrophic engine failure, but there was no evidence in the wreckage. We had an analyst look at the turbine rotors and the wing and fuselage sections we recovered.'

'Who did you use?' Cogan asked.

'Someone from the US National Transportation Safety Board.' She paused. 'There wasn't any obvious damage from gunfire, or shrapnel, or a missile strike.'

'How about high-temperature burns?' Cogan was ahead of her, imagining an Antonov 32 cruising along just outside the no-fly zone at 20,000 feet on a cloudless day, looking for an unsuspecting target in another country.

'Can I tell you about the other crashes?'

'Same sort of thing?'

She nodded. 'Almost. A second one in Turkey last November, and another that we think was from an identical cause in January this year, although it happened out at sea over the Mediterranean. They were both F–16s. Then, two months ago, we nearly lost a civilian aircraft on an internal flight. It landed at Haifa with half its tail-plane missing. The pilot was unbelievably lucky — so were the passengers.'

'So were you.' Cogan had a good idea where this was leading. 'Because it was the first chance your people had to check out the damage on a plane that hadn't disintegrated in mid-air.' He put his beer can on the table. 'And you're going to tell me it looked as though someone had taken a welding torch to the tail, right?'

'Haifa's over two hundred and thirty miles from the Iraqi border,' she said quietly. 'The F–16 that went down at sea was even further away — seventy miles further away. According to our physicists it's impossible for a tactical laser to operate at anything like that range.'

'Or to hit a target if it could,' Cogan said.

'But all of a sudden someone's decided that maybe your physicists are wrong.'

'Two days ago we weren't sure: now we are.' She cleared her throat. 'You must have some idea why that is.'

This time she had the advantage. Cogan didn't have any idea at all. 'What makes you think it was a laser?' he asked.

'Last week Tel Aviv received a coded message from the Israeli Embassy in Washington. It said the CIA were taking over from the NTSB and that we should forget about any further help from the US and redirect our investigations by contacting someone called James Cogan in London. A day later, Tel Aviv had a copy of the information you presented to a meeting at the Pentagon on 22 June.'

'How the hell did you get hold of that?'

'Israel has friends in many places, Mr Cogan. The person who provided it believes the CIA are not acting in the best interests of the US, or Israel, or the wider international community.'

'There were only four people at the meeting,' Cogan said. 'Am I supposed to guess who your friend is?'

'I can't very well say, can I?' She turned her attention to the garden. 'It would be a violation of security, and we're not prepared to jeopardize her position.'

Cogan managed to stop himself from saying anything. By using a deliberate slip of her tongue to reveal who the informant was, Judith Safrai was asking him to respect her confidence, hoping he wouldn't ask again. It was ironic, he thought. The last person he would have expected to leak information was Madeline Isaacs — the only woman at the meeting, and the most hostile of the people there.

'OK,' he said. 'Do you know why the US suddenly decided to stop helping you?'

'Probably because they're afraid Israel might stir up more trouble in the Middle East. The West has learned to live perfectly well without Iraqi oil, and the US and its allies have nothing to gain from an Israeli confrontation with Baghdad — especially if it's over a weapon system that's being developed for defensive purposes — or what the US wants to pretend are defensive purposes.'

'Why would they pretend that?'

'I've just said — so no one makes waves. After the 1998 débâcle over access for UN weapons inspections in Iraq, just about the whole of the Arab world aligned itself against the Americans. Ever since then the US have been trying to recover lost ground. It's even possible they believe an Iraqi laser has no real offensive potential. At your meeting at the Pentagon you said two girls saw a test against a stationary missile. The West isn't going to get excited about a weapon that's designed to destroy a Scud missile in a quarry somewhere. We're not talking about nuclear warheads or nerve gas.'

'What about the aircraft you've lost?' Cogan said. 'Didn't that sound any alarm bells in the States?'

'We can't prove our planes were attacked with an infrared laser. Even if we could, it's too late now the CIA have thrown a blanket over everything.'

'Which is why you've been sent to see me?'

'Yes,' she nodded. 'Can I get you another beer?'

'Let's get this done with. Are you expecting me to tell you where the quarry is?'

'I thought the only person who could do that was Miss Hamilton.'

'She doesn't know.'

'Mr Cogan, I'm not a metallurgist and I couldn't tell the difference between an oxygen-iodine laser and a rocket launcher, but one thing I know a lot about is the Patriotic Union of Kurdistan. If the PUK sent her to destroy a pipeline in Iraq, I assure you she knew precisely where she was going and precisely where she was at every moment of every day she was south of the 36th parallel.'

'Half her damn team were killed in a minefield,' Cogan said. 'The rest of them were taken to the quarry by Iraqi Republican Guards and shot.'

'Is that what she told you?'

'It's what happened.' He paused. 'You want to find the place so Israel can bomb the living shit out of it, right?'

'I didn't say that.'

'What makes you think I'd want to help you?'

She picked up his empty beer can and inspected the label. 'You said one of the American girls is already dead and that the other one is in danger. And now you've come back from the States to find your flat's been bugged. Hasn't it occurred to you that you might be in danger too?'

'From who?' Cogan didn't need her to remind him of the cut across his chest or the sound of bullets ricocheting off the skidder.

'You know who, but you mightn't know all the reasons why.'

'You can tell me why South Africa's involved,' Cogan said. 'If they are.'

'They are indeed. We got our first hint of it about three and a half years ago, after we learned that the South African-controlled

154

state company of Armscor was supplying Iraq with incredibly accurate mirrors made from single silicate crystals.'

'Laser mirrors,' Cogan said.

'Yes. But mirrors are only the tip of the iceberg. After sanctions were lifted in South Africa, Armscor was restructured into a profit-making organization called Denel. The first thing Denel did was to start selling high-technology tank fire-control systems to Syria. When the US heard about it the deal was temporarily stopped, but there were other deals that carried on.'

'So South Africa is still selling equipment to Iraq.'

'Yes, but under enormous secrecy in case the US finds out. You see, the US is pledged to provide the South African Government with aid worth over a hundred million dollars. If anyone ever discovers that South Africa is supplying Iraq with weapon-system technology, the US will cancel their aid package overnight. South Africa won't let that happen — nor will Iraq. Between them they'll do absolutely anything to protect the deal. I think you've already seen how they operate.'

Another piece of the puzzle had slipped into place. The connection between Van Reenan and Khadim was clearer now, and the nationality of Sara's attacker in New York was not the mystery it had been before. But Cogan was neither pleased nor displeased. He felt uninvolved, too far removed from the power struggle in the Middle East to be bothered with it.

'You've got the wrong idea about me,' he said. 'If Baghdad or Pretoria thought I was a problem they'd have done something to fix it before now. And if they want to eavesdrop on my phone calls, that's fine. They won't learn anything because I don't know anything.'

'They want what my government wants — Virginia Hamilton. Will you tell me how I can find her?'

'No.'

'Is she still in Seattle?'

Cogan checked his watch. 'I can't help you,' he said. 'Get someone else or leave things to the US.'

'But you don't believe the Americans will do anything, do you?'

'I don't care whether they do or not.' He stretched. 'I'd better get going. Thanks for finding those bugs in my flat, and for the beer.'

'No, please — wait.' She stood in front of him. 'I haven't explained this at all well. Can't you at least give me the girl's phone number — please?'

'It wouldn't be any use to you.' Cogan

waited for her to move aside.

'If you're not interested in money, what else is there?'

'What do you mean?'

'I just thought — ' She hesitated for a second. 'It's a long way for you to go home, and it's late. You're welcome to stay if you'd like to.'

Cogan felt sorry for her. She'd managed to control her voice, but her cheeks were burning. 'You're trying too hard,' he said. 'There isn't any Virginia Hamilton. Go back to Tel Aviv, finish your holiday and find someone you really want to go to bed with.'

'I didn't say I'd sleep with you.' She allowed him to push past. 'You're lying, aren't you?'

'Yeah, I'm lying. So are the Iraqis, the South Africans and the Americans. And for all I know, so are you. Have a nice assignment. Goodnight.' Leaving her alone on the patio, he let himself out of the house and walked slowly to his car.

The evening had been largely wasted, Cogan thought. Except for confirming the existence of the laser base and explaining why Sara's falcons had been so determined, nothing had changed, and any attempt to solve what remained of the puzzle would be as purposeless as thinking about what might

157

have been. Judith Safrai had her problems and Cogan had his, and unless he made an effort to forget about the last few weeks, the muddle in his head would only get worse.

Telling himself that now was as good a time as any to cut his losses, on the drive back to his flat he made a detour into Hammersmith, intending to stop Bernie from gathering data on the pipeline and to throw away his paperwork on lasers.

He reached the office building shortly before eleven o'clock. Bernie's car was still in the car-park and the ground-floor lights were on, but the electronic lock on the front door was deactivated — either because Bernie was about to leave, or more likely, because he'd forgotten the door was supposed to be kept locked whenever anyone was working after dark.

Neither explanation was correct. Bernie was nowhere to be found, and Cogan's office resembled a rubbish tip.

The contents of his filing cabinets were strewn across the floor, the drawers of his desk stood upturned on the coffee table and, littering the room from one end to the other, were the drawings and reports he'd come to get rid of.

More worried about Bernie than he was about the shambles in his office, Cogan carried out a search, checking all of the other rooms before he heard a faint thumping noise coming from the toilet.

Bernie was in the second cubicle, roped securely to the cistern and wrapped very nearly from head to foot in adhesive tape. There was also a good deal of blood around, spattered over Bernie's shirt, matted in his hair and smeared across the floor.

Telling him to hang on, Cogan went to find some scissors, returning to cut first through the tape and then, with more difficulty, through the rope. When he'd finished he was relieved to see the blood was only coming from a cut on Bernie's head.

'Jesus.' Bernie stared at the floor. 'Is that mine?'

'I think so.' Cogan gave him a handful of paper towels. 'What happened?'

'What the hell does it look like? I'm downloading some stuff when this guy starts banging on the door.'

'What guy?' Cogan said.

'How would I know? I've never seen him before. He said he had a message from you so I let him in.'

'And he smacked you round the head.' Cogan inspected the bruise. It was the size of a golf ball, still weeping blood, but hardly life-threatening.

159

'The bastard must've hit me from behind. Next thing I know I wake up in the toilet bleeding to death with all that tape round me.'

'OK,' Cogan said. 'I'll clean you up a bit, then I'll run you home.'

'You're joking. Here I am with a fractured skull, and you give me pieces of fucking tissue. I'm not going home: I need a hospital.'

In any other circumstances Cogan would have been amused. Instead he was conscious of what felt very much like rage. It had been simmering all evening, fuelled by Judith Safrai's naïve assumption of his willingness to help her, and now by the trashing of his office and the unwarranted assault on Bernie.

Compared with what had happened in the swamp, Bernie had escaped lightly enough. But this wasn't the Okefenokee swamp — this was London, and when neither Jeremiah or Bernie had posed the slightest threat to the governments who had now turned their attention to Cogan, the time for him to lose his temper was overdue.

After making coffee and determining that Bernie's description of the intruder was too vague to be of any use, Cogan went back to his office.

Except for the letter from Peter Kennedy and a copy of his travel itinerary for the trip to Atlanta, he could discover nothing missing. Which made it worse, he thought, a mindless search for information he didn't have and had never wanted — the same overreaction by the men who had sent out Van Reenan and Khadim to hunt down Catherine and Sara.

'Hey.' Bernie was standing in the doorway. 'Have you phoned the police?'

'I will later. How do you feel?'

'Lousy, but I'll be OK to drive myself — do you want me to help you clear up?'

'I'll do it. You get on home. I'll call you in the morning.' Cogan escorted Bernie out of the building and watched him drive away before he switched off all the office lights, locked up and, for the second time tonight, started out on his own drive home.

It was raining when he turned into his street in Hampstead, prompting him to seek out a parking spot as close as possible to his flat.

But for the rain he wouldn't have been looking, and if he hadn't been looking he would never have seen the Rover. It was parked in shadow on the other side of the street a hundred yards from his front gate, a blue Rover with a figure of a man behind the wheel.

For Cogan it was the last straw — a trigger for the release of all his anger.

Leaving the Volvo's engine running, he got out armed with a jack handle and approached the Rover from the rear.

The driver was sleepy, struggling to wake up now he could see someone outside, but failing to react in time.

Cogan directed his first blow at the windshield, swinging the jack handle with all his strength to shatter the glass. His second blow destroyed the side window, allowing him to reach in and grab the driver.

For a second Cogan almost had him, using both hands to force the jack handle hard against the man's throat before beginning to haul him bodily out of what remained of the window.

The driver was stronger than he looked. He fought silently, choking on the steel bar, but suddenly slipping free to reach inside his jacket.

Instinctively Cogan released his grip on the bar, backing away from the muzzle of a gun. It was a short-barrelled revolver, pointing at his stomach, hammer drawn, less than six feet away from him.

But instead of squeezing the trigger, the man started his car with the obvious intention of running Cogan down.

He was just able to spring aside before the jack handle came flying out the window and the Rover grazed his hip.

Had he stopped to think, he could have chosen to let it go, but by now he was committed, remembering Jeremiah trying to repel bullets with his hands, seeing Sara lying white-faced on the creek-bank and remembering how Van Reenan had hunted them through the swamp like a pair of frightened rats.

There had been other opportunities for Cogan to hit back, but never one this good. Before the Rover had reached the end of the street he'd sprinted back to the Volvo and put it into a slithering U-turn, spinning the tyres in the wet as he slammed the door and fumbled with the headlight switch.

He was 200 yards behind at the first roundabout, gaining on the Rover until the driver turned onto the A410 and overtook a small, white courier van on the brow of a rise. Cogan wasn't prepared to take the risk, tucking the Volvo in behind the van just long enough to make certain the road ahead was clear before he floored the accelerator again.

He held the Volvo in third gear, taking the rev-counter needle into the red, confident now that the driver in front was unable to outrun him, determined one way or the other, gun or not, to force the bastard off the road.

But on a wet night in the dark, at speeds approaching eighty miles an hour, disaster was not long coming. Cogan was closing on the Rover fast, changing down for the Northwood intersection when the rattle of gravel warned him of impending danger.

He'd been slow to see the roadworks, but not as slow as the other driver who began to panic.

Instead of correcting for a slide, the driver of the Rover applied his brakes. And instead of trying to maintain a straight line, he attempted to take the corner.

Cogan was luckier. Under control but travelling at over sixty miles an hour on the wrong side of the road, he saw the Rover hit the kerb and become airborne.

As if in slow motion it began to flip end over end, flying through the air for nearly thirty feet before landing on its roof to recommence its slide.

Cogan watched the sparks — brilliant red streaks to accompany the awful sound of tearing metal. He could see petrol too, fountaining out of the ruptured fuel tank to spread across the road.

The driver was more fortunate than he deserved to be. Before the Rover finally smashed into a wall and came to a standstill upside down, the sparks had been extinguished by the rain, and there was no fire.

Leaving the Volvo in the centre of the intersection with its headlights directed at the wreckage, Cogan went to see if the driver was still alive. He was, but only just, hanging limply from the straps of his seat belt. Blood from his nostrils was dripping onto the pavement where part of the roof had been peeled away, and it looked as though his right arm had been fractured.

Of the revolver there was no sign, nor was the driver carrying a wallet or a driver's licence.

Cogan's investigation was cut short by the untimely arrival of the white courier van.

A long-haired youth at the wheel wound down his window, but made no effort to reduce the volume of his radio.

'Do you have a cellphone?' Cogan asked.

'Yeah. Body bag or ambulance?'

'Ambulance, and maybe some cutting equipment too.'

'OK.' The young man pushed buttons on his phone, giving directions to the Northwood crossroads while he leaned out of his window to shine a flashlight inside the Rover.

'Are they coming?' Cogan was watching the blood wash away in the rain.

'Ten minutes. Do you want a hand to pull him out?'

'No. I don't know how bad it is. I'll stay until someone gets here. Thanks for your help.'

'No sweat.' His good deed done, the driver waved a goodbye, leaving without expressing any further interest.

Cogan was half inclined to leave as well, reluctant to be interviewed as a witness, and only going to check out the Rover's glove compartment on a whim.

The search hardly seemed worthwhile until, among the jumble of sweet-wrappers, book-matches and empty cigarette packets, he found a card — a laminated plastic card not unlike another one he'd seen tonight.

He removed it carefully, guessing it belonged to the driver, but only realizing how profoundly he had misunderstood when he held it up in the Volvo's headlights.

The emblem was unmistakable: the eagle-crested heraldic shield and the multi-pointed star — an identity card issued not by any security organization in South Africa or Iraq, but by the Central Intelligence Agency of the United States.

6

In the little bar in Brunswick, Cogan had discovered that the consumption of alcohol was an unreliable way to dull his mind. After a similar failure in an empty motel room in Savannah, and another right here in his London flat last night, he wasn't sure it was worth trying again.

He wasn't sure of very much at all except, perhaps, for his headache and the need to dispose of a leaflet that had come through his letter-box this morning. The leaflet was advertising a new soft drink, an innocent slip of paper lying face-up on the mat in the hall where he'd been careful to leave it because of the picture on the cover — a picture of a pretty girl with a pony-tail and a yellow skirt.

He went to fetch it, taking it with him to the kitchen so he could study the illustration more closely. The girl was laughing, something Sara had done only twice in the whole time he'd known her and, pretty though she was, the girl was too tall and too real to be a pixie. She didn't have the right kind of eyes either; nor was there any discoloration of her skin — which meant she was nothing like

Sara, he told himself. Except that the longer he looked at the picture, the easier he found it to pretend she was.

His recollections of her had been with him for the whole weekend — since the incident with the Rover on Friday night when he'd stood out in the rain, gripping the identity card as though it was a hand-grenade — realizing that whatever Sara had become part of, it was more far-reaching than he had ever imagined.

Because of Friday night, Cogan had spent Saturday and most of Sunday either trying not to think of her or telling himself that conspiracy theories were mostly fabrications, and that if the CIA had decided to bug his phone, search his office and watch his flat, then there was nothing sinister about it — especially when Washington had been so uninterested in the existence of the quarry.

But he was no closer to deceiving himself now than when he'd started. That there was a conspiracy he had no doubt. And because his memories of Sara were as fresh today as they had been yesterday or this time last week, Cogan knew he was rapidly reaching the point where he had no choice but to implement his plan — an ill-formed plan with so many unknowns that if he thought about it analytically the chances of it working were fairly slim, but the only one he'd come up with that seemed to stand any chance at all.

To prepare himself he took two aspirins and drank another cup of coffee. Then, after checking to make certain the bug in the phone had not been removed, he placed a call to the Ministry of Defence and confirmed his acceptance of their offer.

His subsequent preparations were more extensive, involving half an hour in the shower, a change of clothes and a few minutes spent considering how best to present his proposal. By eleven o'clock, with his headache gone and in better spirits, he was ready to leave the flat.

As a precaution, to begin with he headed north in the Volvo, keeping an eye on his mirror until he was sure it was safe to change direction and embark on his drive to Richmond.

Judith Safrai was surprised to see him. She was wearing a cotton dress and had either forgotten to put on her make-up or decided not to bother.

Cogan thought she looked better without it. 'I ought to have phoned,' he said. 'But I didn't have your number.'

'I should have given it to you.' She opened the door wider. 'Come in, please.'

He followed her into the lounge. 'I figure

we might be able to do a deal after all,' he said.

'I see.' She was hesitant, unsure of herself, waiting for him to take the lead.

The lounge floor was littered in photographs — at least two dozen A4-sized prints scattered over the carpet.

'They're for you,' she said. 'I was going to mail them.'

He inspected one, a black and white shot of an aircraft's tail section.

'They came this morning,' she explained. 'A courier brought them from the embassy — because of the report I made over the weekend. I've been told to ask if you'll consider acting for us in a professional capacity. You know, to offer an opinion on whether you think Israeli aircraft have been damaged by a high-energy laser.'

'Does that mean you've given up on Virginia Hamilton?' Cogan asked.

'You said she doesn't exist — or that's what I thought you said.' She paused. 'Are you here to talk about her?'

'Remember that blue Rover you saw?'

She nodded.

'The driver was carrying this.' Cogan produced the identity card.

She took it from him, clearly disconcerted now she could see what it was.

'Looks like you've been on the wrong track,' he said. 'I think the CIA knows damn well what's going on in Iraq.'

She frowned. 'Why would they be watching you though? Why bug your flat?'

'Maybe they need a better fix on the location of the quarry and they think they can get it through me.'

'Or?'

'The reason you said — to make sure I don't make waves in the Middle East by approaching someone like you. The US knows they'll get the blame for any more outside intervention in Iraq whether or not they had anything to do with it. Washington isn't ready for that kind of trouble right now.'

'But you don't know any of that for certain, do you?' She looked at him. 'Or did you have a talk with the owner of this card?'

'He smashed himself up in an accident on Friday night — after someone turned my office inside out and banged a friend of mine around a bit.'

She raised her eyebrows. 'What an exciting weekend.'

'There's something else too. I've just been offered an eighteen-month government contract. Quite a coincidence, don't you think?'

'The CIA won't be operating in the UK without permission. They're trying to take you out of the system, that's all.' She gave him back the card. 'You still haven't said why you came.'

'You've got an assignment to do and there's a young woman in the States who can use all the help she can get. Perhaps the three of us should think about working together.'

'For what reason?'

Cogan smiled. 'Suppose the imaginary Virginia could show your people how to find the quarry? What would happen?'

'If she exists, and if she can, then Israel will take whatever steps are necessary to safeguard its aircraft and secure its airspace. But you said she doesn't know where the quarry is.'

'And you said she almost certainly does.' Cogan inspected another one of the photos. 'One of us is right and one of us is wrong.'

Instead of standing with her hands by her side as she had been, Judith Safrai had begun fiddling with the belt of her dress. 'Would she be willing to co-operate?'

'If I can make her understand it's the best chance she has of leading a halfway normal life. No one's going to be interested in her once the laser base is gone.'

'And what do you get out of this, Mr Cogan?'

'I'll think of something.'

'Why hasn't she told the US authorities what she knows?'

'It's a bit difficult,' Cogan said. 'She ran into a problem in New York — one she doesn't want to talk about.'

'We'll require a lot more information and I'll have to know who she really is. Are you prepared to tell me?'

'Do you want the whole story from start to finish?'

This time her smile was not so artificial. 'I think that would be a good idea,' she said. 'Why don't you talk while I make some lunch. I've been shopping since you were here last.'

Cogan accompanied her to the kitchen and sat down on a bar stool, waiting until she was slicing tomatoes and buttering bread before he started, explaining first how Peter Kennedy's letter had led him to Alaska and then to Georgia in his search for Catherine's friend. He left out little, outlining the reasons why Catherine and Sara had become recruits for the PUK before he went on to describe what had happened to them in Iraq and how, even after their return to the US, their nightmare had continued. He spent less time on the events in Georgia, providing her with an edited account of what had taken place at the motel and in the swamp, saying only that

173

he believed Van Reenan and Khadim would carry on hunting for Sara until they found her.

It wasn't until he'd finished speaking that Cogan saw she'd stopped making lunch. She was leaning against the kitchen table, holding a packet of butter in one hand and a slice of bread in the other, either expecting him to continue or, perhaps, trying to decide whether or not to believe what he'd told her.

'Now do you understand why I'm here?' he said.

'Yes, I do.' She began to butter the bread. 'Your friend Sara was lucky. The Mukhabarat don't make mistakes like that — nor do the Republican Guards. If they'd known she was an Arab, she wouldn't be alive.'

'Are you worried about her being an Arab?' Cogan hadn't missed the implication.

'The enemy of my enemy is my friend. Is that what you expect me to say?'

'I'm just asking.'

'Is she a Muslim?'

'Does it matter?' Cogan said.

'Why should it if you don't know where she is? You said she's disappeared.'

'I found her before so I can find her again. All I need is a bit of help from you.' He paused. 'Assuming you'll do business with someone like her.'

'What if we won't?'

'You and I have a nice lunch together, then you can fly back home to Tel Aviv and I can start my new job for the ministry.'

She busied herself with the sandwiches, saying nothing more until she handed him some plates and a jug of orange juice and asked him to carry them out onto the patio.

'You haven't told me what kind of help you want.' She sat down to face him across the table.

'A new passport for Sara, and large-print advertisements in the personal columns of half a dozen Georgia and South Carolina newspapers.'

'In return for which you'll persuade her to disclose the location of the Iraqi laser base to whoever we specify by whatever means she can. Is that what you're proposing?'

'Right.' Cogan helped himself to juice. 'And if she has to go south of the 36th parallel with some of your people because that's the only way she can find the quarry, I go with her, and you guarantee to get us out again in one piece.'

'Why would you want to go?'

'To ride shotgun. I've been knifed and shot at in Georgia, and jerked around in Washington and London. None of that's going to happen again — not to me, and not to Sara either. She isn't going anywhere by herself.'

'Does that mean you don't trust me or my government?'

'I'm not trusting anyone,' Cogan said. 'Are we going to see if we can make this work, or not?'

'I'll have to check.' She stood up. 'But I'm sure there won't be a problem getting approval for placing the adverts. I'll make a quick phone call while you decide what you want them to say.'

Her acceptance had come too easily, an indication perhaps that he'd underestimated her authority or misjudged the importance of the information he was offering. But so what? Cogan thought. When the alternatives were non-existent, what did it matter? He made himself forget about the plan, concentrating instead on his message for Sara, working on the wording until Judith Safrai returned.

'Everything OK?' he asked.

'I've got full permission to discuss your proposal.' She handed him a note-pad and a pencil. 'What's the advert?'

Cogan used capital letters, printing the words in the centre of the page for her:

SWAMP CHIPPY
MORE FALCONS THAN YOU THOUGHT.
URGENT YOU PHONE BRADY.

She read it over his shoulder. 'I don't understand,' she said.

'You don't have to.' He gave back her note-pad. 'It's for Sara. She'll know who it's from and what it means.'

'I realize she mustn't phone your flat, but she could call you here if that would be any help.'

'I won't be in London,' Cogan said. 'I'll be in Savannah.'

'Suppose she doesn't contact this man Brady?'

'If she sees the advert, she'll call him.' He wondered who he was trying to convince. 'I'd better tell him what's going on. Can I use your phone?'

'Of course.' She glanced at her watch. 'It's nine o'clock in the morning on the US east coast. Is that all right?'

'Should be. I might catch him before he leaves for work.' Leaving her on the patio, Cogan went inside to make the call, checking the area code for Georgia in the directory before he dialled the number and waited to discover whether the ranger was at home.

He was, sounding more suspicious than

surprised when he heard Cogan's voice. 'Where the hell are you?' he asked.

'London,' Cogan said. 'I thought I'd call to say hello.'

'Sure you did. How did you make out in Washington?'

'Lots of words and no action.'

'You didn't get pussy-whipped into taking the girl to England with you, though, did you?'

'She's still in the States,' Cogan said. 'And she should be getting in touch with you some time before the weekend. When she does, will you give her a message?'

'This is the same favour, right?'

'Tell her I'll be at the waffle shop every day at ten in the morning and four in the afternoon starting from the day after tomorrow. Can you do that for me?'

'What waffle shop?'

'She'll know. Say it's important.'

'Listen,' Brady said. 'It's none of my business how often you want to fly backwards and forwards across the Atlantic, but I have to tell you this doesn't sound like a hell of a good idea to me. There're plenty of other nice southern girls in Georgia with long legs and great tits. Why not ask one of them to put a smile on your face if that's what you're after?'

Cogan already had a smile on his face. 'I'll

let you know,' he said. 'Don't forget the message.'

'OK. I'll need some cigars for all this hard work I'm doing for you. A couple of boxes ought to do it.'

If Cogan had thought cigars would guarantee a phone call from Sara he would have gladly provided the ranger with a year's supply, but he knew the odds of her seeing the advert were poor, and that even if she did, there was every chance that she would choose to ignore it. He said goodbye to Brady and returned to the patio where Judith Safrai was shuffling through the photos she'd retrieved from the lounge.

'Would you look at these for me?' she asked.

'There's no need. You know what the Iraqis are doing and so do I. Let's worry about how you're going to stop them.'

'What did Brady say?'

'He's standing by. All I have to do is see if I can catch a flight tomorrow.'

'I'll get the embassy to arrange that for you.' She tucked the photos into an envelope. 'I'd better give you contact telephone numbers for our people in Georgia. You'll need addresses too. I expect you'll have to deliver passport photos for Miss Hamaid to our office in Atlanta.'

'Fine.'

'What name will she want to use?'

'Whatever's best. Just so as it's not Hamilton or Lockhart.'

'Or her own.' She refilled his glass with juice. 'It's funny. You're not at all the sort of person I expected you to be.'

Cogan wasn't certain how to interpret the remark. 'You don't look much like a MOSSAD field agent,' he said. 'And if Sara was here, you'd have a hard time imagining her crawling through a minefield with a rifle in her hand.'

'Is she pretty?'

'Yeah.' He hesitated. 'Look, there's someone else I have to see. If you can let me have those contact numbers now, I'll call you this evening. We can go over the rest of it then.'

'All right. Be careful where you phone from.'

Cogan had long since given up being careful. By coming here today, in addition to breaking the promise he'd made to Sara for the second time, he knew he was starting out on a venture that was as reckless as it was dangerous. A gamble, he thought, based on the assumption that if his own luck ran out he could draw on Sara's because she had enough owing to her for both of them.

Bernie was paler than usual, slumped behind the desk in his office with his eyes closed.

'How's the head?' Cogan enquired.

'Don't ask. Are you working half days?'

'I'm not working at all. Did you get anything on that pipeline?' Cogan had noticed what looked like a print-out of a map lying on the floor.

'You're standing on it.' Bernie opened an eye. 'Are you going to tell me what this is about, or not?'

'When I get back. I'm going overseas again for a while.'

'Where to this time?'

'Here and there.' Cogan sat down on the only part of the desk that wasn't piled high with computer files. 'How do you feel about doing some more work for me? I'll pay double your normal charge-out rate.'

'For what?'

'Same as before. Information — phoned, faxed or e-mailed to wherever I happen to be. I need anything you can find on Russian-built Antonov 32 transport aircraft and I could use some really high-resolution satellite pictures of roads that don't go anywhere near a place called Ba'iji just south of the 36th parallel in Iraq.'

'Nothing on Iraqi presidential palaces?'

'Not for the minute.' Cogan smiled. 'Do a couple of other things for me and you can borrow my car.'

Bernie smelt a rat. He sat up straighter and switched off his computer.

'If anyone starts asking questions, this is what you know,' Cogan said. 'I've landed a government contract to have a look at the failure of unapproved helicopter parts, but the job doesn't start until August. Until then I'm on holiday with a girl called Hazel who you haven't met. We're up in Scotland somewhere together, and you think we're staying in a cottage four miles south of Kinross.'

'What am I supposed not to know?'

'Guess,' Cogan said. 'Lasers, pipelines, Russian aircraft and maps of the Middle East.'

'This sounds like a good way to get myself banged around again.'

'You could tidy up my office for me too,' Cogan said. 'No one's going to bang you around for doing that.'

'When are you off?'

'Tomorrow. I'll be trying to get hold of one of those ultra-compact satellite phones, but don't get excited if you don't hear from me for a few days.'

'If I'm still in one piece, you mean? If some mad bastard hasn't shot me full of holes while I'm driving your car.' Bernie stretched while he weighed up the risks. 'OK,' he said. 'You have a nice time in Scotland and I'll see what I can do here, but no promises and if things get out of hand you're on your own.'

It wasn't hard for Cogan to imagine things getting out of hand. Justifying his return to Savannah because of a four-line poem and a leaflet showing a girl in a yellow skirt might be foolhardy. But becoming involved with Judith Safrai could be a mistake on a different scale altogether.

He spent a few more minutes talking to Bernie then, with the groundwork for his plan complete, he left the building, his thoughts no longer centred on the potential for mistakes, but on the possibility of recovering lost ground and of discovering just how genuine the sentiment in the poem might turn out to be.

7

Had he been less on edge, Cogan would have been enjoying his return to Savannah — a gracious, sunlit city of trees, broad avenues and sub-tropical vegetation — a place so different and so far removed from London that it was easy to imagine himself running into Sara on a street corner or finding her sitting in the shade on a park bench somewhere. But, after four fruitless days of waiting for her at the waffle shop, his confidence was ebbing away and he was beginning to question his reasons for being here.

This afternoon, with the last of the advertisements appearing in the Charleston and Savannah newspapers, he was feeling particularly pessimistic, reluctant to start off on the walk from his hotel in case it turned out to be another wasted trip.

To avoid the crowds of the city market he headed straight for Bay Street, taking one of the narrow, cobblestone alleyways down to Factors Walk before he turned left into the riverfront district, trying not to pre-judge his reaction if today was to be like all the other days.

Sandwiched between a boutique and a tavern, the waffle shop was set back from the sidewalk to provide room for customers to sit at outside tables. In the morning, the tables were invariably unoccupied, but by four in the afternoon a queue for waffles had usually built up and there was rarely anywhere inside or outside for people to sit down.

Today, because it was Saturday, an untidy line of tourists and locals was spilling out into the street, and the shop was even busier than it had been during the week.

Cogan was already looking, endeavouring to pick out Sara from the crowd when his view was blocked by a passing truck. It was moving slowly, the driver threading his way through groups of pedestrians who had to move aside to let the vehicle through.

As they parted, Cogan saw her. She was in the centre of the street, coming towards him, her attention on the shop-front.

Hardly daring to believe it was really her, he stayed where he was until he could be sure. Then he went to say hello.

She was out of breath from hurrying, standing awkwardly with her hands clasped together now she'd recognized him.

Cogan searched for the right words, uncertain of what to say or do because she was refusing to meet his eyes. 'I'd given up on you,' he said.

She raised her head but seemed too embarrassed to answer him.

'You didn't have to run out on me,' he said.

'Why have you come back?'

'You know why.'

'Because there are more falcons?'

'They're not yours any more. I'm taking them over; they're mine now.'

'You're not making any sense.' She bit her lip. 'Why do you keep looking at me like that?'

Cogan did what he should have done earlier. Oblivious to the people in the street, he lifted her bodily off the ground and buried his face in her hair.

For a second she remained rigid, then suddenly melted, wrapping her arms round his neck and clutching him to her until he told her to let go so he could put her down.

She smoothed back her hair, composing herself before she spoke. 'I didn't expect to see you again,' she said.

'Serves you right for writing me that note. When did you see my advert?'

'Yesterday. It was in the *Savannah Morning News*, but I didn't speak to Brady until today.' She paused. 'I'm not imagining this, am I?'

186

'I don't think so.' After eight days and eight nights of wondering if his memory had been playing tricks on him, there was no disappointment. Every single thing about her was as he remembered it — the fragrance of her hair and her skin, the shape of her mouth, each curve of her figure and the unblinking way she had begun to return his stare.

This afternoon, instead of having a pony-tail, her hair was loose, and instead of her yellow skirt she was wearing jeans. She was also wearing a long-sleeved white blouse and a necklace he hadn't seen before.

'You haven't been back to your place in Brunswick, have you?' he asked.

She shook her head. 'I bought all new stuff. I haven't been anywhere except the awful trailer-park where I'm staying. I haven't done anything either — except for trying to decide where I should go. I've run out of money too.' She smiled. 'You can say it serves me right again if you want. I know what happened is my fault — for letting you go to Washington, I mean.'

'And for not trusting me,' Cogan said.

'What I said in my note was all true. You know that, don't you?'

She didn't need to ask. Just seeing her again had dispelled the last of his doubts. 'A fair bit's gone on since then,' he said. 'You've got some catching up to do.'

'While we stand here in the middle of the road?'

'Where shall we go?'

'Depends on what kind of catching up you have in mind.' She took his hand.

'You can decide after I've told you about my new girlfriend.'

'I didn't know you had one. What's her name?'

'Judith Safrai. She flew all the way from Tel Aviv to see me in London.'

'But she didn't take you to a cabin in the woods, did she? And she didn't catch you fish for breakfast, or take you to a prairie where the eagles fly.'

'No,' Cogan said. 'Come on, let's get out of here, then I can explain who she is.'

'Not until I've reminded you of who I am.' As if to reassert her claim on him, she stood on tip toe and brushed her lips across his mouth.

So light was her kiss that he was barely aware of it, a reminder not only of the very first time she'd kissed him, but of the definition of a pixie. A small, imaginary enchantress, his dictionary had said, a warning of how careful he'd have to be not to blink if he was to avoid losing her a second time.

Having his stitches removed was proving more pleasant than Cogan had expected it would be.

She was sitting astride him, straddling his hips with her legs, holding a pair of scissors in one hand and pushing him back onto the bed whenever he tried to see how she was getting on.

'These should have come out over a week ago,' she said.

'You put them in so I figured you ought to take them out. Why do you think I came back?'

'After what I've heard this afternoon I think it's just so you can show the lovely Miss Safrai how clever you are.' She used the tips of the scissors to snip through more stitches, pulling out the twists of fishing line delicately with her fingernails. 'Am I hurting you?'

Cogan shook his head. 'When are we going to talk about the deal?'

'Tomorrow. I don't want us to have an argument today.'

'We won't.' He stopped her for a moment. 'You haven't said why you lied about knowing where the quarry is.'

'Catherine and I promised each other we'd never tell anyone. We couldn't think of any

189

other way to protect ourselves. I didn't lie to you. I don't know the latitude or the longitude or anything else. All I can remember is what the terrain's like, and how far the minefield was from the Dijlah river and the railroad to Ba'iji.'

'What about map co-ordinates?' Cogan was finding it hard to concentrate, endeavouring to keep his eyes off her when she leaned forwards.

'The PUK issued us with two hand-held global positioning units, but we lost them both in the minefield, and the Republican Guards took all our maps.'

'But you knew exactly where you were before you were captured?'

She compressed her lips. 'More or less.'

'And you've got some idea how far the truck travelled before it reached the quarry, haven't you?'

'Yes. I suppose if I had to find the place again, I could. But I don't have to find it again so I don't see why I should.'

'You're wrong,' Cogan said. 'We only get one crack at this. If we don't take the chance we'll both be looking over our shoulders everywhere we go. You don't want to carry on like that, nor do I.'

'You're making it sound as though it's the only way we'll be able to live happily ever after.' She paused. 'If that's what you mean, we don't need Judith Safrai. We can do whatever we want without any help from her. Once she's organized my new passport, we can just disappear. Anyway, if the Americans know all about the Iraqi laser base like you say, sooner or later they'll do something to destroy it. If Israel can't wait for that to happen they'll have to try and find the quarry by themselves, won't they?'

'While Khadim and Van Reenan keep on searching for you? What if the CIA thinks you'd be better out of the picture as well?'

'Why should they?'

'Because the US have got their own agenda. They were trying pretty hard to keep their eye on me in London.'

'We're not supposed to be talking about this. You said we'd come back here to your hotel so I could have a shower and so we could have dinner together, but all you've done is go on about Judith Safrai and the CIA.'

Cogan was as anxious as she was to end the conversation, but not until he'd obtained at least a hint of a commitment from her. 'Do you want to talk about us instead?' he asked.

'No. Everything's all tangled up — you and me, Jeremiah and Catherine and all these

191

different people who want different things to happen.'

'Nothing a suitcase full of Semtex won't solve. One good bang and everything's fixed overnight. All you need to do is show the Israelis where to put the charges or where to drop a bomb.'

'And you'd go with me?'

'Part of the deal,' Cogan said.

'Isn't your friend Judith worried about me being an Iraqi?'

'She knows you were in the PUK. That means you're not exactly a nice Muslim girl with a picture of Saddam hanging on your bedroom wall.'

'If I was a nice Muslim girl I wouldn't have been driving a skidder in the Okefenokee swamp, and I wouldn't be letting you look down my blouse in a hotel room either. Tell her that if you're going to phone her.'

'What else should I say?'

'Whatever you like.' She took out the last of the stitches and placed the scissors carefully on the bedside table. 'I'm not sure about us. Why don't you ever talk about your wife?'

The question caught Cogan off-guard. 'Ex-wife,' he said. 'What do you want to know?'

'Did she have a name?'

'Karen.'

'Who walked out on who?'

'I was overseas a lot. One day I came home and she wasn't there.' He made an effort to change the subject. 'Brady thought I'd taken you to London with me.'

'Why?'

'Something about me being pussy-whipped.'

'Oh.' She began to smile. 'You should be so lucky.'

'Are you going to sit on me all evening, or are we going to eat?'

'I haven't decided.'

'You haven't decided about anything yet.' Cogan looked at her.

'Yes I have.' She climbed off him. 'I'll be in the shower. Don't go away.' She started off towards the bathroom, but stopped and turned round. 'I wasn't telling the truth about seeing those advertisements you put in the papers for me. The trailer-park isn't the sort of place where papers are delivered. I hadn't read one for a week.'

'If you didn't see the advert, what made you call Brady?'

'To ask him if he knew your London phone number. I only got a paper after he'd given me your message.'

Because the question she hadn't answered was by far the most important, Cogan used a more direct approach. 'Why did you want to phone me?' he asked.

'To see if I could really be like everyone else after all — you know, by making my own luck.' She took a deep breath. 'Of course, it could've been just to remind you about your stitches. You'll never be quite sure, will you?'

He swung his legs off the bed, but she was too quick for him. Before he could reach her she'd slipped into the bathroom and locked the door.

Nothing had changed, he realized, except, perhaps, that she was less self-assured and the hard edge to her seemed to have gone. But whatever it was that made her so captivating was the same as it had always been. He'd been conscious of it from the first moment he'd seen her on the river-front this afternoon — her ability to start a fire Cogan had given up trying to extinguish because every time he tried she would do something to fan the flames.

He went to get himself a drink of water, almost succeeding in controlling his imagination until he heard her call out to him.

If the open bathroom door hadn't made her proposition obvious, the half-smile on her lips eliminated any confusion. She was naked, standing immodestly in the shower with water streaming in rivulets over her shoulders and between her breasts.

'Remember the first day you saw me?' she said.

'Why?' Cogan was in trouble, unable to recall anything very clearly.

'I've never apologized, have I?'

'For what?'

'This.' Putting her head under the shower nozzle, she took a mouthful of water and spat it at him. 'Remember now?'

'What if I do?'

'Well, that day in the swamp I wanted you to go away and leave me alone. Now I don't so I thought if you soaped my back, I could say I was sorry.'

The idea was as suggestive as the way she was standing, an invitation for Cogan to show her how truly irresistible she was, and a means for her to show him what she wanted him to know.

She made room in the shower, giving him the soap but continuing to face him, hurriedly removing his clothes while she allowed him to lather not her back but her breasts. By the time she had finished undressing him she was smothered in suds, drawing her nipples sideways across his chest, rewarding him with a flurry of the same gentle kisses when he slipped his hands between her legs.

To begin with she seemed content to be submissive, standing quite still in a world of her own with her eyes closed, offering nothing but her lips until Cogan became more enterprising.

Forming a channel for the water with his wrists, he worked the bar of soap between her thighs.

She responded at once, aroused initially by the stream of warm water and then by his fingers, slowly spreading her legs for him and breathing faster now.

Soon her eyes were wide open, and instead of butterfly kisses, she was busy with her whole mouth, grasping him with both hands as she began to move, seeking her enjoyment more eagerly with every breath she took.

Cogan was equally eager, knowing that, like him, she was incapable of curbing her real demands for very long, but intoxicated by the thrill of touching her, willing her to give all of herself to him so he could more thoroughly caress the soft, moist centre of her each time she relaxed to let him do so.

For a while she continued riding shamelessly upon his wrists, pressing her body forwards until the need for greater intimacy began to overwhelm her.

To stop him teasing her, she made him drop the soap then lifted herself into his arms and wrapped her legs around his waist.

'Now,' she whispered. 'Go on.'

Because she was slippery with suds, her words of encouragement came too late. Before she was ready to accept him, Cogan had pushed her back against the wall and taken her uncompromisingly for himself.

He thought he might have hurt her, but when she tipped back her head to allow water to spray onto her face again, he saw that instead of pain, her expression was one of exhilaration — of a desire that was building second by second to carry her towards the release she was preparing to share with him.

Her climax was no less explosive than his own, a hedonistic surge of pleasure that made her cry out as she joined with him in the consummation of what they both had sought.

It took Cogan some time to regain his sense of perspective and to realize she was still clinging to him, murmuring something he couldn't hear.

He turned off the shower, but she made no attempt to let go of him or to repeat whatever it was she'd been saying.

'Are you all right?' he asked.

'I don't want to be alone,' she whispered.

'You're not.'

'I don't mean now. I mean tomorrow, or

the day after, or next week.'

'It's OK,' he said. 'You won't be. I promise.'

'You can't promise. You don't know when the next bad thing'll happen to me. It doesn't matter how much you want me today, I'll never be sure about tomorrow — especially when I don't know what you truly think.'

'I'll tell you,' Cogan said. 'Right now I think you're getting pretty damn heavy.'

'Oh. Oh, I see. I'm sorry.'

He lowered her to her feet. 'Shall I make the phone call?' he said quietly.

'I don't think it's that easy.' She pulled her hair back from her face. 'Nothing is.'

'Let's find out. A new passport and trip to the Middle East gets rid of all the bad things forever. I've got a friend in the UK who'll be watching our backs while we're away, and you won't be going anywhere by yourself. Two or three weeks and it'll be over. Then all you'll have to worry about is me catching you in the shower like this every day.'

'So I'll really be able to live happily ever after?' She smiled at him.

If this was a fairy tale and she was a pixie, there would have been no need for her to ask the question — confirmation of something Cogan had known for a long time — that in the real world, a happy ending was likely to depend more on the intelligence skills of the Israeli military than on the luck which had brought her back to him on this warm, serene Savannah evening.

8

Charles Greenwald was having a bad day. It had started at 6.15 a.m. after the red phone beside the bed had rung, and his wife had cut off the caller in her haste to pass him the receiver. Since then things had not improved. Subsequent phone calls had confirmed how little progress had been made, and the tone of this morning's meeting had already been set by the abrasive manner of the young man who had come to see him.

Hartley Porterfield was not yet in his thirties, a rising star in the State Department, and one of the new, fresh-faced appointees that Greenwald particularly disliked.

'Well?' Porterfield enquired. 'Convince me. Have the Iraqis developed a tactical, high-power airborne laser, or have they not?'

'You've read the reports,' Greenwald said. 'Baghdad have been running a joint development programme for over three years.'

'With their good friends the South Africans?'

'Indeed.'

'And there's no doubt their programme is

ahead of our own? I'm supposed to believe they've got something more powerful than our two million watt Mid-Infrared Chemical Laser, am I?'

Greenwald nodded. 'If Iraq's testing lasers against static missiles under thrust, I think we can assume their technology is fairly well advanced.'

'You said *if* they're testing. For Christ's sake, we've got KH-12 satellites up there costing over a billion dollars each, and we're not sure what they're doing?'

'We know a good deal,' Greenwald said. 'If you'd care to listen instead of asking questions perhaps you'll understand better. We have evidence of at least four Israeli aircraft being attacked at long range from inside Iraqi airspace. We have enhanced satellite data showing what are almost certainly infrared laser beams emanating from an Antonov 32 aircraft flying at high altitude south of the 36th parallel, and we have intelligence that leads us to believe the Iraqis are maintaining some form of underground development facility in the desert north of Ba'iji.'

'But we still don't know where the facility is, do we?' Porterfield's voice was scathing. 'Because you haven't found the girl, and because the elusive Mr Cogan is as elusive as he ever was.' He paused. 'Then, of course, there's the possibility of South African and Iraqi terrorists operating in the country. I don't think the White House is going to be very pleased.'

'When lasers aren't classified as weapons of mass destruction under any UN resolution that I'm aware of, I fail to understand why the White House should be interested.' Greenwald was being careful now. 'Or has someone simply decided an Iraqi laser might be a threat after all?'

'It's more complicated,' Porterfield said. 'More wide-ranging — an initiative the State Department wants to approve as long as we can get the right guarantees. I've been asked to carry out a risk assessment — you know, see what level of support your agency can offer.'

'In regard to what?' Greenwald remained cautious, waiting for the punchline.

'Middle East policy,' Porterfield said. 'Or what passes for it. Here's the situation as we figure it. Iraq is still developing anthrax, botulinus and aflatoxin — stuff we never got close to wiping out in 1998. They're also developing mustard gas, sarin and VX nerve gas. They've stockpiled around thirty thousand tons of biological agents, and according to our most recent information, they've still got around four thousand tons of precursor chemicals hidden in Iraq waiting to be turned into chemical poisons. You know that, I know that, the White House knows, the British know and so do a handful of other countries in the West.'

'What's your point?' Greenwald asked.

'It's not my point. It's fact — the fact that the US never had any real support from anywhere for military intervention. We still don't have. Places like Syria, Jordan and Iran don't like us interfering in the Middle East on principle. Other countries have always resented America playing globocop, and the rest of the world doesn't give a shit what Iraq is stockpiling because they think it doesn't affect them.'

'Are you saying the US is considering acting unilaterally again?'

'As long as we're not talking about any big deal, what have we got to lose? The UN inspection programme is a joke. Saddam's making nasty stuff faster than anyone can find it, and there's nothing we can do to stop him because since the 1998 impeachment crisis the US has blown its credibility. Outside governments think our foreign policy revolves around the president's prick.'

'And the White House is anxious to change this perception?' Greenwald removed his glasses and began to polish them with a handkerchief.

'They're more interested in waking up the international community to the real threat from Baghdad's biological and chemical weapon programmes. It's a project that's been on the wish-list for a while. That's why I'm here — to discuss how we might bring about a little redirection of world opinion.'

'Is that all?' Greenwald's expression was impassive. 'What exactly does the State Department or the White House have in mind?'

'Well, let's see, shall we?' Porterfield began to walk around the room. 'The US has three choices: sit on our butts and wait for Saddam to gas a few more thousand Kurds so we can make a big fuss, or we can poke him with a stick and hope he goes over the top with his response, or we can give him a longer piece of rope to play with. Which do you favour?'

'I think I favour seeking an analysis with rather more depth to it.'

The remark stopped Porterfield from pacing. He returned to the table and sat down again. 'Just hear me out,' he said. 'I need your help.'

'Then perhaps instead of giving me the benefit of your insight into Middle East politics you should explain what kind of assistance it is you want.'

'OK. This is how it goes down. Waiting isn't an option because the White House is tired of waiting. Provoking Baghdad into some sort of precipitous military action isn't an option either. Short of a full-scale war, Iraq isn't going to deploy chemical or biological weapons it claims not to have. So we're left with the rope — we offer Saddam an opportunity to use his airborne laser — an invitation he can't refuse.'

'His laser?'

'Right.' Porterfield nodded. 'Sucker him into attacking a US aircraft that's supposed to be carrying some heavyweight VIP passengers. While you do whatever you have to do to get satellite coverage of the event, we arrange the flight for somewhere over the Middle East and leak the route information.'

'How very innovative,' Greenwald said. 'Please go on.'

'Officially, if the plane crashes, the passengers escape with their lives. If it doesn't crash, as well as having a pair of shit-scared diplomats, we get an aircraft with a fucking great burn hole in it. Either way, once the media gets hold of the story, Saddam's going to look like an international pariah all over again. If that doesn't refocus world attention on his other weapon systems, nothing will.'

'I take it there'll be no actual passengers on board,' Greenwald said. 'What about the pilot?'

'We can rig for completely automatic operation if we have to. That isn't the problem. It's the satellite coverage we're worried about. If your people don't know where the quarry is, how can we be sure of tracking the Antonov when it takes off? We need a hell of a lot more than fuzzy, high-altitude pictures of a piece of desert with an infrared streak going from one place to another. We need quality shots of the right Antonov and the right target — good high-resolution prints.'

'Then you'll have to hope we do better than we did detecting the nuclear tests in India, won't you? What other steps are the administration intending to take?'

'What do you mean?'

'You know very well what I mean.' Greenwald hadn't expected an answer, but he was gratified to see the change in the young man's expression.

'Look,' Porterfield said, 'can we get good satellite shots or not? Yes or no? That's all I need to know.'

'I'll call you this afternoon,' Greenwald said.

'It has to be before three o'clock.'

'You'll have the information when I'm ready to provide you with it. I said this afternoon, so that's when you'll get it. Now good morning to you, Mr Porterfield. The longer you intrude upon my time, the longer it will take to get your answer.'

For several minutes after Porterfield had left the room, Greenwald remained seated alone at the small table, wondering why someone twenty years his junior should even try to pull the wool over his eyes, and why, nowadays, nothing was ever as it seemed to be.

* * *

Five thousand miles away at a PUK camp high in the northern mountains of Iraq, Cogan, too, had decided that things were far from being what they seemed to be.

By Kurdish standards the camp was tiny, sheltering a few hundred refugees who had set up home here for the summer, a collection of tents on a bleak, rock-strewn piece of mountainside where men, women and children from villages in Iraq mingled with Turkish refugees who had fled south in recent months.

But there was another side to the camp, one he was only just beginning to appreciate, partly because he hadn't been looking properly until this evening, and partly because his briefing had failed to paint a picture of what a place like this was actually like.

The briefing had started when Judith had met them off the plane in Ankara, continuing during their internal flight to Malatya and for much of the 200-mile drive to the Turkish border. Cogan had paid little attention, too preoccupied with his own thoughts when he hadn't been intervening in the arguments between Judith and Sara which had quickly sprung up. As a result, he'd been unprepared for the squalid conditions at the camp.

Yesterday, arriving sweat-stained and foot-sore from their six-hour climb from Zakhu across a moonscape of crevices, crags and rocks, Cogan's opinion of the camp had been coloured by what he'd seen and smelled of it before nightfall. But after a day here, he recognized how wrong he'd been.

The difference came from what could be seen and what couldn't be, the difference between the harshness of life outside on the mountain under canvas, and the compara-tively comfortable environment provided by the caves.

There were five caves in all, their entrances concealed by piles of boulders to make them invisible from the air, a legacy of the days when the Iraqi Air Force had been allowed to travel this far north to bomb and strafe anything that moved.

So far Cogan had explored only three of them, wandering in unannounced to discover that news of visitors had already spread to every corner of the camp.

Fierce-looking rebel fighters in turbans and baggy trousers had offered food and drink, provided tours of the medical facilities and, on more occasions than he could count, asked whether the two American women were his wives. The warmth of the welcome had been surprising, but the contents of the caves were more surprising still — enough heavy artillery, grenades and small-arms to equip a modern army of several thousand men.

Over the course of the day he'd also come to realize that, just as it had been Sara's idea to head for the camp to obtain transport, it was Sara who understood these people and who had their respect. Judith Safrai might have pulled the strings to get them here, but for the moment at least, the girl with the pony-tail and the big eyes was the one who was doing all the talking and attracting most of the attention.

An hour ago, Cogan had left her deep in conversation with a senior member of the

PUK, an English-speaking Shi'ite major called Zebari who, despite clearly disbelieving her story, had volunteered his son as a guide for their onward journey south.

The way she was accepted, and her own easy acceptance of conditions in the camp was a reminder for Cogan, proof of how she was more at home in a place like this than she had ever been in Savannah, and of how readily she could slip back into what she termed real life. Except that this was no more real life than the swamp had been, he thought. And the sooner she realized it, the better for everyone.

Nodding at children and returning the smiles of some Kurdish women who were carrying water from one of the hillside springs, he carried on with his exploration, trying to locate another cave in the fading light.

He was still searching when he heard Sara call out to him. She was hurrying, nearly tripping over a generator cable in her effort to catch him up.

'Where have you been?' she asked.

'Here and there. Where's Judith?'

'Organizing. You know how she is. She wants us to leave tomorrow.'

'Have we got wheels?' This was the first Cogan had heard about tomorrow.

'We're borrowing that Mercedes truck you were looking at this morning — in exchange for fifty boxes of our tetracycline.'

Despite having to carry the antibiotics overland from Zakhu, Cogan's reservations about bringing them had long since evaporated. In a country where there were a hundred Kalashnikovs for every packet of aspirin, the need for medical supplies was greater than the need for food, and he knew that the farther south they travelled the more valuable the drugs would become.

'What did you tell the major?' he asked.

'That you're a journalist with a big international magazine. You're doing a photo story covering my search for my parents. I said they were living in Ba'iji before they disappeared. It was the only way I could think of to explain why I was once in the PUK — you know, because it's sort of true.'

'Your parents didn't really live there, though, did they?'

'No. Their home was in As Samawah — in the south on the Euphrates.' She kicked a stone. 'Judith says there are people in Syria who have underground links to Baghdad. She thinks I might be able to trace my parents through them.' She paused. 'One day.'

'Are you OK?' Cogan tried to see her face.

'What do you think? One minute I'm living

211

in a Savannah trailer-park, and the next minute I'm back where I started — back in a PUK camp full of refugees and *peshmergas* in another country.'

'Are *peshmergas* the fighters?'

'Those who confront death. Kurdish militiamen.' She turned to look at him. 'Cogan, I don't know what I'm doing here. I don't want to go tomorrow. I can't.'

'Why? What's wrong now?'

'I'm not sure. Maybe because I can't see any point in doing this. You believe it's to stop Van Reenan and that man Khadim, but that's only part of the reason I agreed to come — you know it is. The other part had to do with Catherine and Jeremiah — because of some stupid idea I had in my head. But it's gone. I don't know how or why it has, but it's not there any more. All I want to do now is forget.'

'Perhaps this is the best way to.'

She bit her lip. 'How can it be? How can this help me forget? Suppose I find the quarry? Suppose Judith gets what she wants so Israel can send a fighter-bomber in under Iraqi radar like she says? It doesn't help Catherine or Jeremiah, does it? And I don't think it's going to help me. I can't understand why I ever thought it would. Look around you — just look.'

Cogan remained silent, wishing he'd recognized the warning signs earlier.

'There are camps like this everywhere,' she said. 'All across the north, right across the south. You saw what's happening along the border with Turkey; thousands of soldiers, thousands of refugees and starving children. If it isn't bands of Republican Guards it's Kurdish Turks fighting Iraqi Kurds. Cogan, there are people dying in their hundreds every day. I'm not part of this. I might've been once, but I'm not now. I can't handle it.'

Twelve days ago on their last night alone together in Savannah, Cogan had been faced with a not dissimilar hurdle. The trigger then had been the delivery of her new passport, her realization that with a fresh identity there were other options. This evening, though, her reasons were more fundamental and, in the circumstances, more difficult to counter. His own doubts had been growing too, a feeling that the mission carried with it a disproportionate level of risk — a sledgehammer to crack a nut when all he was trying to do was keep her out of harm's way, or perhaps, if he was truthful, keep her safely for himself.

The notion was disturbing, compounded by his own unease and by the sense of danger that seemed to permeate the whole camp. This wasn't a place for either of them, Cogan realized. But it was a bit late for second thoughts, and hard to imagine abandoning everything when the three of them had come this far.

He put his arm round her, knowing from experience that any attempt to lift her spirits would either backfire or make her more introspective than she was already.

To the west, where a blood-red sun was balanced on some distant and equally inhospitable mountain ridge, so thick was the air with dust that it was impossible to pick out any detail, and, for a second or two, Cogan could picture himself being on another planet. The evening was much cooler now — a prelude to the sudden plunge in temperature that would soon convert the blast-furnace of day into the deep-freeze darkness of night. At this altitude nothing was gentle, and for the people who lived, fought and died here it never would be, he thought. But when an entire nation was on the run, survival was enough because, for the *peshmergas* and the refugees of Kurdistan, survival was the equivalent of winning.

Still with his arm around Sara's waist, he watched the sun sink lower, waiting for her to reopen the conversation, half-expecting her to ask the one question he was not yet ready to answer. But like him she remained silent, staring into the distance, standing motionless beside him until the sun had vanished completely before she took his hand and started out on a slow walk back to the tent.

Judith was already there, sitting outside in front of an open fire, cooking what appeared to be pieces of goat meat on a long, steel skewer. She glanced up at Sara. 'I don't think I've got this quite right,' she said. 'But as far as I can make out, you look like an aunt.'

'What do you mean?'

Judith placed more twigs on the fire. 'There's a bit more to it as well — something you both need to hear.'

'What are you talking about?' Cogan asked.

'Ayisha,' Judith called. 'You can come out now.'

A child emerged from the tent, a golden-eyed little girl, no more than seven years old. Despite being severely malnourished and having a stump where her left hand should have been, she was unusually pretty, neatly dressed in jeans and a blue sweater.

'Well, hi there.' Sara knelt down. 'How much English do you understand?'

The girl pointed at herself. 'Ayisha,' she said.

'OK.' This time Sara began to speak in Kurdish, but was interrupted when the girl took a crumpled photograph from her pocket and launched into what sounded like a complicated explanation.

'Oh, I see.' Sara smiled at her. 'Well, I can try for you, can't I.' She switched back to Kurdish, patting the ground to persuade the child to sit down.

'What did she say?' Cogan had been trying to follow the exchange, but with little or no success.

'Ayisha came to the camp to look for her father. He was taken prisoner by the Mukhabarat, but there was a rumour that he'd escaped. He isn't here, though, so she's going home tomorrow.'

'Is that a photo of him?'

'No.' Sara shook her head. 'It's of herself. She's been told I'm an American, so she's come to ask if I'd take it back for an aunty she has in Philadelphia. It's terribly sad. She wants her aunt to send a helicopter for her — one of the UN helicopters she saw when her family were living in Mosul.'

Discomforted by the little girl's request, Cogan reached out for the photo, but found she was unwilling to show it to him.

Judith too was straight-faced. 'I wasn't allowed to see it either,' she said. 'I think Sara's the only one of us who passes as a real American. Ask Ayisha what happened to her hand. She didn't mind when I tried before.'

Sara pointed to the girl's arm, speaking in a matter-of-fact way to avoid embarrassing her.

The girl picked a twig from the fire and swept the glowing end through the air before she embarked on another long explanation, using the same twig to draw a picture in the dirt when Sara asked her another question.

'Did she say lightning?' Judith inspected the drawing. 'That's what I got when I asked last time.'

'Hot lightning.' Sara threw the twig away. 'She was travelling in a refugee convoy near a village called Ain Zalah. There were eight trucks and some horses. She was trying to draw a dead horse for me.'

Endeavouring to discount a possibility that was too sickening to contemplate, Cogan was studying the girl's eyes. They were truly golden, innocent young eyes reflecting the colour of the firelight. 'How long ago?' he asked.

'About a year. She says the lightning came from the sky. It started at the front of the convoy and moved along it burning up all the trucks and the horses and the people. Her mother and grandfather were killed. That's when she lost her hand. Apparently the same thing had happened to other convoys before.'

'Jesus.' Until now, not once had Cogan considered that anything like this had been going on. 'Ask her if she saw the lightning?' he said quietly.

'I already have. She didn't. She says no one ever sees it. But she felt the heat, and she heard it — the same noise I heard after the missile had exploded in the quarry.' Sara paused. 'So now we all know how Ayisha's mother and grandfather died, don't we? And we know why she only has one hand.'

'No international outcry because there's no evidence.' Judith stabbed at the fire with the tip of her skewer. 'Better than shrapnel or nerve gas.'

'Just a lot of dead people and maimed children.' Sara got to her feet. 'I'm taking Ayisha back to her tent. Her grandmother's supposed to have an address for her aunty.' She took the girl's hand. 'Then I want to be by myself for a while. Don't wait up for me.'

Before the girl departed, as though wishing to communicate the importance of her message to another westerner, she came to stand in front of Cogan, staring at him so earnestly that he found it hard to smile goodbye to her.

Even after she'd tripped away in the darkness, her expression stayed with him, evidence if he needed it, not only of how cheap life could be for the refugees, but of the hopelessness that Sara had tried to make him understand.

If Judith had guessed what he was thinking she was being careful not to show it. She went to the tent, returning with two plates on which she deposited the portions of cooked meat.

'Do we have a problem?' she asked.

'We?'

'I mean is something upsetting Sara?'

'She'll be OK.' Cogan started eating, keeping his attention on the embers of the fire. 'What's the programme?'

'Major Zebari's lending us a truck. His son will take us down through Nineveh to Erbil. After that we'll be on proper roads so we shouldn't get lost.'

'Until we head off into the desert,' Cogan said.

'How can we get lost with satellite phones, GPS units, compasses and more maps than we can carry? All we need is Sara's local knowledge.'

'Have you told her we don't need to get close?'

Judith nodded. 'She knows. She knows I've borrowed a mine-detector too. I don't see what else I can do.'

'You could stop being so bloody patronizing. She's not here to help you; she came for her own reasons — to help herself.'

'No she didn't. She came because you talked her into it.'

Cogan wasn't going to argue. 'Look,' he said, 'I know this trip matters to you, but you didn't spend three weeks of your life in some godforsaken piece of desert with Republican Guards after you. Sara's wound up because she's started remembering what it was like before.'

'It's not that. It's because two of us are women. Things would've been easier if you'd stayed behind in London, or Savannah or Ankara — anywhere.'

'How about here?'

'If you're happy with the idea, why not ask Sara if she is? She's perfectly capable of looking after herself. She doesn't need you to baby-sit her.'

Cogan slid his plate to one side. 'I'll tell you exactly what she doesn't need,' he said. 'She doesn't need you telling her what to do, and nor do I. We're going to finish this together — you and me and Sara. Have you got that?'

'Yes.' Judith Safrai was tight-lipped. 'I have to contact Tel Aviv this evening. Are there any messages you want them to pass on for you?'

'I'll send my own messages, thanks. You can do something else, though; see if

Madeline Isaacs knows if the Americans have cancelled their trace on me.'

'Why do you want to know?'

'No reason.' He stood up. 'I don't much like people looking for me, that's all.'

'In the same way you don't like women telling you what to do?'

'Depends who they are.' He smiled. 'I'd better go and find Sara. Thanks for dinner.'

'I thought we'd leave early.' Judith gathered up the plates. 'If that's all right.'

Cogan wasn't ready to commit himself. It was a question of trust, he thought, whether Sara still believed he could exorcize her falcons, or whether by returning to Iraq she had convinced herself that the attempt was no longer worth the risk.

He spent the best part of the next hour endeavouring to discover where she'd gone, mixing with the *peshmerga*, asking if anyone had seen her and trudging to the far north outskirts of the camp in the moonlight before abandoning his search and returning to the tent to catch up on some sleep.

★　★　★

The crump of a mortar was the first sign of trouble. Cogan woke with his heart banging, forcing himself to listen while he tried to

221

decide where the danger was coming from.

He had the presence of mind to dig Sara in the ribs and was yelling at Judith when a incoming shell exploded somewhere on the mountain. A minute later the camp was in turmoil. People were shouting, there was the sound of rifle fire, then suddenly, drowning out everything, came the chatter of machine-guns.

Outside the tent under a full moon that had turned the night to silver, men were either starting trucks or scrambling to drag field-guns from the caves. Others were dispersing into gullies or ditches carrying armfuls of ammunition.

The scene was a repeat of one Cogan had hoped to never see again, a re-enactment of the night raid on the Afghan rebel camp where he had been held captive three years ago. Everything was the same — the roar of artillery, the vivid flashes of light, spiralling geysers of dust and the familiar acrid smell of cordite. The dryness in his mouth was familiar too. But tonight there was a difference: tonight he was not a prisoner, and tonight he had Sara with him.

More shells were landing now, most exploding harmlessly near the springs on the north-east edge of the camp, or hitting higher on the mountainside where the danger from them was not great. The real threat was coming from elsewhere — from the bullets ricocheting off rocks and zipping through the air in increasing numbers.

Head down in a shallow trench behind the tent, Cogan was holding Sara's wrist with one hand and gripping Judith's belt with his other.

'We can't stay here,' he shouted. 'Wait for a lull then head for the caves.'

Almost as soon as he'd given the instruction the gunfire seemed to die away. Where a second ago the night had been filled with noise, now there was nothing — an eerie silence broken only by the bubbling sound of a man dying somewhere in the darkness.

Not certain what was happening, Cogan stood up cautiously to listen. 'OK,' he said. 'One at a time. Keep in the shadows from the tents.'

Sara went first, her tiny figure disappearing among the rocks as she made her way to the safety of the nearest cave. Judith was more hesitant, hanging back until he told her to go.

Cogan continued to be wary, delaying his departure long enough to grab his satellite phone from the tent before he started out on his own eighty-yard sprint across the camp.

Inside the mouth of the cave, Major Zebari

was waiting for him to arrive.

'Good evening.' The major laid down his rifle. 'I apologize for this disturbance of your sleep.'

'What the hell's going on?' Cogan refused the offer of a cigarette. 'Who is it?'

'Sometimes the Iraqi Army send soldiers, but tonight we think these are guerrillas from the Kurdish Democratic Party. Before winter the KDP will try to occupy this position, so each month they test to see what strength we have.'

'What's made them stop?' Cogan held up a hand to prevent Sara interrupting.

'They cannot approach us from above where there is no access. From below it is easier, but impossible for them to depress the muzzles of their big guns to such an angle. It is one reason why we camp here. Now you have seen how the shells fly high, you will understand they are to frighten us only — to divert our attention so we may be attacked with automatic rifles at close range.'

'Why have they stopped then?' Cogan asked.

'Ah,' the major smiled. 'Because in the darkness my men have passed among them with sharp knives. But the KDP will try again — perhaps in one hour, perhaps tomorrow.' He turned to glance at Sara and Judith. 'By then it will be better if you and your women are gone, I think.'

Cogan thought so too. 'Are you sure it's OK about the truck?' he said.

'I am sure. If you will collect your equipment and prepare yourselves, I will instruct my son on how he is to take you through the pass.'

Sara's curiosity had got the better of her. 'I want to know what's happening,' she said. 'If there are Republican Guards out there, you have to tell me.'

'The major thinks it's the KDP.' Cogan brushed some sand off her face. 'We're leaving right away. I'll fetch our stuff, you wait here with Judith.'

She began to say something, but appeared to change her mind.

He left her where she was, telling himself the gunfire would not begin again while he returned to the tent to pick up their belongings. It was too quiet, Cogan decided, too easy to believe no one was watching him over a rifle sight somewhere.

But there were no more shots, only some shouting in the distance during his journey back, and a glimpse of light flickering among the boulders on the north boundary where the attack had first begun.

Outside the cave where a Mercedes truck

was parked with its engine running, Sara was engaged in a heated discussion with the major's son. Although the boy was only about sixteen, he was a good foot taller than she was. He was also heavily armed. Resting against the truck was a well-used AK47, two Scorpion machine-pistols hung on straps from his shoulder, and he was endeavouring to give Sara what looked like a large-bore semi-automatic shotgun.

'You ready?' Cogan asked her.

'If we have to do any shooting I can do better with a rifle. He won't believe me.'

The major intervened. 'The shotgun is for the mines,' he said. 'Please understand. We make these trips many times.'

Cogan was in no mood for an argument. 'Sara, just get in the damn truck,' he said.

Snatching the gun from the boy she hauled herself into the cab, refusing an offer of assistance, but turning to help Judith once she was installed.

Cogan checked to make sure there was room for them all to squeeze across the seat, then, after stowing their packs in the rear, he went to say his goodbye to the major.

Zebari shook hands. 'If you will forgive me, there is a question I wish to ask,' he said. 'Among my people there is a saying that for a man to enjoy two women he must have four hands. Please, how is it you are successful in this?'

'I'm not.' Cogan grinned at him. 'Good luck with the KDP.'

The major shrugged. 'We will wait for them. Please keep the truck for as long as you wish, but tell my son he must return here within four days. From Erbil he will be able to make his own way.'

'OK.' Cogan climbed up into the cab, slamming the door as the truck began to move away in a series of lurches.

Across the camp now, although the shadows were longer, forming pools of blackness on the ridge outside the caves, the mountainside itself remained bathed in the same unearthly moonlight that was still transforming rocks to chunks of metal and still turning dust into swirling particles of silver.

If the light was unchanged, beside him in the cab Judith Safrai most certainly was not. Gradually, since their departure from Ankara, she seemed to have abandoned the role she had initially assumed, deferring more and more frequently to Cogan when he disagreed with her, choosing instead to relieve what he thought was her frustration by aggravating Sara whenever the opportunity arose. It had made an awkward situation worse, creating unnecessary tension until Cogan had lost his temper with her during their hike across the mountains from Zakhu. From then on she had been quite different. In place of the efficient field agent she had tried hard to portray, a rather vulnerable young woman had emerged, someone who had either underestimated the rigours of travel in northern Iraq, or who had badly overestimated her own capabilities.

But attributing her behaviour to inexperience had been a mistake, Cogan realized. It wasn't that at all. She was frightened, scared witless, probably because for the first time in her life, she'd found out what it was like to be shot at on a dark night in a country where nobody cared whether she lived or died. Which wasn't going to help things a hell of a lot, he thought, especially if the shooting was to begin again.

Wondering if Sara shared his misgivings, he put aside his concern, trying instead to pretend that the worst of the danger already lay behind them.

At the wheel of the Mercedes, the boy was preparing to change gear, increasing his speed along a track only a little wider than the truck itself. He had not yet switched on his headlights, preferring to rely on the moon and his knowledge of the terrain to guide the

228

vehicle along a series of rock-faces on the uphill edge of the camp.

'How far's the pass?' Cogan asked.

'One thousand metres — maybe less,' the boy answered, without taking his eyes off the track. 'When I open the windshield you will please be ready.'

The windshield was hinged, Cogan saw, a means of providing unrestricted access for guns if guns were going to be needed.

Sara was already working the action on the shotgun, emptying the shells onto her lap before reloading them into the magazine. When she'd finished she handed Judith a machine-pistol, then reached across to give the other one to Cogan.

'This is crazy,' she said. 'How can we do anything about mines we can't see?'

'They will lie on the surface,' the boy answered. 'In the pass the rock is too hard to bury them.'

'And we have to clear them out of the way,' Cogan said. 'Is that the idea?'

'Perhaps there will be none. But if so, we have also what I think in America is called a catcher for the cows.' The boy nodded towards a button on the dashboard. 'Soon I will lower it. Then we must ask Allah to protect us.'

Judith was not reassured. She was fumbling

with the machine-pistol, glancing nervously first at Sara then at Cogan.

'Here.' He took the pistol from her, checking the safety before he showed her how to chamber the first round. 'Use both hands,' he said. 'Don't worry about the muzzle flash and as soon as the barrel starts to kick up, take your finger off the trigger.'

Sara frowned at him. 'You're supposed to be a metallurgist,' she said. 'What do you know about Polish pistols?'

He had no chance to explain. Before he could reply, the Mercedes went into a slide as the driver braked heavily, switched on the headlights and hit his dashboard button.

A second later, while the boy was kicking open the windshield, the high-pitched whine of a hydraulic pump was replaced by the sound of a steel blade grinding against the ground.

Now the windshield was open, dust from the scraper was pouring into the cab, severely obscuring Cogan's vision. But he could see the pass, a deep cutting through the rock no more than seventy yards ahead.

The boy had sharper eyes. 'There.' He pointed.

The mines were close, half a dozen squat red cylinders arranged in a line across the track.

'You try.' The boy held the truck in second gear, making no further attempt to reduce his speed.

Hard though it was with the truck bouncing around, Cogan did his best. The first long burst from his Scorpion ricocheted off the road surface only a few inches short. His second attempt was more accurate.

A series of flashes and ear-splitting bangs told him that by hitting one mine he had triggered a chain reaction in the others.

He was only partly right. Nearer the cutting there were more — more than Cogan could begin to count. 'We're going too bloody fast,' he shouted. 'You'll have to slow down.'

The boy shook his head. 'It is what they wish.' He pointed again, this time at some shadows where a man was preparing to level a grenade-launcher.

The Mercedes was not an easy target. Unharmed, travelling in its own dust cloud, it lurched onwards, approaching the entrance to the pass at over thirty miles an hour.

A crackle of small-arms from somewhere was accompanied by the full-throated roar of Sara's shotgun as she opened fire. To get a better view she was leaning forwards, being slammed back by the recoil with each shot, but refusing to stop.

Cogan provided her with cover, sweeping

the Scorpion's muzzle from one side of the cutting to the other, holding down the trigger until the truck ran into a wall of flame.

On this occasion the mines appeared to detonate together. The explosion was impressive, a blinding burst of light and a blast severe enough to lift the truck several inches off the road. It came down heavily, slewing sideways, but by then the danger was over.

Clearly pleased with himself, the boy spat out a mouthful of grit before he retracted the scraper and pulled the windshield shut. 'So now you see how to do this,' he said. 'One day they will learn to dig a trench across the road. Then it will be more difficult for us.'

Cogan didn't bother to answer. High on his list of places to avoid in the future were the refugee camp and the track from it leading south. Now the adrenalin had stopped running it was hard to imagine why he'd ever believed this was a good idea, and equally hard to imagine doing it again.

Squashed alongside him on the seat, Judith was still gripping her gun in both hands. The Scorpion was unfired, the safety catch still on, its muzzle pointing at the floor.

'Better let me have that.' Cogan took it from her. 'Are you all right?'

'I suppose.' She spoke so quietly that he

could barely hear her above the noise of the engine.

It was Sara who brought her round, talking to her for the next four or five minutes as though the incident had already been forgotten.

Cogan was careful not to interfere, keeping his mouth shut until they were through the pass and travelling in more open country, only then reaching behind Judith to touch Sara on the shoulder.

'Not much of a start,' he said.

'No. I tried to tell you what things might be like — right from that very first night at the cabin.'

The distrust was in her eyes again. Even in the moonlight he could see it. 'It's your turn,' he said. 'You can say I told you so, if you want.'

'I don't know what I want. I know you thought you could take away the bad things, and I know it's not your fault you can't. But this isn't going to work. I'm not brave enough any more.' She stopped speaking for a moment. 'Maybe I just want you to stop making me promises you can't keep.'

Hidden in her statement was an echo of the message she'd written in Savannah, a repeat of everything she'd ever said, a plea for him to leave her alone because in her heart she'd never believed he could deliver on his promises.

And so there was another decision to be made, one that Cogan knew he couldn't put off much longer.

A hundred yards ahead, a jackal had paused on its journey across the road. Uncertain of whether to continue, its eyes glowed briefly in the headlights before it retreated, slinking off in the direction from which it had come.

Instinct, Cogan thought. When you don't know where the hell you're going, don't hang about, and always take the safest option.

9

Three days in Erbil had been three days too many. Parts of the town were still clinging to the old ways, radiating some degree of prosperity, but in general the atmosphere was dreary and depressing.

Cogan's first impression had come at daybreak on the morning of their arrival. On the outskirts of town, a giant mosaic portrait of Saddam riddled with bullet holes had been a warning of what to expect, a symbol of the decay that extended from simple urban housing right through to the Kurdish Parliament building, a once handsome piece of architecture now trashed and gaping with shell holes. And everywhere, on every street corner in every district, Cogan had seen the effects of a UN embargo that was strangling the people of Erbil to death.

Even Sara had been shocked by the deterioration that had taken place since she had been here last. Like Cogan on that first morning, as the boy had driven them into town she had sat silently in the truck, trying not to notice the barefoot children with their stringy limbs and pus-filled eyes — some of

235

them already victims of marasmus and kwashiorkor, diseases brought on by a level of malnutrition usually reserved for places like Ethiopia or the Sudan. And like Cogan, slowly she too had come to terms with the poverty and the sickness because she knew there was nothing she could do about it.

To begin with she'd been reluctant to leave the accommodation the boy had arranged for them before he left, a small, detached house on Ain Kawa street in a predominantly Christian neighbourhood where the presence of westerners was not uncommon, although the few that Cogan had encountered had been careful to avoid eye contact and none had bothered to say hello.

But the house was clean, inconspicuous and, apart from having the disadvantage of an inquisitive landlord, it was a safe enough place for them to catch their breath.

This morning, for reasons Cogan could only guess at, Sara had decided it was time they spoke in private. She'd been insistent, nagging at him until a few minutes ago when he'd brought her outside and escorted her to the truck.

'Did you tell Judith where we're going?' she asked.

'I don't know where we're going.' Cogan climbed into the cab. 'She won't care anyway

— not as long as we're out of her hair. She wants to contact Tel Aviv again, and she's not keen on us listening in.'

'Why are we taking the truck?'

'Because I need to phone someone too. I don't fancy making the call from a park bench somewhere.' He started the engine, checking the mirror for non-existent traffic before he pulled away from the kerb and began fighting a gearbox that was either full of gravel or dangerously low on oil.

Now they were underway, Sara's eyes were brighter and she was trying not to smile. 'You should've let me drive,' she said.

'Because you can drive anything?'

'You know I can.'

'The boy did better than you could've done through that pass.'

'He'd made the trip a hundred times.' She settled back in her seat. 'I spoke to him before he left. It was like talking to Catherine again — you could almost feel the hate. He's been fighting since he was twelve years old.'

'Does he know what for?'

'Sort of. He's got his own reasons. He said that when the Iraqi Army overran his village they strapped Kurdish babies to the front of their tanks. One of them was his sister. He swears he'll never forget.'

Cogan had heard similar stories at the

camp. 'His father won't forget either,' he said. 'If I was an Iraqi tank commander I wouldn't want to meet Major Zebari on a dark night.'

Now the truck was moving faster he risked another gear, searching for a road that he hoped might lead out of town. 'Judith was wrong,' he said. 'We shouldn't have come down through Turkey at all. Jordan would've been better — or even Syria maybe.'

'Then we wouldn't have this nice truck. And we wouldn't have that nice Scorpion pistol you bought from the boy, would we?'

Cogan had no idea she'd witnessed the purchase. 'Insurance,' he said.

'Against what?'

'We're a long way from home.'

She compressed her lips. 'You might be, but I'm not. I was born here — remember?'

'What does that mean?'

'It doesn't mean anything — not in the way you think it does. Did you buy the pistol because you want us to carry on to the quarry?'

'We're damn nearly there.' Cogan didn't look at her. 'Judith says it's probably no more than fifty or sixty miles away.'

'We're only in Erbil because of what happened the other night. If there hadn't been a raid on the camp we could just as easily have turned round and gone home.

We're here by accident, not because it's halfway to the quarry. Anyway, have you asked Judith if she still wants to go? I don't think she does.'

'To hell with Judith,' Cogan said. 'It isn't her decision, it's yours and mine. If you've had enough, that's fine, but we're going to have to think this through. You can't very well go home, can you?'

'Why not? I can get another job where no one'll find me, or I could take my clothes off again every week for Uncle Abu. Then I wouldn't need to work, would I? And I wouldn't need you either.'

'Don't start,' Cogan said.

'All right. We'll go to London. You said I'd be safe there.'

'That was before the CIA started looking for you — or us.'

'So that leaves where — Australia, South America? I suppose Alaska's no good because Catherine was killed there. How about the Seychelles? Did you know people speak Creole in the Seychelles? I've always wanted to go someplace where they speak Creole.'

'Don't push your luck.' He was pleased her spirits had returned. 'For all you know, Uncle Abu might have lost interest,' he said. 'I can call him any time to find out for you.'

'On your clever satellite phone?'

'Right.'

'Go on then. I'll give you the number.'

Having finally coaxed the truck up to the same speed as the rest of the traffic, Cogan was endeavouring to steer it in a straight line. 'How's the bruise from the shotgun?' he asked.

'It's stopped hurting.' She unbuttoned her shirt. 'Look.'

Sara had not undone her shirt to show him the bruise on her shoulder; Cogan knew it, and so did she. The reason was more complex, a not so subtle excuse to remind him that this was their first opportunity to be alone together since their departure from Ankara. It had been six days, he realized, most of them spent on the road or at the camp where privacy had been a luxury.

'If you don't want to see, why did you ask?' She slid away from him on the seat. 'Would you rather check out Judith?'

'I don't think she'd appreciate that, do you?'

'You might be surprised. She likes you. Haven't you noticed?'

Cogan hadn't. Nor was this the time to discuss it one way or the other. He continued driving, heading north-west in the general direction of Mosul, wondering if there was still a chance of talking Sara round, or whether, like the jackal on the road, she was right in wanting to take what she believed was the easiest option.

There was a good deal more traffic now. Dilapidated tractors towing trailers were being overtaken by modern four-wheel-drive vehicles, while trucks and tankers running contraband from the borders to Baghdad were starting to appear more frequently. Although a few of the trucks were new, most were in no better condition than the Mercedes, overloaded, blowing smoke and struggling on even the slightest incline.

Twice Sara pointed out Nissan Patrols bearing the UNICEF insignia on their doors, and twice when she had seen army vehicles parked at the roadside she had become visibly uneasy.

Anxious not to spoil her mood and to avoid squandering fuel, Cogan began searching for somewhere to stop. He chose a narrow, no-exit side road leading up to what looked as though it might once have been a sports ground. It was overgrown with weeds that had succumbed to the heat, but it was quiet and with a group of scrubby trees growing at one end.

He parked beneath them in the shade, then opened the windshield to let out the engine fumes.

Laid out in the distance, Erbil was shimmering in the morning haze, the minarets of its mosques rising like so many swollen needles from the conglomeration of flat-roofed houses. The countryside was hazy too, a uniformly wheat-coloured background, broken only by sparsely wooded foothills to the east where the atmosphere was clearer and the sky a deeper blue.

From this far away, Cogan's impression of the place was different. Baking under the summer sun, the town appeared to be asleep. But he knew it wasn't. It was in hibernation, its people going about their business day by day, week by week, while they waited for the UN to relax the sanctions so Erbil could re-awake and become again what it had been before.

It was a slim hope, he thought, one that was unlikely to be realized when Baghdad was still making all the wrong noises and doing its best to drive the Kurds into oblivion.

To get more air into the cab, Sara reached across to push open his door. 'What about your call?' she asked.

'I'll try now.' Taking the phone from its case, Cogan flipped up the lid and gave her the handset to hold.

'Can you really talk to anyone in the world

242

on this?' She sounded doubtful.

'As long as there's a geostationary INMAR-SAT satellite hanging around somewhere. We've got nine to choose from so I don't think we'll have a problem getting through to the UK.' Cogan smiled. 'Getting through to Bernie might be more difficult. I haven't used one of these before.'

'Have you worked out the UK time?'

'It's first thing in the morning there. Bernie'll be at the office — or he should be.'

'Unless you've made a mistake, and it's Sunday like it was that day in the swamp.' She returned the handset to him. 'Why do you have to phone him?'

'You can listen on the speaker.' Cogan punched in his identification code, followed it with the number then waited to discover if the system was going to function or not.

After a delay of several seconds Bernie answered, sounding more weary than usual when he gave his name.

'I thought I'd better find out if my car's OK,' Cogan said. 'How are things?'

'Shit. I knew I should've stayed home today.' Bernie's voice became slightly more alert. 'Are you still up in Scotland?'

'I'll be here another week. Anyone been asking for me?'

'The ministry phoned on Friday and a

couple of guys called round to see you three times last week. I told them you were on holiday with Hazel.'

'What did they want?'

'How the hell would I know? I didn't ask. They were both from military intelligence, nice and polite, but so full of bullshit they had trouble believing each other.'

Cogan decided to gamble on the phone line being clean. 'OK,' he said. 'How did you make out with the maps?'

'I've downloaded everything that isn't classified. I've got enough stuff to wallpaper your office — mostly photographic coverage that was done for the Gulf War.'

'And?' Cogan said.

'Waste of time if you're looking for roads that don't go anywhere north of Ba'iji. Either there aren't any or the US have pulled the high-definition stuff out of circulation. I've come across a few other holes like that. Buy yourself a Michelin map instead.'

Because Sara had always claimed that the quarry road would be unidentifiable from the air, Cogan wasn't surprised. 'What about the other information?' he asked.

'I've got half-a-dozen pretty pictures of the Russian plane, and that oil pipeline into Turkey shows up on a couple of the maps.' Bernie hesitated. 'Have you been too busy playing with Hazel to read the newspapers?'

'Why? Have I missed something?'

'You might have. There's been a lot of noise about the US getting their balls in a knot over the Iraqis flushing out their pipelines to slow down corrosion. The Americans are saying the whole thing's a crock of shit, so they're putting pressure on the Turkish Government to stop them buying any Iraqi oil at all.'

'How are they going to do that?' Cogan saw Sara raise her eyebrows.

'Hang on and I'll tell you.' Bernie's voice faded for a moment. 'This is an article from yesterday's *Telegraph*,' he said. 'I'll read it. 'In both Britain and the US there is again concern over Iraq's non-sanctioned oil sales to Turkey which are, according to diplomatic sources, increasing almost daily. These sales are in violation of UN resolutions permitting pipeline flushing on a limited scale only. Senior US State Department official Gordon Ferris will be flying to Ankara on 23 July for special meetings with the Turkish Government. Ferris, who is presently in Damascus on unrelated business, is expected to present an American and British plan that will leave Ankara little room to compromise regarding the purchase of Iraqi oil supplied under the guise of pipeline flushing'.'

'OK,' Cogan said. 'I've got it.'

'Do you want me to fax the maps?'

'No. It's a bit difficult right now. Is there anything else in the papers?'

'Usual stuff — you know, how Baghdad is stockpiling enough nerve gas to paralyse the universe. I think the West's gearing up for another 'let's throw rocks at Saddam' week. Still, if you're up in Scotland, what the hell do you care?'

'Go back to work,' Cogan said. 'I'll call you in a couple of days.' He replaced the handset slowly, wondering if the flurry of interest in Iraq was anything other than a coincidence.

Sara too was puzzled. 'It's weird,' she said. 'Why should the US suddenly want to stop the pipelines from being flushed when they've known about it for years?'

'It might just be that someone's decided it's time to have another go at Saddam like Bernie said. What do you think?'

'I think I ought to know who Hazel is.' She slipped out of the cab and went to stand by herself under one of the trees.

'Hazel isn't anyone.' Cogan spoke through the open windshield.

'You'd better come and explain. It's nicer out here anyway.'

She was right. He hadn't realized how hot the cab had become until he left it and walked across to join her in the shade.

'Well?' She leaned back against the tree.

'If there was a Hazel I'd be in Scotland. But there isn't, so I'm stuck here in Iraq with you.'

'It's not my fault. This is your idea not mine.' She compressed her lips. 'Once upon a time you had a wife called Karen, then you pick up Judith Safrai and now there's someone called Hazel.'

'You've forgotten Shannon Lockhart.'

'No I haven't. You're the one who's forgotten — because you don't want to remember me like that, do you?'

Her clipped speech was as familiar to Cogan as the approach she was employing — the method she invariably used to provoke him whenever she was uncertain of herself or believed she was being left out of things.

His own reaction was equally familiar — amusement, followed by a feeling of having let her down before he recognized the signs for what they were. Today, because of her expression, he decided to end the charade early.

Pinning her shoulders against the tree, he held her there while she struggled to turn her face away.

'Sir, where are your manners?' She spoke in her southern accent. 'Please remove your hands.'

'Or what?'

'Or I won't let you make love to me.' She wriggled free then stood on her toes to kiss him on the mouth. 'It's no good pretending you don't want to because I know you do.'

'Not here I don't.' The musk of her skin was heady, and her breath was fresh and warm against his cheek.

'I didn't mean here. We can do it in the truck. No one'll see us.'

In almost any other circumstances Cogan would have been unable to say no. She was as bewitching as ever, fidgeting while she waited for him to agree. But over the last few days, more aware of being a stranger in a strange land than he had been for some time, he had begun to rely consciously on his instincts. This was not, and never could be, a place for them to make love. He knew it intuitively, just as he knew that the longer they postponed their departure from Erbil, the harder it would become to convince her to journey further south.

When he tried to reason with her she was disappointed, returning to the cab without saying anything, but snuggling up beside him on the seat as soon as he had the truck on the road for the drive back to Ain Kawa street.

They had gone less than a quarter of a mile when a police car passed them travelling fast in the opposite direction. Where it was headed Cogan couldn't be sure, but its presence reminded him again of how important the lesson of the jackal might yet turn out to be.

⋆ ⋆ ⋆

Judith's anxiety was showing. After attempting to disguise her concern for most of the afternoon, it had finally surfaced now Sara had accused her of being secretive.

'I don't think you're in any position to judge,' she said. 'Look at yourself sometime.' She left the kitchen and disappeared into the other room.

'You better see what's going on,' Cogan said.

Sara remained where she was at the sink, continuing to rinse the rice she'd bought as though nothing had happened.

'Find out,' he said.

'Ask her yourself. She won't talk to me.'

Cogan went to the lounge where Judith was standing at the window with her back to him.

'I didn't realize you and Sara were lovers.' She spoke defensively. 'You never said.'

'What makes you think we are?'

'I'm a woman. And I'm not stupid.'

'Why should it make any difference?'

'It does when the two of you try to make all the decisions. You haven't even asked what I think about going on to the quarry.'

'Shouldn't it be Sara who decides?'

'She agreed to come.' She swivelled round. 'If we use the truck it'll only take us two or three days — unless I've been silly.'

'Over what?' He pulled up a chair. 'Let's have it. What's happened now?'

'Nothing. Well, not really; only that I could've been overheard while I was on the phone to my section head this morning.'

'Who the hell was listening?'

'Mr Barzani, that nasty little man who owns the house. It was so hot I had all the windows open. When I went to open the door too, I found him outside. He said he'd called round for the extra money we promised him. I don't know how long he'd been there, I don't know how much he heard, and I don't even know if it matters. I just wish I'd been more careful.'

'Did you mention Sara's name, or infrared airborne lasers, or who you are?'

She shook her head. 'It wasn't about that exactly.'

'What was it about?'

'Something else has gone wrong between Washington and Tel Aviv. Once we'd got co-ordinates for the quarry we'd planned to launch a low-level air attack on it from a Turkish air-base. But now we'll have to send in a ground team because the Americans have suddenly refused permission for any aircraft to enter the Iraqi no-fly zone. The US are making the same sort of fuss over Iraqi oil sales, but we don't know why they are.' She attempted a smile. 'I keep telling myself our landlord wouldn't have understood anything because I was speaking in Hebrew.'

Cogan was more relieved than annoyed. 'You've got yourself wound up over nothing,' he said. 'All Barzani's interested in is our cash. How much did you give him?'

'Another two hundred. He said if we have more American dollars he'd be pleased to introduce Sara to someone who can trace her parents, but I think he was just fishing. He gave me the creeps. I don't trust him either.'

'Because he's an Arab?'

'Because he's an Iraqi.'

'Sara's both,' Cogan said.

'It's not the same. She grew up in the States.'

'Look,' he said, 'if it'll make you feel better, I'll go and have a chat with him sometime tomorrow.'

'I thought we might leave tomorrow. There's no reason for us to stay here any longer, is there?'

'Do you really want to go on?'

She nodded. 'I know you think I'm scared, but it's not important. I'm different to you and Sara. I'm working for my country and there are people relying on me back home.' She stopped abruptly. 'I'm sorry. That must sound awfully pretentious. What I'm trying to say is that I can't do this by myself. I need your help.'

'How about telling me the truth, then?' he said. 'You haven't done anything like this before, have you?'

'No.'

'So who had the bright idea of giving you the job to begin with?'

'My section head thought it would be best to send a woman to talk to Sara. It went on from there. I'd been doing desk research on the PUK, and I knew a lot about the laser strikes on our aircraft, so as soon as you said Sara might be prepared to help us, I sent a fax recommending a low-risk, exploratory mission into Iraq.'

'And someone sitting behind a desk in Tel Aviv asked you to organize it?'

'I was told to. I wanted the job anyway. I suppose I should've realized what I was letting myself in for, but I didn't — not then.'

Cogan wasn't entirely unsympathetic. She was unable to conceal her discomfort, nervously smoothing back her hair. 'You'd better talk to Sara,' he said.

'She'll do whatever you tell her. She only pretends to be difficult to make herself more attractive to you. She understands exactly why we have to go, in the same way she knows you're the one who can get us there and back in one piece.'

'Why the sudden note of confidence? Has Tel Aviv told you to pull your head in?'

'No. It's just that I've stopped believing you're a metallurgist or an air accident investigator. You're not either of those things, are you?'

'Yes he is,' Sara spoke from the doorway. 'Ask him again, then see if he'll tell you about his wife and what happened in Afghanistan. You won't get any answers, but he might tell you things he hasn't told me. Then you'll know more about him than I do.'

Cogan had heard enough. Close to losing his temper he stood up, kicking his chair to one side before he took control. 'Right,' he said, 'you can both shut up. I'm sick of your games. We're here to do a job, so, whether you like it or not, this is what we're going to do and how we're going to do it. We travel at night starting at nine tomorrow evening. We take the main road through Ash Sharqat, which means the pipeline will be to the west running more or less parallel with us, and the river will be a couple of miles away on our eastern side. If we can cross the river in the truck before we reach Ba'iji, that's what we do. If we can't, we go by foot. From here on I don't want any more arguments or smart remarks, so if you have something to say, this is when you spit it out.'

'What if I won't go?' It was Sara who asked the question. She remained in the doorway, her voice brittle and with her hands on her hips.

'You don't have a choice. I'm bigger than you are and I've got the truck keys. I'll just tie you up and throw you in the back. How's that?'

As if to confirm Judith's opinion of her, she frowned at him for several seconds before she answered. 'When I was a little girl, my uncle bought me a book on the Crusades,' she said. 'If I was ever unhappy I'd sneak it into bed with me so I could look at one of the pictures. It was a painting of a man on horseback — sort of half heroic and half scary.'

Cogan interrupted her. 'Save it,' he said. 'If this is about your white knight tell me another time.'

'No. I'm going to tell you now — because there was something else in the picture. I'd forgotten about it until Catherine read me that poem she'd found. You see, the knight had a falcon on his arm.' She smiled very slightly. 'And to think I stopped believing in him when I was nine years old.'

★ ★ ★

Cogan's early night was already a failure. The lounge floor was hard, the ceiling fan was doing little to lower the temperature and, for some inexplicable reason, during the few, odd minutes when he'd been able to sleep, his dreams had been of Karen.

She'd been mocking him, standing legs apart on the bed, holding her skirt up around her waist because she knew he was too jet-lagged and too burned-out to make love to her. It was a familiar dream that Cogan's mind had invented for him, a means of justifying what had happened to his marriage and an excuse for him to become angry.

There were two endings to the dream, both of them very similar. In one he started throwing things at her immediately; in the other he delayed until she led him downstairs where she offered herself to a waiting lover.

Usually he woke up once the dream had run its course. Tonight, though, there was a more pleasant and altogether different ending involving Sara. She was drawing her palm over the knife wound in his chest, and he fancied he could feel her hair brush across his face as she spoke his name.

'Cogan.' She shook him again. 'It's me.'

To make sure it was, he reached up and locked his hands together behind her neck.

'Don't wake up Judith,' she whispered. 'Are you all right?'

'I'm fine.'

'I heard you talking to someone.' She lay down on the floor beside him. 'It's cooler out here than in the bedroom.'

'You ought to have brought your bed with you, then.'

'It's not big enough for you as well.' She made herself comfortable. 'You're supposed to say it's because I don't take up as much room as anyone else.'

Cogan abandoned any idea of going back to sleep. 'You might as well come right out with it,' he said. 'What's the problem?'

'Judith's the one with a problem. She still doesn't believe you're a metallurgist. After what happened at the camp she thinks you might be a mercenary or something. She can't understand why you weren't scared. I can't either.'

'Don't be bloody silly,' he said. 'I was as scared as you were.'

'How do I know that's true? You've spent

weeks asking questions about me, but you never say anything about yourself unless I drag it out of you. I couldn't tell Judith she was wrong because I don't know if she is.'

Cogan attempted to see her face in the dark. She was lying on her stomach with one arm draped over his chest. 'Is this about Karen again?' he said.

'No. It's about me finding out the truth. I want to hear what happened to you in Afghanistan. If you don't tell me I won't go with you tomorrow.'

'It was a long time ago,' he said.

'No, it wasn't. Three years isn't a long time.'

'I explained when we were in Savannah. A STOL, F–39 transporter on a cargo flight from Peshawar in Pakistan went down twenty miles short of Jalalabad in Afghanistan.'

'That doesn't explain anything. Was the pilot hurt?'

'He died in the crash — after he'd radioed to say he'd lost all power. The company that designed the plane asked me to go and inspect the wreckage. It was just a routine investigation.'

'If the plane was only carrying freight and there was no one else on board, why investigate?'

'Because it's bad business if you don't.

257

There are over five hundred F–39s in operation in eighty countries. Manufacturers always need to know why their aircraft crash. They got permission from the Afghan Government for me to have a quick look and paid for a helicopter to fly me in. It was supposed to be a one-day trip.'

'Which went wrong?'

'Yeah.' He searched for the right words. 'It was at the time when the Taliban rebels were hammering hell out of Kabul. The hills were crawling with mujahedin and Islamic holy-warriors. We'd only been at the site for half an hour when a whole bunch of them jumped us. They thought we were on a surveillance flight for the Rabbani Government. We were trying to get back to the helicopter when they blew it to bits with a rocket.'

'And they were the men who captured you?'

'Not just me; they got my pilot too — a guy called Rick Maitland. They threw us in a hole in the ground at their camp. Then, on the night they were going to execute us, there was a big raid on the place, and we got away. End of the story. Are you happy now?'

'If that was the end you wouldn't be rushing to say so.' She paused. 'But you haven't come to the important part yet, have you? How did you get home?'

'There isn't an important part,' Cogan said, 'unless you count Rick. Before he became a charter pilot he was in the SAS. If he hadn't been, we'd never have made it back to the border. We lived up in the mountains like a couple of animals, stealing guns, hunting for food and killing anyone and anything that moved. We both got pretty good at it.'

'For how long?'

'We travelled sixty-three miles in twenty-nine days. I've managed to forget most of them.'

'Except in the middle of the night when someone starts asking you questions you don't want to answer.' She propped herself up on an elbow. 'What happened to Rick?'

'He came to see me about a year afterwards. Then he settled down somewhere in the Caribbean. You can guess who with.'

'Oh. Oh, Cogan, I'm sorry.'

'You don't have to be sorry.' He was surprised how easy it had been to tell her. 'If things hadn't ended up the way they did with Karen, I probably wouldn't have gone poking around the Okefenokee swamp.'

'And Shannon Lockhart would have missed out on living happily ever after?' She leaned forwards. 'Is that what you mean?'

Cogan didn't know what he meant.

Unsettled first by his dream, and now by recollections he had no wish to remember, he was certain of two things only — that by visiting the swamp he had finally closed the door on the past, and that the kisses she had begun showering on him were not intended to lull him back to sleep.

10

Having used up the space on the kitchen table, Cogan had begun spreading maps out on the floor, knowing the exercise was largely a waste of time, but still hoping he might discover something he'd overlooked before.

The geographical maps were the best, providing some indication of how difficult the terrain was likely to be, although so far Ba'iji had appeared on only one of them, and for the most part the scales were too small. Surprisingly, the road maps were even less useful, showing none of the detail that he was looking for.

Sara came to kneel beside him. Except for preparing lunch, and later helping Judith pack food for the trip, for much of the day she had kept to herself, avoiding any mention of last night, and until now showing little interest in what he'd been doing.

'Bernie was right,' she said.

'About us buying a Michelin guide?'

'Mm. Now you can see how important I am. Without me you'd get lost five minutes after you left the road.'

'Not with GPS units I wouldn't.' Cogan

261

gave her a pencil. 'Draw in the airstrip and the quarry — go on, have a guess.'

'I need a map with the pipeline on it.' She searched for one, choosing a computer-enhanced satellite photograph that Judith had obtained from somewhere.

'Start from the minefield,' he said.

'OK.' She traced a finger along the pipeline, stopping when she reached the junction of the Dijlah river with a waterway running west from the Dokan dam. 'That's the Zab As Saghir,' she said. 'It's another river.'

Cogan looked over her shoulder. 'And the minefield was between the pipeline and the meeting point of these two rivers?'

'Maybe a bit further north, where the railroad's closer to the Dijlah.'

'But you never found the pipeline, did you?'

'No.' She shook her head. 'We were close though. And I know we were south of an oil refinery because we could see the flame from it burning at night.'

Cogan put his finger on a symbol denoting what he thought was an industrial site. 'Is that it?'

'I don't know.' She drew a small circle. 'If I had to guess, I'd say the minefield was about there.'

'So where's the quarry?'

She shrugged. 'Six or seven miles to the east perhaps. I've been trying to work out how fast the truck was travelling, but I'm not sure. We had wounded men and a whole lot of Republican Guards shouting and screaming at us. Catherine would've remembered. She wasn't as frightened as I was.'

'Do you think the mines were supposed to stop terrorists attacking the pipeline?'

'I did to start with. But now I think it was to protect the road to the quarry.'

'Which doesn't exist.'

'It was sand — all the way there.'

'Geotextiles,' Cogan said. 'It's a coarse-woven plastic cloth that you can lay in mud or silt to stabilize the surface. If it was buried a few inches deep no one would see it. You might even be able to chuck it on the top and let the wind do the rest. I've seen it used to make runways out of nothing on waterlogged ground.'

'The runway was concrete. It was the same colour as the sand, but it was concrete. I saw it three or four times.'

'Maybe it doesn't show up in photos because of its colour. You said it wasn't very long, didn't you? Just a strip leading away from the quarry.'

'Away from the rock-crushing plant — the

hangar where they kept the Antonov.'

'We'll have a look for wheel tracks,' Cogan said. 'They can't be flying in all their supplies.'

'Why not?' Judith had come into the room. 'The Iraqi Air Force can fly wherever they like below the 36th parallel.' She studied the map. 'Wouldn't it be simpler for them to fly things in?'

'No.' Cogan had been thinking. 'They need aviation fuel and chemicals for the laser. I don't know how much hydrogen peroxide and chlorine an oxygen-iodine laser uses, but it'll be a hell of a lot for one the size we're talking about — especially if the Iraqis are pumping oxygen faster than the speed of sound.'

'Is that why it's so powerful?' Judith cleared away some maps and sat down on the table. 'Why nobody else has been able to build one?'

'Partly. You need clever mirrors too — the single crystal silicate mirrors the South Africans are making for them.'

'I don't understand where the oxygen comes from,' Sara said. 'Whenever we start talking about the laser you change the subject.'

'Try this,' Cogan said. 'Step one, find yourself a twin-engined Antonov and fit it out with chemical holding tanks. Step two, build a laser cavity with some smart mirrors at each end, and buy a couple of super-high-speed pumps. Bolt on some electronics for beam guidance, and you're in business. All you have to do then is mix hydrogen peroxide and chlorine together to make oxygen and inject it into the cavity along with a bit of iodine. That generates a chemical reaction. The iodine atoms get excited and produce an almighty pulse of light. Bounce the light off the mirrors and you can amplify it to the point where it'll escape as a beam of completely pure infrared energy. The faster you pump oxygen, the more power you get.'

'How much power?' Judith asked.

'You already know. A couple of million watts — enough to burn through an aircraft fuselage two or three hundred miles away.'

Sara got to her feet. 'Or enough to melt a hole in the skin of a Scud missile,' she said. 'Or incinerate a convoy of Kurdish refugees.'

'Never mind the laser.' Cogan was anxious to bring the discussion back on track. 'We're trying to find a quarry.' He held up the satellite photograph. 'Are you certain you can't remember any landmarks?'

'Only some mountains in the distance.'

Sara's voice was defensive. 'You don't have to keep asking.'

Knowing better than to push, Cogan gave up on his questioning. 'Right,' he said. 'I'm going to fill the truck with diesel and check the gearbox oil before the garages close. You can figure out where we ought to cross the river.'

'What about the landlord?' Judith asked. 'Aren't you going to see him? You said you would.'

'Do I still need to?' Cogan had all but decided not to bother.

'It'd be a good idea, don't you think? You could tell him we're staying on here for a while — you know, to give him the wrong information — just in case.'

'OK. I'll call in on him.'

Sara was putting on her shoes. 'I'll go with you,' she said. 'Mr Barzani's English isn't very good.'

'I can manage,' Cogan said. 'You stay here.'

'No. I want to go.'

'Why?'

'Well.' She looked away. 'He wouldn't have said he knows someone who could trace my mother and father for me unless it was true, would he?'

'He's just after your money,' Cogan said gently. 'As far as I can make out, everyone in

Iraq knows somebody who's in the missing people business. Major Zebari said the same thing.'

'I can ask him anyway. Why shouldn't I?'

Unwilling to discourage her, Cogan headed for the door. 'Come on, then,' he said. 'Bring the pack with the antibiotics in it. If Barzani's as tricky as Judith thinks he is, maybe he'll do some kind of black market deal.'

He waited for her outside, conscious of the late afternoon sunlight, knowing that in a few hours they would be embarking on the last and most important leg of their journey. But instead of being optimistic he was aware only of a vague feeling of disquiet — a defence against the possibility of failure, he decided. Or because he could see through Sara's confidence — because the closer they got to the damn quarry, the less certain she seemed to be about her ability to find it.

'Are you angry with me?' She interrupted his thoughts.

'No. Are you ready?'

'Mm.' She accompanied him to the truck, throwing the pack up into the cab before she climbed inside. 'There's a garage on the block where we saw those UNICEF cars the other day,' she said.

Cogan already knew where to go. Driving slowly, he turned left at the end of the street, negotiating his way through what passed for Erbil's rush-hour traffic until he reached the garage forecourt where he drew up beside a battered pump displaying a diesel sign.

The youth who came to serve them was uncommunicative and surly, making no effort to understand when Cogan asked him to fill the tank and check the gearbox oil. Only after Sara got out to explain did he become more helpful, glancing at her surreptitiously while he manned the pump and smiling when he emerged from beneath the truck to announce that the oil level was normal.

The boy's reaction was one Cogan had seen a hundred times, and one of the reasons for Judith's resentment of her, although today he fancied he could detect signs of a truce between them.

He paid for the fuel, waited for Sara to climb back in then pulled out onto the road again.

'What about the transmission?' she said. 'You don't think it's going to hold up, do you?'

'It might. Keep your fingers crossed.'

'But not my legs?'

'Cut it out.' Cogan was looking for the right road. 'Do you remember how to find Barzani's place?'

'Down there.' She pointed. 'It's only about

a mile. Do you know he owns four other houses? He told Judith.'

'He told Judith a lot of things.' What interest Cogan had in their landlord was rapidly disappearing. He was also uneasy with the idea of Sara recruiting a stranger to help trace her family. Although her perseverance was understandable — particularly when her first attempt had ended in disaster — he knew this was not the time to reopen a search that would more than likely end up in a graveyard if it ended up anywhere at all.

'There it is.' She pointed again. 'The grey house.'

On the morning of their arrival in Erbil, Cogan's attention had been elsewhere and he was relying on her recollection of Barzani's house being better than his own. But he was still not sure she was right.

'How do you know?' He parked the truck on the opposite side of the road.

'I recognize the iron gate. Do you want to go in by yourself first — to see what you think?'

Cogan grinned. 'Who was it that had to come to translate?'

'I will if you want.'

'I'll give you a shout if I need you.' Leaving her alone in the cab, he walked over to the gate, discovering that it was chained and padlocked to one of the posts.

He resisted the temptation to turn away, climbing over the gate instead, half hoping the lock meant that the owner was not at home.

The window blinds were drawn, there was no sign of a car in the garage or in the driveway, and no response when Cogan rang the doorbell.

He waited for a moment then returned to the truck where Sara was stuffing boxes of tetracycline back into the pack.

'You're pleased, aren't you?' she said. 'You didn't want me to talk to him.'

'Look,' he said, 'let's get the quarry over with. Then we'll see if Judith's people can pull some strings for you.'

'Judith only cares about herself.'

He ignored the remark, nudging the truck forwards over the kerb to turn round before driving back down the street. In the few minutes that the vehicle had been stationary, the temperature inside had risen to the point where, even with the windows down, Cogan was becoming uncomfortably hot.

He slowed for the next intersection and was endeavouring to admit more air by opening the windshield when Sara shouted at him.

'What?' He applied the brakes.

'We have to stop. Now.'

'What for? What the hell's the matter?'

'I've just seen someone. The little girl from the camp. She was in a car that went right past in front of us.'

'It wasn't her.' He knew it couldn't have been.

'It was. Cogan, I know it was. She was in the back seat with her grandmother. I saw them both.'

He remained sceptical, discounting the possibility because, even if by some coincidence the girl and her grandmother happened to be in town, the chances of seeing them were too improbable to be worth considering.

'Why won't you believe me?' She stared at him.

He didn't answer.

'It was them.' She punched his arm. 'They're here in Erbil.'

'If you're right they're not just here,' he said. 'They're less than half a mile away from where we are.'

'Ain Kawa street,' she said. 'Major Zebari's son — he knew.'

'Why would he tell the girl? Why tell anyone?'

'Perhaps Judith knows.'

'We'd better ask her then, hadn't we?'

More disturbed than he was prepared to admit, he executed another U-turn, and began searching for somewhere to temporarily hide the truck.

In his mind, a worst-case scenario was taking shape, a scenario based on the assumption not only that something had gone wrong, but that his complacency of the last few days had been misplaced.

Sitting tight-lipped beside him, Sara had evidently come to a similar conclusion. She said nothing when he swung into a narrow side-street and eased the truck into an even narrower alleyway between a derelict factory and a partially demolished concrete wall.

'Check the pack,' he said. 'Judith's binoculars should be in there.'

She handed them to him. 'Do you believe me now?'

'No.' He held his door open to let her out his side. 'We'll go and make sure, though.'

It took them nearly a quarter of an hour to reach the south end of Ain Kawa street, and another two or three minutes to select the doorway of a corner shop from which to view the house. By then, Cogan's worst-case scenario had turned into a nightmare.

Soldiers were at the roadside, a white van and three late-model cars were parked nearby, and on each side of the driveway, armed men stood guard in the garden.

'Oh God.' Sara shrank back into the doorway. 'Tell me this isn't happening.'

Equally dismayed, Cogan was cursing their misfortune, trying not to guess how Judith might be coping.

'Mukhabarat,' Sara whispered. 'And Republican Guards. How did they ever find us?'

A reply was unnecessary, nor was there any need for him to use the binoculars.

A man had emerged from the front door, a small, neatly-dressed man who, half an hour ago, instead of being at home, had almost certainly been on his way here.

'Jesus.' Cogan watched Barzani walk to his car. 'Why the hell didn't we guess?'

'Judith did.'

Cogan was thinking furiously, groping for solutions to an impossible problem.

Sara too was thinking. She was tense as well, relaxing only slightly now Barzani had driven away. 'This is crazy,' she said. 'Why report us when he had no idea what we're doing or where we've come from?'

'Judith's phone call. And we're westerners — or he thinks we are.' Another picture formed in Cogan's mind. 'And there's someone who knows exactly where we came from.'

'Ayisha?'

'She was due to leave the camp the morning after us.'

'Cogan, for God's sake, she's only six or seven years old.'

'You've forgotten the Mukhabarat have got her father locked up somewhere. Blood's thicker than water. If she's here, you can bet it's because her grandmother's been in touch with them.'

'She wouldn't do that. Ayisha's Kurdish. So is her grandmother.'

'It hasn't stopped them. Look.'

This time there were no surprises. On the steps outside the front door a woman was brushing back the hair of a little girl who had only one hand — the innocent, golden-eyed child from the camp.

A man escorted them to one of the waiting cars. He nodded pleasantly at the woman and smiled at Ayisha, waving goodbye to her through an open window as the car moved off.

Too upset to watch, Sara had turned her back. 'How could she?' she said bitterly. 'How?'

Cogan was less disillusioned, knowing that in any country, let alone one as unstable and war-torn as Iraq, a child would willingly sacrifice strangers in exchange for a mother or a father.

Sara, though, was still refusing to accept the situation. She was pale, leaning against the wall in the doorway, arms by her side, fists clenched. 'I could be in there,' she said. 'They could've found me as well as Judith.'

Cogan didn't need reminding. 'It's my fault,' he said. 'I didn't listen to her properly.'

'About Barzani?'

'Yeah. We can thank him for this. If he's renting out other houses he's probably got a nasty arrangement with the local police.'

'That doesn't explain what Ayisha and her grandmother were doing here.'

'Yes it does.' He kept his eyes on the street. 'As soon as Barzani told the Mukhabarat there were foreigners in town they'd have wanted to know who the hell we were. If they got a call from Ayisha's grandmother at the same time, they'd have been real suspicious.'

'Why bring Ayisha to the house?'

'Identification,' Cogan said. 'To make sure they'd got their hands on the right people.' He paused. 'Except only Judith was home.'

'She'll have already told them who you are, who I am and where we were going.'

'She's tougher than that. She's a MOSSAD field agent.'

Levering herself away from the wall, Sara took hold of his wrists. 'Cogan, listen to me,' she said. 'You don't understand. I promise you she'll answer every single question they ask her. Being an Israeli makes it worse. You can't even begin to imagine what they'll do to her.'

He didn't want to imagine. Faced with soldiers, guards and an indeterminate number of men, he was as sickened by the idea of what could be happening inside the house as he was powerless to do anything about it.

For nearly a minute he considered his options, then he took the truck keys from his pocket. 'Go back and get the Scorpion,' he said. 'It's under the seat on the right-hand side.'

'No. I shouldn't have said what I did. They won't have hurt Judith. They're waiting for us to show up.'

Cogan wished fervently that he could believe her, but he couldn't. The soldiers in the street were evidence enough. They were no more expecting to capture the other two westerners this evening than they were expecting him to mount a one-man rescue mission — the only edge he was ever going to have.

'Fetch the gun,' he said. 'Go on.'

'No. You're mad.'

'We're not going to leave her.' He used the binoculars to scan the garden, searching for a route that would provide a degree of protection and, with luck, some small element of surprise.

'We have to wait,' she said.

'For what?'

'I don't know.' She glanced at him. 'Until it's dark. Until we come up with a plan that doesn't get us both killed.'

Common sense told him she was right. But she was buying time as well, refusing to let him take the risk because, like him, she recognized that, even under the cover of darkness and with all the luck in the world, his chances would be as slim as Judith's.

So the choices were straightforward, he thought. Now, while it was still daylight, and his approach would be easy to detect, or later tonight when in all probability, for Judith Safrai, any rescue attempt would be too late.

* * *

A month ago, on his first evening back in Georgia, Cogan had watched the sun go down on the Savannah waterfront. He had stayed there for an hour afterwards in the company of several hundred other people. They'd been of all ages, casually dressed, drifting in and out of coffee shops and bars, laughing and enjoying the soft, night air.

He had felt lonely then, but tonight, concealed in a dark doorway at the end of a street in a foreign town in a foreign country, his loneliness was being overridden by fear. He was worried about Sara too, concerned that she'd deliberately not returned with the machine-pistol in order to keep it from him, or worse still, that she'd encountered some kind of trouble.

On both counts he was wrong. Without warning she slipped out of the shadows, reappearing as if from nowhere.

She handed him the gun. 'Has anything happened?'

'No. Did you get lost?'

'I was careful. You told me to be careful.'

Where she'd been holding the Scorpion the receiver was warm and slippery with her sweat, making it difficult for him to work the action.

'I'll see you later,' he said. 'Better wish me luck.'

She touched his cheek. 'You don't have to go,' she said quietly. 'But I don't know how to stop you.'

Cogan's mouth was dry, and he could feel his heart thumping. He searched for words to reassure her, but could find none. 'Give me half an hour,' he said, 'then you get the hell out of it.'

Fifty yards away, the house was in darkness except for a ray of light streaming across the front lawn from one of the windows. But the light was weak and the shadows too deep for him to pick out the men who had been there earlier. Nor could he see any of the soldiers. Because they were wary, he wondered? Or in the van? Or simply waiting for him elsewhere?

Gripping the machine-pistol in both hands, he crossed the street diagonally and began to make his way cautiously towards some rubble that workmen had piled up beside a low stone wall.

The futility of what he was doing was becoming more apparent with every step he took. There was no cover to speak of, he had no means of breaking into the house when or if he got that far, and in a matter of minutes the rising moon would start to play its part.

Unwilling to believe that the street could really be deserted, he crouched behind the heap of rubble, closer than he had been to the parked vehicles, and with a clearer view of the garden.

Now, Cogan told himself, while the adrenalin was still pumping, while he was still able to pretend he could do this.

But he was already too late. Before he could summon the courage to continue, the porch light came on and the front door suddenly opened.

Four soldiers were the first to leave — Republican Guards, sauntering unhurriedly over to the white van.

A second later Judith was brought out. She was naked and barely conscious, being supported by two men. Her upper and lower lips had been split open, cigarette burns disfigured her breasts, and she was bleeding between her legs.

One of the men was Massoud Khadim. The other was Van Reenan.

11

Cogan was striding out, making it hard for Sara to keep up with him.

'We're going too fast,' she said. 'What if they have people out looking for us?'

'They haven't. They know they've screwed up.' Grim-faced, fighting to suppress his anger, he was ready for a confrontation, half-hoping he'd have an excuse to use the Scorpion before he reached Barzani's house.

But the streets were empty, and in the ten minutes since Judith had been taken away, not a single car had passed them by. For the first five of those minutes he had stayed where he was beside the wall, waiting despairingly for an opportunity that had never come, while Sara had remained hidden helplessly in the doorway, both of them appalled at what they'd witnessed, and both of them aware of how dreadfully they had failed.

By now, though, the full impact of Cogan's carelessness had hit home, and he was responding to a mixture of bitterness and rage, goaded into embarking on what he knew was another ill-considered undertaking, but unable to think of anything except the need to stop what was happening to Judith.

That she was alive at all was justification enough for what he intended to do. But it was the identity of the men who were responsible for her suffering that was fuelling his anger — reminding him of the knife wound across his chest, of the cold-blooded execution of Jeremiah and of Sara's determination to survive in the cloying wilderness of the swamp.

Why Khadim and Van Reenan had been in Erbil, was not hard to guess. Guessing where they were going was another matter, a question on which Judith's life could depend, and one Cogan intended to have answered before her predicament became more wretched than it was already.

He carried on walking without slackening his speed. 'We'll use the back door,' he said. 'If there is one.'

'Suppose he went somewhere else?' Sara had given up trying to slow him down.

'It's gone eleven o'clock. He'll be there.'

'Barzani won't know anything. He's just an informer.'

'We'll see.' It was best to keep his suspicions to himself, he decided. Then, if he turned out to be wrong, nothing would be lost.

Over the next quarter of an hour, to guard against surprises he became more alert, glancing over his shoulder at each street corner, listening for the tell-tale squeal of tyres and maintaining his watch for headlights until, for the second time that night, he found himself outside the house with the iron gate. On this occasion, a car was parked in the driveway, and the gate was unsecured.

'Lights,' Sara whispered. 'At least he hasn't gone to bed.'

'Might be better if he had.' Cogan opened the gate. 'OK,' he said. 'Don't speak English when you say hello and stand to one side where he can't see you. Leave the rest to me.'

He let her go first, staying close behind her as she made her way round to the rear of the building and approached a door surrounded by some trellis-work.

'Now?' she mouthed.

Cogan nodded. He took a deep breath, slipping the Scorpion out of his shirt, ready to adopt the technique that had been used to break into his Brunswick motel five weeks ago.

She knocked twice, blinking nervously when more lights came on.

The sound of footsteps was followed by the noise of a bolt being drawn. But Barzani was a cautious man. The door opened no more than an inch, not wide enough for Cogan to check for a safety-chain, although he could just see the outline of a figure through the crack.

For a second he waited, hearing Sara begin to say something. Then he launched himself forwards, bursting the door open with his shoulder.

The lack of a chain was his undoing. Off-balance and moving too quickly, he was ten feet inside the house before he could stop. He spun round, catching a glimpse of Sara in the hall, realizing too late that Barzani was behind the door, bleeding from his nose, but already advancing on her.

Sara had seen the danger. She evaded him by stepping aside, neatly kicking the door shut before she twisted his arm behind his back to slam him face-first into the wall.

Surprised by how easily she'd dealt with someone much stronger than herself, Cogan went to take over. 'Here.' He handed her the gun. 'Make sure there's nobody else around.'

She said nothing, disappearing into one of the rooms, leaving him to consider the best way to begin his interrogation.

Although the Arab was not a large man, he was wiry, cursing fluently as he fought to relieve the pain in his arm.

To stop him struggling, Cogan increased

the pressure. 'If you want me to break this for you, I will,' he said.

'You are a fool. Already the Mukhabarat are coming. They will make you watch when they do to the girl what they have done to the Jewish bitch.'

The remark was a mistake. Instead of intimidating Cogan, it antagonized him. With some difficulty he resisted the urge to overreact, disregarding a threat that was almost certainly as hollow as the lie. 'How much did you get paid?' he asked.

'Fuck your mother and fuck the daughters of your mother. Ask the Mukhabarat.'

The time for exchanging pleasantries was over, Cogan decided. 'Well,' he said, 'until they arrive it looks like I'll have to make do with you, doesn't it? Where have they taken Judith?'

'To a place where she will be happy to tell them what they wish to learn.'

Sara had returned, her face still pale, her knuckles white where she was gripping the gun. 'No sign of anyone,' she said. 'Is that all he's been saying?'

'Along with some other crap.' Cogan was having second thoughts, wondering if he'd come here for nothing after all. 'Maybe I figured it wrong.'

'Let me try.' Speaking in Arabic she

approached Barzani, slipping the Scorpion muzzle down into the gap between his stomach and the wall.

The inflexion in her voice was peculiar, and she was too controlled — so much so that Cogan moved to intervene.

'Hang on,' he said. 'What are you doing?'

'I've told him Judith's my sister, but I've promised not to kill him.'

'Why the hell tell him that?'

'Because I've said I'll make him into a eunuch instead. It'll be real quick — just one shot. But I don't think he believes me.'

Cogan didn't believe her either. To prevent a misunderstanding, he shook his head before he spoke. 'OK,' he said. 'Do it. Never mind the noise. Then maybe he'll change his mind.'

No further inducement was required. Faced with the prospect of losing his manhood, Barzani immediately became a different person, swivelling his head round to speak, anxious now to cooperate in any way he could.

'Please to take away the gun,' he said.

'In a minute,' Cogan said. 'Where is she?'

'You must understand I cannot be sure of this. Once only the tall man has spoken of a *mahhgar*, but I believe it is not right I hear of such a thing.'

Cogan had come across the word *mahhgar*

often enough to recognize it, but the tip-off had been volunteered too readily, he thought. Which could mean Judith was *en route* to somewhere other than the quarry and raised another possibility — that the information had been deliberately leaked to Barzani in the hope that he might be pressured to pass it on.

If Sara had similar concerns, she was keeping them to herself. 'You know what *mahhgar* means, don't you?' she said.

'Yeah.' He was trying to pull the threads together, wondering if she understood that Judith could have become bait for a trap. 'Did you see a phone anywhere?' he said.

She nodded.

'Rip out the cord and bring it here. We need something to tie him up with. See what you can find for a gag too.'

She extricated the machine-pistol, but remained standing where she was. 'So we can do what?'

'So we can figure out if he's lying or telling the truth.'

'I don't see it matters.'

'Because Judith could be dead?'

'I didn't say that.' She turned to go. 'Ask Barzani if he thinks she is.'

Barzani's thoughts had been centred on something quite different. He had been waiting for Sara to move, waiting for the right opportunity to overpower her. Now, as she walked away, without warning he spun round, ducking and breaking free.

He was fast, lunging at Sara while she still had her back to him, simultaneously kicking the Scorpion out of her hands and reaching inside his jacket.

This time he was successful. Before she could protect herself, he seized her by the throat. And this time he had a knife.

He had miscalculated.

Cogan was already watching the blade, already back in the mountains of Afghanistan, unconsciously drawing on his rage, welcoming it, confident of relying on skills he thought had been forgotten.

As if in slow-motion he saw Barzani's knife-hand travel back and saw it pause in preparation for the thrust.

By then Cogan had him, wrenching him away, swinging him round like a rag-doll to finish what should never have begun.

There was no struggle. Outclassed in a contest in which Barzani had stood no chance, he paid a fatal price for threatening the one person in the world he should have left alone.

The end was mercifully swift. He died on his knees, slumped against the wall, coughing blood, unable to remove the steel blade that was buried between his ribs.

At the end of the hall, Sara had frozen with her hands at her throat. Her face was without expression, her eyes as wide as Cogan had ever seen them.

'It's OK.' He went to her. 'It's over.'

'You didn't have to do that.'

'I know.' He picked up the gun. 'Come on. Time we were out of here.'

Once he'd helped her to the door and checked that it was safe for them to leave, he stood outside beneath the trellis for a moment, breathing in the night air, staring at the moon, willing himself to believe that even with everything unravelling overnight, he could still keep Judith alive, and somehow still fulfil his commitment to the girl who was waiting so untrustingly in the dark beside him.

★   ★   ★

The events of the last few hours were beginning to take their toll. It had been nearly an hour since they had retreated here to the comparative safety of the truck, but Sara remained withdrawn, seemingly preoccupied with something she was unwilling to discuss. Cogan had tried to discover what it was, but so far he had made little progress.

She was not in shock. Of that he was sure. Nor did she appear to be distressed — mainly, he thought, because she'd learned how to insulate herself from the worst of the horror and the violence she'd experienced in her life. But, with time ticking away, the need to bring her round was becoming more pressing. Enough uncertainty lay ahead without him having to worry about her feelings, and he knew that the longer he put off telling her what they were going to do, the less likely he was to win any argument about it.

To break the impasse he handed her the backpack. 'Have a look through that,' he said.

'Why?'

'To see what we've got.'

She unzipped the top, tipping out the packets of tetracycline onto the seat before she checked. 'Not much,' she said. 'A half-empty bottle of water, your satellite phone, the binoculars, two bars of chocolate, one of the GPS units, a dirty T-shirt and a pair of my jeans.'

'No maps?'

'They're all back at the house.'

'And no range-finder?'

She shook her head.

The absence of a map was going to be a problem, he thought, but the phone and the

GPS unit more than made up for it. He took the T-shirt from her, using it to wipe his hands and to remove any spots of blood he'd left on the steering wheel or on the doorhandle. It was a ritual he'd inherited from Rick: first clean your weapons, then clean yourself — a means of closing off the past because unless you could forget about today, you wouldn't be ready for tomorrow.

Three years ago the ritual had worked well. Tonight it didn't. Cogan knew he was still wound up, continuing to dwell on what had happened instead of concentrating on what had to be done next.

To get some fresh air, he wound down the window, smelling only the aroma of diesel leaking from the truck, listening for sounds that weren't there, unable to see anything except shadows in the alleyway.

Like Erbil, the whole outside world was asleep, he decided. Only Sara was awake, and only Sara would be able to guarantee success tomorrow.

He was about to announce his proposal when she tucked her legs beneath her and turned to face him.

'I need a new trick,' she said. 'After I ran away from New York and went to work for SCL, I really believed I was Shannon Lockhart. It was easy. All I had to do was keep telling myself that all the time I was Shannon, I'd be all right — you know, because I'd made her into such a strong person. Now when I try to be her, it doesn't work.'

'She's still back in the swamp. I'll go and get her when we're finished here.'

'After we've decided what to do about Judith?'

'Right.'

'Cogan.' She took his hands. 'If Judith's at the quarry, we can't help her. You must know that.'

'Maybe her people can get her out.'

'Why should they? She's nobody. She doesn't matter to them. Israel won't risk sending in a team to rescue Judith. It'd be too dangerous, and it's too far for them to come.'

'Unless they've got a team coming anyway — for another reason.' He'd been allowing the conversation to take its course. Now he braced himself for the crunch. 'Judith said the US have blocked all air traffic from entering the no-fly zone. That means the Israelis can't launch an attack from a Turkish air-base, so they'll have to destroy the quarry from the ground. As long as they're sending troops they might as well try to find Judith before they blow the place.'

'You mean as long as I can tell them

exactly where to look for her. I'm not sure how much of the place I'll be able to recognize.'

Cogan was disconcerted. Instead of her being negative, she seemed to have accepted what he'd said without question — perhaps, he thought, because she'd misinterpreted the implications.

'You realize what I'm saying, don't you?' He tried to see her expression in the moonlight.

'Yes. You're saying the only way we can help Judith is by giving the Israelis what they want — the location of the quarry.'

Gently, Cogan thought. Don't force the issue and let her make the running. 'I can phone the co-ordinates through to Bernie,' he said.

'So he can pass them on to Tel Aviv?'

'Or to Madeline Isaacs in the States. She can get in touch with the right people in MOSSAD, and she knows who I am. She probably knows who you are by now.'

'Mm.' Sara twirled a strand of hair around her fingers.

'It's the best shot Judith'll have. And it fixes the problem we came here to fix.'

'You don't have to explain.' She started repacking the boxes of antibiotics. 'I suppose going south won't be any more dangerous than going north. They'll be looking for us everywhere.' She paused. 'We'll go back and get Barzani's car. It'll be safer than using the truck.'

'No.' Cogan had already rejected the idea, knowing that, in spite of the size and slowness of the truck, it was always going to be a better bet. 'The minute someone finds Barzani, there'll be a description out on his car,' he said. 'And if we have to go off-road or run into trouble I'd rather we had some heavy-gauge steel around us.'

'The mine-detector's still back at the house.' She zipped up the pack. 'With all our other stuff.'

'Including some of your friends from the Republican Guards. I only saw four of them leave. We've got bigger problems than the mine-detector — no money and no damn maps.'

'You've forgotten I've been here before,' she said. 'There's more than one road south.'

Cogan was beginning to think he'd misread the situation. After what had taken place tonight, and after spending weeks attempting to convince her that the location of the quarry was the solution to everything, her endorsement of his plan had been as unexpected as it was out of character.

'Money.' She handed him an envelope. 'It

was on a dresser in Barzani's kitchen. I think it's what the Mukhabarat paid him for turning us in. I don't know how much there is, but it'll be enough — you know, for food and the other things we'll need.'

'Let's go back a step,' Cogan said. 'Why all the sweetness and light? What the hell's going on?'

' "Or never will the river run".'

'What?'

'It's a line from the second verse of Catherine's poem.'

'I didn't know there was a second verse.'

'I never gave it to you. It's not yours: it belongs to me.'

'What's the bloody poem got to do with you suddenly agreeing to go on?'

'You wouldn't understand.'

Cogan had no intention of trying. 'Look,' he said. 'If you don't believe we can do this, you say so right now. And if you think Judith doesn't stand a snowball's chance in hell, get that off your chest as well.'

'I don't know whether they'll keep her alive or not. I'm not going because of Judith, I'm going because of the poem — for myself, or for you and me — I'm not sure which. But I'm fairly sure I can find the *mahhgar* and I know how to get us out of Erbil. We'll have to wait for daylight, though, otherwise I won't be able to remember the way.'

The way to where? Cogan wondered. Headlong into a trap? Or the way to a distant, rock-filled hole in the ground that had already cost the lives of Catherine, Jeremiah and Barzani, and where for Judith, if she was being taken there at all, time would fast be running out.

12

Last Saturday their journey in to Erbil had been straightforward and direct; their journey out was not. They had started at dawn with Sara at the wheel, slinking out of town on a route that had taken them past the ruins of Erbil's ancient hilltop fortress before they'd turned south into a rabbit-warren of shops and mud-brick houses. From there, somehow or other, she'd managed to find the road to a disused marble-cutting factory that had been converted into an indoor and outdoor market.

The place was already crowded when they arrived, but over the last ten minutes, so many people had turned up that by the time they'd found a parking space, Cogan had changed his mind about stopping.

'We'll try somewhere else,' he said. 'You're going to stand out like a sore thumb with a pony-tail and your hair uncovered.'

'How about this?' She took the dirty T-shirt, ripping it in half to fashion a scarf to put over her head.

'We don't have to buy stuff here,' Cogan said.

'We have to ask about the ferry. It'd be silly to drive for miles and miles, and then find out it isn't operating any more.'

The ferry was Sara's idea, a means of crossing the river without having to rely on bridges which might or might not have been rebuilt since the war, and where roadblocks could have already been erected.

'Do you want to stay in the truck?' she asked. 'I'll only be a minute.'

'No.' Pushing the Scorpion back under the seat with his heel, he climbed out and waited for her while she locked the doors. 'Where to?' he said.

'This way.' She headed off towards the centre of the market, walking quickly as though she knew exactly where she was going.

Cogan was less confident, keeping a watchful eye out for uniforms as he followed her through the crowds, enjoying the fresh, earthy smell of vegetables, fruit and garlic, but relaxing only marginally.

Here on the outskirts of town, Erbil's economic hardship was not so noticeable. The atmosphere was nothing like as dreary as it had been nearer the city centre, and there appeared to be no shortage of produce, the stalls crammed with sesame cakes, slabs of sheep's-milk cheese, dried prunes and an endless variety of olives. There were walnuts and almonds as well, baskets full of them hanging alongside plastic bags containing cloves and honey of all colours. Even a stuffed jackal was on offer, a delicacy Cogan hurried past in order to avoid the clouds of flies that were being attracted to it by the smell.

Despite himself he was beginning to unwind, he realized, still cautious, still unable to think of Judith without his stomach knotting, but the feeling of despair had gone, and with it had gone much of his pessimism. On a bright, sunlit morning amidst the hustle and bustle of the market, and with Sara no longer so withdrawn, his perspective on the night's events was becoming clearer.

Thoughts of Judith continued to haunt him, but the need to concentrate on what lay ahead was helping him deal with his misgivings about her future. His misgivings about himself were harder to handle. Last night he'd been able to rationalize Barzani's death, writing it off as an understandable if unfortunate mistake. Since dawn, though, it had become more difficult to justify what he'd done, and although the coldness inside him had not yet gone away, he'd begun to search for a better explanation.

Sara interrupted his thoughts. 'Have you

got the money?' she asked. She was standing at the counter of a food-stall where a wizened old lady in a chador was waiting with her hand outstretched.

'What did you buy?' Cogan tried to see.

'What we said. Lots of mineral water and some dates and some bread. I can get figs and raisins, too, if you want.'

'Dates are fine.' He gave her the envelope and watched her count out the dinars, aware all over again of how quickly she could adapt to unfamiliar places and situations that anyone else would have found bewildering. She was as at ease here as she'd been in Savannah, or at the PUK camp — treating the market in the same way that she treated everything in her life, except for her involvement with him which seemed to vary in complexity from one day to the next.

'Why are you looking at me like that?' She handed him a paper bag to carry.

'Don't ask. Did you find out about the ferry?'

'The lady says it used to cross every two hours, but it's been losing money, so now it only runs when there are enough cars or people to make a trip worthwhile. Apparently the Republican Guards wanted to close it down last year, but they never got around to doing anything.'

'What if they've suddenly got interested again?'

'No one would be expecting us to use it. It's only a little flat-topped barge.'

'Big enough to take the truck?'

'I don't know. The PUK only told us about it. We were further east.'

Cogan decided to take the risk. 'OK,' he said. 'We'll give it a try.' He smiled his thanks at the old lady, then began trailing Sara back through the crowds, remaining watchful until they were safely reinstalled in the truck and underway again.

It was some minutes before Sara decided which of several roads she should take. Like Cogan, she, too, was slowly beginning to unwind, settling down to her driving once she was certain they were travelling in the right direction.

'Can I ask you something?' she said.

'Depends what it is.'

'Do you think Barzani was just trying to get out of the house, or did he really want to kill me?'

'Van Reenan or Khadim might have had a talk with him. If they did he could have fancied his chances of turning us in to make some more money.'

'Or earn more Brownie points from the Mukhabarat.' She swung the truck left onto a gravelled road and changed gear. 'What are we going to do if we see a roadblock?'

'Maybe there won't be any. By now the Iraqis will have found out that you and Catherine didn't ever know where the quarry was.'

'From Judith?'

'They'd have guessed anyway,' he said. 'You wouldn't have turned up on their doorstep again unless you had good reason to — unless you were looking for something. It must've been a hell of a shock when they realized you were never the problem they thought you were.'

'Are you saying they might not bother searching for us at all? I don't believe that.'

Cogan didn't either. 'They've got two choices,' he said. 'They can either forget about us and hope we'll go home, or they can assume we're going to carry on.'

'That we'll carry on because of Judith, you mean?'

'Van Reenan isn't stupid. He wouldn't have mentioned the quarry in front of Barzani by accident.'

'You're making it sound as though we're walking in to a trap.' She took off her headscarf. 'As though they're playing a game with us.'

'What about the game you're playing? You

302

know as well as I do what we're walking in to. But you don't care any more, do you?'

'I told you why.'

''Or never will the river run'?'

'Yes.'

'How does that make you not care?' Cogan knew she wasn't going to tell him.

'It's too complicated to explain.' To end the conversation she changed gear again, holding the Mercedes in the centre of the road as it accelerated and began to gather speed.

Already the countryside was changing. With Erbil well behind them, they were travelling through a fertile region of shallow valleys and well-watered foothills that showed little sign of becoming the desert Cogan had been expecting to see.

Laid out on each side of the road, the slopes were the same colour as the valley floor, a dusty, uniformly wheat-green tapestry of orchards, date-groves, vineyards and open grassland sprinkled here and there with copses of slender, silvery trees. The farmhouses and their barns were equally dusty, dun-coloured, nestled among the trees or standing beside the irrigation ditches leading from the river.

Picturesque though the scenery was, Cogan's appreciation of it was superficial, spoilt by the need for him to stay alert. He watched the fields and the hills roll past, conscious of the rising temperature now the sun was higher, trying not to listen to the whine from the gearbox, wondering if the Iraqis were really expecting Sara to continue her search, and if so, when and where they would set their trap.

Sara herself seemed untroubled. She asked no more questions, handling the truck effortlessly, apparently content to let Cogan forewarn her of any danger, although he saw how her hands tightened on the wheel when other vehicles slowed down or pulled out in front of them.

For the most part, the traffic was slow and unmotorized, consisting of handcarts, donkeys and the occasional horse-drawn wagon, all of them keeping well to the side of the road as soon as they heard the Mercedes coming or caught sight of its attendant cloud of dust.

Whether or not they were making good time, Cogan wasn't sure. The road was gradually deteriorating, the little hamlets along it appearing less frequently than they had done earlier. There was also a marked change in the colour and richness of the soil. In the last half-hour the landscape had gone from being green to a pale, washed-out brown, and in place of vineyards and orchards, now there were only goats roaming around rocks in search of anything that the sun had not yet shrivelled up to nothing.

Far away to the east, the mountains had assumed a different colour too, still tinged with vegetation in places, but otherwise barren, arid and unfriendly. Only the river was the same, either spread out in front of them around a bend, or sparkling in the sunshine when they looked down on it from the crest of a rise.

Soon the road began to climb, becoming so steep in places that the combination of washboard and loose gravel made it almost impassable on hairpin bends and on some of the sharper corners. Not until it straightened out at the end of a cutting did the surface improve, and only then was Cogan able to see how far they'd come.

'Hey.' He pointed. 'Over there. Isn't that your pipeline?'

She slowed the truck, keeping it rolling in first gear to avoid losing traction until she could find somewhere flatter to stop. 'Where?' She used both hands to shield her eyes from the sun. 'It's just the railroad — the one we saw before.'

'Further to the left, between the railroad and the river.'

'Oh.' She tried again. 'Oh, yes — two pipes, side by side.'

'Not hard to see in daylight.' Cogan handed her the binoculars. 'Pity you didn't bring a couple of kilos of C4 with you.'

'The PUK gave us a lot more explosives than that. But we didn't know there were two pipes. They look so easy to find, don't they?'

'They only stand out because we're up high,' he said. 'And because the sand's been blown away from them.'

'They weren't supposed to be buried — well, we weren't told they were.' She scanned the area with the binoculars. 'I can see the ferry landing — look, where the railroad starts to curve away.'

Cogan couldn't pick it out until he made himself trace what he thought was the outline of the road, a faint trail leading across the flats to an open, rock-free piece of ground alongside the west bank of the river.

'Can you see it?' she asked.

'Yeah, I think so. I can't see any barge, though.'

'Perhaps it's over on the other side. The main thing is that there aren't any soldiers around.'

A good sign, Cogan thought, although the absence of waiting passengers was less encouraging, an indication that if the ferry was operating at all, the next crossing was still some time away.

Sara switched off the engine. 'Do you know where we are?' she asked.

'On a mountaintop somewhere in Iraq.'

'We're out of the no-fly zone. We're south of the 36th parallel.'

Cogan received the news with mixed feelings. Discovering that they'd made better progress than he'd believed was one thing; being in the region where they could be spotted by the Iraqi Air Force was another.

'How about some lunch?' he said. 'It doesn't look like we'll have to hurry to catch the ferry.'

'We can see it from here anyway.' She gave him a handful of dates and one of the small, unleavened loaves she'd bought. 'You're worried, aren't you? You think we're taking too much time.'

'Depends how long Judith's got.'

'Catherine and I were kept locked up for six and a half days, and Judith's a lot more valuable than we were. Iraq can exchange her for prisoners, or even parade her on television if they want — you know, as an Israeli terrorist — like they did with those British pilots who were shot down in the Gulf War.'

'Or they could carry on with the cigarette burns and doing God knows what else to her.'

'If they believe she's told them the truth, why would they do that?'

Cogan had no answers. There were too many possibilities, all of them bad and all of them based on the presumption that Judith was still alive.

He tried to eat, but his mouth was too dry for him to swallow the bread. 'How many more miles after we've crossed the river?' he asked.

'It's hard to tell. Once we're on the other side I'll have a better idea. I've never been in this part of the country. The PUK told us about the ferry, but we didn't use it because they said it wasn't safe.'

'Do you know which road we have to take?'

She shook her head. 'There aren't any. We have to drive cross-country through one of the gorges.'

'Aren't we supposed to be looking for a desert?'

'Yes — well, sort of — a rocky desert. There's nothing for miles and miles around the quarry — no water — not even any scrub. Catherine knew how to find water, but there wasn't a single spring. We didn't see goats or anything either — just snakes and scorpions.'

'So how are you going to decide which way we have to go?'

'By the mountains — by their shape. I'll remember them. But we're not close enough yet. I'll have to wait until we're further south.' She raised the binoculars again, studying some of the peaks before directing her attention back to the ferry landing. 'Cars,' she said. 'And a tractor with a trailer behind it.'

'How many cars?'

'Two — like those four-wheel-drive Nissans we saw the other day.' She gave him the binoculars. 'I wonder if they're the same ones?'

They weren't Nissan Patrols. Cogan could see them clearly. They were white Toyota Landcruisers, and the insignias on their doors were not those of UNICEF, but of the United Nations.

'Surprise,' he said. 'We're going to be in good company.'

'What do you mean?'

'I think it's some kind of UN Weapons Inspection team, or part of one. God knows what they're doing here in the middle of nowhere.'

'If they're going to a quarry we can follow them.' She nearly managed a smile. 'We'd better join the queue. There's the ferry.' She pointed. 'See?'

Emerging from the rushes on the far side of the river, a barge was pushing its way diagonally upstream to combat the current, leaving a white smudge of a wake behind it. From this distance it hardly seemed large enough or powerful enough to make the crossing empty, let alone return with vehicles on its deck.

Sara watched it for several minutes before she restarted the truck and eased it back on the road. 'Do you think the UN inspectors will be Americans?' she asked.

'If they are, don't talk to them,' Cogan said.

'Why not? We can explain what's happened.'

'Sure. We'll tell them Judith's a Girl Scout who's been kidnapped by a South African terrorist and that she's being held prisoner at an imaginary, underground Iraqi laser development base somewhere in the desert.'

She frowned at him. 'Don't talk to me like that. It was only an idea.'

The downhill descent was proving as hazardous as the climb had been. With each application of the brakes all four wheels were slipping on the gravel, forcing Sara to rely entirely on the engine to hold their speed at a manageable level.

Towards the bottom of the hill where the rubble was thicker, her job became more difficult, but the road soon straightened allowing her to coast the last few yards to the landing.

Their arrival was met with little or no interest from the occupants of the UN vehicles. None of the men got out to say hello or pass the time of day, either indifferent to the presence of two sweat-stained fellow travellers or preferring to remain in the air-conditioned comfort of their Toyotas because of the heat.

Cogan could understand their reluctance to open a door or wind down a window. The bonnet and the mudguards of the Mercedes were already too hot for him to touch, and even this close to the water, the air was windless, oppressive and laden with fine dust that the truck had brought down to the landing with it.

The tractor driver was evidently insensitive to the temperature. He was smoking a cigarette, half-asleep, half-watching the approaching ferry as the man at the helm lined up the bow-ramp with the shingle beach.

Now the barge was closer, Cogan could see it was more substantial than he'd originally believed. It was a rusty, steel-hulled vessel powered by an Evinrude outboard motor that was either on its last legs or running on the wrong mixture.

So bad was the exhaust smoke that long before the Landcruisers, the tractor and the truck had been driven on board, the entire landing was shrouded in a thick, blue haze — a signal for any troops on the other side to prepare themselves, Cogan thought.

But there were no soldiers hiding in the rushes, no Republican Guards and no welcoming committee from the Mukhabarat. The river crossing was as uneventful as their journey from Erbil had been, providing a brief respite from the dust and an opportunity for Sara to sluice some fresh water over her face and through her hair, but otherwise doing nothing to make Cogan believe that the worst of their trip was behind them.

At the landing on the east bank, after each driver had negotiated payment for the crossing, the UN cars and the tractor disembarked, moving off one after the other towards the solitary exit road or track. Sara, though, made no attempt to follow. Instead she spent two or three minutes speaking to the ferry-man, pointing repeatedly to the south, and twice mentioning Ba'iji — the only word Cogan recognized.

When she eventually drove off the barge and was able to see past some of the taller groups of rushes on the east boundary of the landing, she swung the truck to the right, squinting into the sunshine as she tried to decide on a route across the foothills.

'We have to look for a valley with blue-veined rock on its western slope,' she explained. 'It's supposed to be hard to find, but it might not matter too much. The ferry-man says that over half the valleys interconnect in different places.'

'To hell with the valleys,' Cogan said. 'There has to be some kind of road.'

'There isn't. Not to where we want to go.'

'What about those two Landcruisers? Did you ask him about them?'

'He thinks they might have special permission to inspect a military air-base about ten kilometres away where the Iraqi Army are storing old warheads.' She swerved to avoid a ledge where some grass was growing. 'All we have to do is be careful we don't cut out our tyres on the rocks.'

Which wasn't going to be easy in country like this, Cogan thought. In the distance, waves of mountains with jagged, tooth-like peaks and saw-backed ridges were glowing yellow against the sky. A mile away, the valleys to the south were less forbidding but leading off in all directions, some already in shadow, others shimmering so much in the heat that they could just as easily be mirages.

How Sara would decide which of them had

dead ends, he couldn't imagine. The valley entrances gave no clues, nor was it possible to guess which ones might interconnect at some point further in to the range.

She was working hard at the wheel, guiding the truck across the bed of a dried-up tributary, heading for the mouth of a wide ravine where he could see traces of blue strata.

'We have to hope one of the gorges goes right through,' she said.

'Through to the quarry?'

'Well, to the plain. It's south of this ridge of mountains. We have to go out onto the plain first. After that I'll know where I am.' She paused. 'Or I should do.'

Cogan wished he shared her optimism. Unable to offer any advice, he braced himself against the door to counter the lurching and the bone-jarring bouncing, letting her choose how fast, how far and which direction they should travel.

He should not have been so trusting. By six o'clock in the afternoon he'd begun to question her judgement, and by 6.30 his doubts had become serious enough for him to call a halt. Both of them were filthy, drenched in perspiration and, despite trying to maintain their water intake, already suffering headaches from dehydration.

She stopped the truck without protest, perhaps guessing what he was thinking, or because she, herself, recognized the uselessness of what they were endeavouring to do.

This was the fifth valley or ravine they had explored, and one of only two that had showed any promise. The end of it was not yet in sight, but in the last ten minutes it had begun exhibiting all the characteristics of leading nowhere, the side slopes becoming progressively steeper, and with the scree at the bottom forming a layer of debris on which Sara had been forced to drive.

At the end of her tether, frustrated and almost too exhausted to speak, she was slumped over the wheel, her hands raw, her hair caked with sand and grit.

'Better let me take over,' Cogan said gently. 'You need a break.'

When she didn't reply he reached across to help her sit up, only then noticing that her face was streaked with tears.

'Hey.' He wiped her cheeks with his palm. 'It's OK.'

'No it isn't. It's my fault we're lost. You shouldn't have listened to me.'

'We're not done yet,' he said. 'It's getting cooler, and we've still got plenty of fuel.'

'I didn't stop to save fuel. I've stopped because I don't know where to go any more.

It's like being buried. I can't see the mountains, I can't see the sun and none of the ravines end up where I think they will. I don't recognize any of them.'

'What about this one?'

She shook her head.

'We'll stretch our legs for a bit. Then I'll drive.'

'To where?' She pushed open her door.

'Your call. We can either go on, or we can backtrack.'

Backtracking was not going to be an option. He had his hand on the ignition key ready to switch off the engine when the rear window splintered into a thousand pieces.

'Get going,' Cogan yelled. 'Move.'

He punched out more glass to obtain a clearer view. As he did so there was the scream of a second bullet ricocheting off the bodywork.

The shots were coming at an angle, the first exiting through Sara's open door, the second howling off the roof above her head. He waited for a third, holding his breath, trying to locate the gunman among the rocks.

But with the truck already accelerating, dust swirling up from the wheels was obscuring his view, and it wasn't until Sara put the Mercedes into a series of evasive slides that he caught sight of the last thing he'd wanted to see.

Behind them, 250 yards away, an armoured vehicle was in pursuit. It was a tracked vehicle painted in desert camouflage, either a light tank or a personnel carrier that had been fitted with a forward-mounted machine-gun.

'Go for it,' Cogan shouted. 'Don't weave. We'll outrun them.'

By putting her foot hard down, for a while Sara was able to maintain their lead, but there was a limit to how fast she dared to go. Fighting for control at nearly thirty miles an hour on a surface that would have been treacherous at half the speed, she'd abandoned her attempt to conserve their tyres, wrenching at the wheel, changing into a lower gear whenever they lost momentum and keeping the Mercedes in the centre of the ravine where she could gain maximum traction.

Her efforts were in vain. On tarmac or a gravelled road, the truck might just have had the edge; on a surface of loose stones and coarse sand it was no match for a vehicle with tracks.

Cogan watched the gap begin to shrink, counting down the seconds until they'd be in range of the machine-gun, certain that it was the army who had stumbled upon them or even followed them into the ravine.

The earlier shots had come from a rifle, accurate, long-distance shots against a stationary target. But in a chase like this, a rifle would be next to useless, and he knew that the machine-gun would be the weapon of choice.

He tried to estimate how long it would be before he'd have to tell Sara to get her head down, praying that the ravine would become no narrower and struggling to decide what the hell he was going to do with her if it did.

Being frightened for Sara was not a new experience. In the same way he'd been concerned for her safety in the swamp, at the PUK camp and last night when Barzani had drawn the knife, so was he fearful for her now, but this time without the means to do anything about it.

He'd been right about the machine-gun. Above the roar of the Mercedes' engine he heard the stuttering noise begin and saw the ground to their left erupt in a line parallel with the truck. The bullets were landing less than six feet away, smacking into the scree or burrowing, throwing up fountains of dirt to warn Sara of the danger.

She changed course abruptly, compensating for a slide before she shouted and pointed ahead.

Instead of narrowing, the ravine was

318

opening up. A minute ago the walls had been so steep and so high that they'd been blocking out the sunlight. Now, at the very moment when Cogan had thought their luck had failed, the ravine had become a valley.

Sunshine was replacing shadows, and instead of the ground being littered with scree it was much firmer and smoother, allowing Sara to increase their speed.

Soon the west wall had all but melted away, offering her a chance to bear right onto a flat, cream-coloured plain.

But before she could change course, another burst of fire tore up more dirt beside them.

'Which way?' she yelled.

Cogan wasn't sure. He was waiting for a second option — hoping against hope that a left turn would take them into broken country where there would be more cover.

In the end the decision was made for him.

The pursuit vehicle had stopped gaining, but the driver hadn't given up. He was anticipating the direction Sara would choose, diverting right to cut her off.

'Left,' Cogan shouted. 'Go left.'

Immediately she put the Mercedes into a long slithering curve, swinging wide of the valley mouth so she could see where to go.

Cogan stuck his head out of the window to

get a better view, desperate to discover whether or not the manoeuvre had been successful.

The plain extended to the east as well, but to his relief, along the northern boundary of it, the protruding remnants of foothills had created a wasteland. Two-hundred-foot-high escarpments rose vertically from the desert floor, buttressed by outcrops of solid rock, their bases piled high with giant boulders and sandstone blocks. Dark areas of shadow between them contrasted with a background whiteness so dazzling that he was unable to see how far the plain might stretch.

More confident now, he wiped the sweat and grit from his eyes before he tried to re-estimate their lead.

Sara had the same idea, using her mirror in order to make up her own mind.

'They've gone,' she said. 'What's happening?'

'They haven't gone. They've stopped.'

'Oh my God.' She became rigid, staring at him, her arms locked on the wheel.

Fast though he was to slam his hand down on the dashboard button, in the time it took for the hydraulics to lower the scraper, the truck had travelled another thirty feet.

There was a judder as the blade began to do its job. Then, without any warning at all, they hit the first of the mines.

The blast was off-centre, a sharp detonation and a flash of light followed by the clang of the blade being flung upwards against one of the chassis rails.

Knowing they could run over another one at any minute, he shouted at Sara, telling her to keep going while he quickly checked for damage.

The front tyres were intact, and he could detect no hissing from the radiator. The suspension, too, felt as though it was still in one piece, and the needle of the oil pressure gauge was steady in the right position.

In his haste he'd forgotten about Sara who was near to panic, ignoring his instructions and rapidly reducing speed.

He glanced over his shoulder again. 'Don't slow down,' he yelled. 'Wait until we're out of range.'

'Cogan, for God's sake. We're in a minefield. We can't go on.'

'We can't stay here either — not unless we want to get shot to pieces. We'll take our chances with the mines.'

'That was only an anti-personnel mine. They're only tiny. What happens if we hit a big one?' She was refusing to look at him now, concentrating her whole attention on the ground in front of them. 'They herded us,' she muttered. 'Like sheep.'

But they'd underestimated the Mercedes, Cogan thought. Like the KDP six days ago, they hadn't realized that beneath its rusted-out exterior there was sufficient steel plate to deflect shrapnel and shock loads. Whether the gearbox would continue handling the strain was more doubtful. It was whining badly, struggling against the increased resistance of the scraper blade even though by now their speed had dropped to almost nothing.

'Nice and easy,' he said. 'Just keep moving.'

They came under no further fire either from rifles or from the machine-gun. Instead they faced a new, more insidious hazard, never knowing from one second to the next whether they were in danger or not, unable to tell whether they were driving deeper into the minefield or on the point of leaving it.

For Cogan, the experience was nerve-racking enough. For Sara it was worse. Charting what she thought was the best route, she was edging the truck closer to the escarpments where the scree was deeper and where the likelihood of hitting mines was less.

The idea was good. But it didn't work.

The second explosion was more savage, lifting the right front wheel off the ground and throwing her sideways onto Cogan's lap.

She scrambled back across the cab, managing to depress the clutch pedal a second before the engine stalled.

The incident destroyed what little confidence she had left. She was shaking, bleeding from a gash on her forehead, almost too distressed to know what she was doing.

'We have to stop,' she said.

'No we don't. Just hang on. Another fifty yards and we'll be past the first bluff where no one can see us. All you have to do is get us there.'

'Then what?'

'Then we disappear for a bit.' He used a piece of the T-shirt to prevent the blood from running into her eyes. 'We're only about ten miles south of that Iraqi air-base.'

She remained silent.

'They sent aircraft when they were hunting for you and Catherine,' he said. 'So we'll play it safe until dark.'

'They'll still find us. They'll use helicopters — like last time — helicopters with spotlights.'

'Well, they're going to be shit out of luck. We'll either lose ourselves in another ravine, or see if we can fit into one of those bloody great cracks.' He pointed to the end of an escarpment that seemed to be on the verge of splitting open.

Huge though the fissures were, they were barely wide enough to take a man, let alone a truck, but ahead there were more escarpments and more cracks, some of them half-blocked, the entrances of others flanked by house-sized boulders that had tumbled out of the cliff-face.

If Sara had been listening to what he'd said, she either disagreed with his plan or was too apprehensive to consider whether it was flawed or not.

'We'll be out of this by morning.' He'd tried to sound convincing, but one look at her face told him that his attempt to reassure her had been the failure it deserved to be.

She was smothered in blood from the cut on her forehead, biting her lip and flinching with each bump. 'It'll be harder for us after dark,' she said. 'It'll be too dangerous to use headlights, and if we don't know where we are or where to go, how are we ever going to find our way anywhere?'

Cogan had no idea. Behind them to the west where the sun was beginning to set, lay an endless desolate plain patrolled by the Iraqi Army, while to the north there was nothing but mountains, rocks and a military air-base. Which left the south and the east, he thought; two choices out of four, giving them a fifty per cent chance of choosing the right direction — but only if they could stay alive until nightfall, and to do that, first they had to find a hiding place in the middle of a minefield.

13

Since the moon had risen, the helicopter pilots were having an easier job, but the frequency of the flights was still irregular. For the last three hours Cogan had been trying to predict the timing of them without once being right. The search patterns themselves were equally random, occasionally beginning at the mouth of the valley, but following no pre-arranged route although the pilots usually flew lower and spent more time hovering out of sight some distance to the east.

The chopping noise was coming from there now, sounding closer than it was because of an echo off the cliffs. He listened, endeavouring to decide whether the echo was growing louder before he turned to look back at the escarpment for the hundredth time.

The end of it was about ninety yards from where he was standing, a massive wall of stone divided almost down the middle by the cleft in which the truck was concealed. He could see the entrance of the fissure, and he could see the front of the Mercedes, but only because he knew it was there, he told himself. The rocks he had laboured so hard to pile on the bonnet and the roof were adequate camouflage to prevent detection from above, but a low altitude sweep of a searchlight could pick up a stray reflection off the windshield if the beam came from the right direction. Which meant they had to continue relying on their luck, Cogan thought, if they hadn't already used it up in the minefield.

Before dark they had run over only one more mine during their journey east — another small, anti-personnel mine buried not far from the mouth of the first fissure that had been wide enough to accept the truck. By then, any hiding place would have done, and even Cogan had been unwilling to search for somewhere else that might have offered more protection.

He listened again for a second, then trudged back to the truck in the moonlight, hoping to find Sara still asleep.

She wasn't. She was preparing dinner, stuffing dates into the hollowed-out halves of loaves which she'd placed in a row on the dashboard alongside the two semi-liquid chocolate bars she'd retrieved from the rucksack.

'We have to eat,' she said.

'It's nearly midnight.'

'I know, but it's no good us just drinking water.'

Cogan inspected the cut on her forehead. It had stopped bleeding, although without stitches it looked as though it could open up again at any moment. 'How's your headache?' he asked.

'I'm all right.' She gave him one of the half loaves and a bottle of water. 'Did you see anything?'

'Only lights. We won't be going anywhere yet — not while they're still out there.'

'We could give them the truck,' she said. 'Why don't we just put a rock on the accelerator pedal and let it go with the scraper blade up?'

'And hope it gets knocked out by a couple of mines?'

'Yes. They'll think we're dead.'

'What do we do then?'

'Wait for the Israeli ground team to arrive.'

'If we can't tell them where the quarry is, why the hell would they show up? All we can give them are the co-ordinates of a minefield where they're as likely to get blown to bits as we are.'

'They could follow our wheel-marks, couldn't they?'

'You've missed the point,' Cogan said. 'They need a reason to come. Judith isn't enough. Anyway, there aren't any wheel-marks. You don't leave tracks on this stuff. I can't even see where the scraper blade's been.'

'Oh.' She paused. 'So what do we do?'

'Make a run for it back to the ravine — after things have quietened down.'

'You don't mean that. What about Judith?'

'What do you want me to say?' He was angry with himself and angry with her, knowing he had no solution that stood the slightest chance of working.

'I'm sorry.' She stared at the floor. 'I know all this is my fault, but everything I said was true. If we'd got closer or chosen a different valley I'd have been able to recognize something — I know I would. I'm not stupid and I haven't forgotten what the mountains looked like.'

'So where are we?'

'I'm not sure.'

'Guess,' Cogan said.

'I can't. I've already told you — I don't know where we are. I'll try again when it's light.'

'If we last that long. If they don't start using heat-sensors to find us.'

She raised her head. 'Can they do that?'

He'd mentioned heat-sensors to ram home the seriousness of their situation, but her expression made him realize he was only making things worse. 'We'll be fine,' he said.

'Infrared detectors give false readings near rocks that have been warmed up by the daytime sun. We'll be out of here as soon as they get tired of flying their helicopters round in circles.'

'No,' she said. 'I'm not ready.'

'You don't have to drive.'

'It's not the driving. It's because if something goes wrong, I don't want it to be tonight — not after everything that's happened to us — not until we've had more time — you know . . . '

'Time for what?'

'Well.' She was embarrassed, stumbling over her words. 'I just want us to be together for a bit longer as though we were ordinary people doing ordinary things. I know it's silly and I know you don't understand, but I can pretend.'

There had been no hidden meaning in what she'd said, but if Cogan had ever needed a reminder of how thoroughly he'd let her down, he had it now. By making such a simple request it was as if she had thrown all of his broken promises in his face.

'We're not going to run out of water,' she said. 'And it's nearly thirty-six hours since we had any sleep.'

He didn't need persuading. As well as being dog-tired, he knew he was in no better

shape than she was to make a move tonight.
'OK,' he said. 'You get some rest. I'll keep
watch.'

She was pleased, snuggling up against him
so he could put his arm around her. 'You can
have my chocolate bar,' she said. 'I saved it
for you.'

Placing a finger on her lips to shut her up,
he tried to make himself comfortable, looking
out over the moonlit plain while he listened
for the thump of rotors and waited for her
eyes to close.

★　★　★

A ray of sunshine had found its way into the
fissure, slanting across Cogan's face to drag
him out of a sodden sleep.

He freed his arm and rubbed it to bring
back the circulation before he shook Sara to
wake her. 'Breakfast-time,' he said.

'Ouch.' She blinked in the light.

'How do you feel?'

'Awful. Did the helicopters come back?'

'No.' He examined her cut, washing away
the congealed blood with some mineral water
so he could check for signs of infection. 'Do
you want to come with me while I have a look
around?'

'I have to pee first. You fix the waffles and

put on coffee. I'll only be a minute.' She opened the door, but got no further.

'What's the matter?' Cogan said.

'Listen.'

He could already hear the noise, a rumbling coming from somewhere nearby. It was getting louder, building rapidly until it became a deep-throated roar — the unmistakable sound of a heavy aircraft preparing for take-off.

'Cogan.' She slammed the door shut. 'It's the Antonov.'

So crucial were the implications that in his hurry to get out he nearly forgot to check the sweep hand of his watch.

'Come on,' he shouted.

'No.' She remained in the cab. 'They know we're here. They'll do to us what they did to that convoy of refugees. They're going to burn us out with the laser.'

'No they're not.' He reached for her hand, hardly able to believe they'd been on top of the airstrip all along.

If they weren't quite on top of the airstrip, they were certainly not far away. He was in the process of pulling her outside when the noise changed, convincing Cogan that the aircraft had started to taxi.

Towing Sara behind him, he clambered over rocks to the mouth of the fissure where their outlook was unobstructed.

'Right.' He checked his watch again. 'You have to guess its take-off point. Keep your eyes on something that's in line with the sound — a stone — anything.'

She knelt down beside one of the larger boulders. 'What are you going to do?'

'I'll tell you later. Go on — now. The bloody thing'll be here any second.'

This time he hadn't exaggerated. No sooner had he finished speaking than the Antonov came into view, struggling to gain altitude, the pilot not even attempting to climb until he had gained more airspeed.

It thundered across in front of them, thirty tons and 5,000 horsepower of military aircraft, nearly close enough to touch, travelling west at right angles to the end of the escarpment.

'Cogan!' Sara shouted above the howl of the big turboprops. 'Can you see the pod?'

It was hard to miss. The Antonov was painted in olive-drab except for an ugly yellow bulge along its fuselage, extending rear-wards from the leading edge of the wing almost to the tail.

By now Cogan had the information he needed to work out the approximate position of the airstrip, but the temptation to find out whether the aircraft would change course was impossible to resist. He walked out into the sunshine, watching it continue on its early morning flight across the plain until it was nothing more than a dot, climbing steadily and heading west.

Sara had given up trying to pick it out against the sky. 'I wonder where it's going,' she said.

'On a long haul. That was a hell of a load it had on board — more than just fuel.'

'Like hydrogen peroxide and chlorine and iodine?'

'Probably.' He smiled. 'Do you still think it's after us?'

'I'd only just woken up.' She looked at him. 'Well, now you know where the quarry is, don't you?'

Cogan was mentally calculating its position, estimating the Antonov's take-off speed so he could multiply it by the elapsed time on his watch.

'We're only about a mile away,' he said. 'You couldn't have got us much closer.'

'I could if I hadn't made so many mistakes. You don't have to try and make me feel better.'

'I'm not trying to do anything. It was your idea to stay. If we hadn't stayed we'd have missed it. Did you get a fix on the sound?'

She pointed to the south-east. 'The pilot

was following the road,' she said.

'OK. I'll go and get a quick GPS reading.'

'For what?'

'For the road. We don't want Judith's people winding up in the minefield like we did. They'll need two sets of co-ordinates, one set for the base and one set for the road. That'll let them plot a line on a map and give them a safe route in.'

'So you and I are still going to the quarry?'

'Tonight,' he said. 'A nice easy trip there and back on a nice road without any mines to worry about.'

'Oh.' She turned round and began to walk away.

'I'll get the reading,' Cogan said. 'You stay here. Come and rescue me if a mine blows off one of the wheels.'

'I don't want to stay here.' She spoke with her back to him.

'Go and have your pee then. I'll get the truck started. We might as well get on with it in case the Antonov's not going as far as I think it is.'

Although there was no indication that it would return in the near future, Cogan was still wary, anxious to confirm the position of the road, but determined to minimize the risk now that their luck seemed to be improving for a change.

After reversing the Mercedes out of its hiding-place, he waited for Sara to join him then lowered the scraper and began driving directly south.

'Say when you think we've reached the road,' he said.

'When we're underneath the flight-path? Is that what you mean?'

'Yeah. How about here?'

She shook her head. 'Further — another fifteen feet - maybe twenty.'

He stopped where she said, leaving the engine running in case they needed to retreat.

'Don't you want this?' She held up the GPS unit.

'You do it.' He climbed out. 'Just hang on while I have a look for something.'

He knelt down and started removing stones, excavating a shallow hole in the scree and the grit until he felt his fingers touch a slippery layer of woven plastic.

'Take the readings,' he said. 'Don't forget to push the memory button and double-check that they've been recorded.'

'Have you found that geotextile stuff you were talking about?' She leaned out the window. 'Is it there? Are we on the road?'

'Yep.' He stood up, relieved that he'd been right. 'Have a look at the mountains. If you don't know where you are now, you never will.'

She was reluctant to try, stowing away the GPS unit and waiting until he was back behind the wheel before she directed her gaze at the skyline, studying the eastern range of razor-sharp ridges and rocky spurs for nearly half a minute before she said anything.

'It makes me think of Catherine.' She shivered slightly. 'Just being this close gives me the creeps.'

'Are we too close?'

'If anyone's looking we might be. We're right in line with the airstrip. That peak with the sloping top isn't far from the boundary of the quarry either.'

'OK.' Keeping the scraper blade lowered for insurance, he turned the truck round on what he hoped was still the road, then drove back to the escarpment in second gear, maintaining his speed until they were once again secure and out of sight in the cool shadows of the fissure.

Short though the excursion had been, it had provided Cogan with a badly needed boost of confidence. After despairing of ever locating the quarry or of finding their way back to Erbil in one piece, he was more encouraged than he'd been for days, starting to believe that with Bernie's help and a continuation of their lucky streak there was at least some chance of helping Judith and of getting Sara out of the mess he had created for her.

Over the next few hours, in order to build up a picture of the quarry in his mind, he asked her to describe it in as much detail as she could, prompting her to remember things she'd forgotten so he could draw a layout in the sand, only breaking off his questioning when, shortly before 10.30 they heard the Antonov returning from wherever it had been.

It followed an identical flight-path, coming in low over the plain, giving Cogan the opportunity to refine his estimate of the road's width and for him to check how long it took the aircraft to touch down after it had crossed in front of them.

His afternoon was less productive, much of it spent on his back searching for damage beneath the truck to make certain they still had transport should they need it in a hurry.

By four o'clock he was as prepared as he was ever going to be. Sara, though, was steadily becoming more nervous, either wandering off alone to explore the fissure or standing at its entrance, staring out at the dancing heat-haze as though looking for some unseen, distant landmark.

Like her, Cogan was keeping his thoughts to himself, postponing the one, awkward step he had yet to take. Now that the Antonov had finally revealed the position of the laser base, he'd been presented with the option of either taking her with him tonight or of leaving her behind for the last return leg of their journey.

For the very first time since he'd met her, there was the chance to isolate her from any danger — a chance to keep her safe as long as she agreed and didn't change her mind at the eleventh hour.

He should have known better than to mention the idea. Despite waiting until after dark to pick what he believed was the right moment to make the suggestion, so swift was her rejection of it that he might just as well have saved his breath.

He decided to try again later, intending to reopen the subject closer to the time of his departure when the moon was up, and when she'd had longer to think things through.

But with the rising of the moon came the beating of more helicopter rotors, and by then he'd begun to realize that the option of leaving her behind was too dangerous to consider.

14

The return of the helicopters had been more than a setback. For three-quarters of the night the search had persisted, forcing Cogan into a late start and making a mockery of his prediction that the trip would be easy.

With no compass and with the moon already below the horizon, he was guiding Sara by instinct, praying they wouldn't stray off what he believed was the road, travelling blind in a race against daylight.

'Cogan.' She stopped walking. 'We're not going straight.'

'Yes we are.' After looking back over his shoulder in an unsuccessful attempt to pick out the silhouette of the escarpment, he began kicking a hole through the stones, hoping to find the layer of geotextile fabric.

'How do you know we're not on top of a mine?' she said.

'Because we're still on the road.' He made her kneel down to feel the plastic sheeting. 'We're OK.'

'Except that we're running out of time.' She brushed the grit off her hands. 'We're not going to make it there and back. It'll be light in half an hour.'

'So we stay. That might give us a lead on Judith.'

'Hide somewhere, you mean?' She sounded doubtful.

'What about those ledges you were talking about? You said the whole east wall of the quarry's made up of ledges where the overburden's been excavated.'

'I only told you what I saw from the window of the shed where I was locked up. It'd be hard for us to get onto a ledge.'

'Suppose we did? Would we be out of sight?' He started walking again.

'From the base of the quarry we would, but not from helicopters — well, probably not.' Her voice was flat, and she was hanging back.

'Look,' Cogan said. 'I know this is as tough as hell for you, but you can't give up now. We're ten minutes away. Once we're where we want to be, all we have to do is phone the co-ordinates through to Bernie and keep our heads down for one more day.'

'Then leave when it's dark?'

'Right. No one's going to find the truck now. If it was easy to find, they'd have sniffed it out on the night we arrived. We can hole up in it for as long as our food and water holds out, or we can head off back through the valley tomorrow night. We could even try the road now we know where it is.'

'Why don't we wait until Judith's people do something? If they come down through Turkey like we did, they could be here by Sunday.'

Cogan was careful not to answer, knowing that the Israeli military would be no more inclined to rush things than they would be concerned about the loss of an inexperienced, female field agent.

He continued walking, telling himself that the road would soon become an airstrip, waiting for the texture of the ground to change or for some other sign that the minefield was behind them.

It was Sara who came across the wheel-marks, two pairs of black streaks where the Antonov had touched down yesterday. They were just visible in the dark, faint but unmistakable.

To expose the concrete she scraped some sand away with her shoe. 'We're right in line with the hangar,' she said. 'If it was daytime we'd be able to see it.'

'How far?' Instead of examining the wheel-marks, Cogan was looking for lights.

'Not very. It's only a short airstrip. If we're going to climb up to the back of the quarry, we'll have to decide which way to go from here.'

'You decide.'

'All right.' She thought for a moment. 'It'll be quicker if we go north.'

'Then skirt round behind it?'

She nodded. 'I didn't think I'd ever be doing this. It doesn't seem real somehow.'

'You're sure there's no barbed wire, no fences or guards?'

'There isn't anything. I've told you. The whole place has been made to look derelict. All anyone would see on a satellite picture is a big pit cut into the side of a hill, some old sheds and the building where the rock-crushing plant used to be.'

'The hangar building?'

'Yes. Everything else is underground.'

'OK,' he said. 'Let me have the Scorpion. I'll put it in the pack with our other stuff so we've only got one thing to carry between us.'

She handed over the machine-pistol, waiting nervously while he made certain it wouldn't rattle against anything.

Ahead of them the sky had begun to lighten, allowing Cogan to get his first glimpse of the surrounding terrain. Although the quarry itself was still nothing more than a void in the dark hillside at the end of the plain, the top edge of it was just visible, and further in the distance he could see the sloping top of the peak that Sara had pointed out to him yesterday.

He accompanied her to an incline at the base of the hill, relieved to be clear of the minefield at last, hoping now that her nerve would hold, and that this time she knew where she was going.

He should not have been concerned. Once they began their climb she took the lead, clambering cat-like over the slab-sided rocks and boulders that littered the quarry's northern flank.

In daylight the climb would have been reasonably easy. It was steep, but with the rocks forming what was almost a natural stairway, there was no need for her to pick any particular route. The problem was speed.

Sure-footed though she was, by hurrying to beat the dawn she was taking risks, twice using her hands to pull herself up because she was so small, and on one occasion having to wait for Cogan to lift her bodily onto an overhanging rock-shelf. She was also running out of energy, but refusing to slow down until he made the effort to overtake her.

'If you don't take it easy, you're going to burn out,' he said.

Too exhausted to speak she pointed to the sky. It was a deep red colour, a sign that within the next five minutes the sun would start to appear over the peak.

To the west, except for a shadow cast by the quarry wall, the plain was drenched in the same red light, extending for as far as Cogan could see. He could see into the quarry too — not clearly yet, but clearly enough to know that they'd either have to stay where they were or find somewhere better in a hurry.

'This way.' She fought for breath. 'Come on.'

He'd expected her to continue climbing, but he was wrong. She struck off to her right, following the curve of the quarry's rim before suddenly vanishing from sight.

The reason for her disappearance was not hard to find. At some time in the life of the quarry a narrow section of its upper edge had collapsed inwards, creating a miniature ravine, and an avalanche of debris that had lodged on the first of the excavated ledges.

Fifteen feet below him, Sara was already on the ledge, holding onto the twisted steelwork of a gantry.

She waved to make him hurry, then began moving rocks, stacking them in a row in front of her while Cogan embarked on his descent, sliding down feet-first on his back with the pack clasped to his chest.

Arriving on the ledge in a shower of gravel, he released the pack and struggled to his feet.

Laid out before him now the quarry was an enormous chasm nearly a quarter of a mile across to the other side where sunlight was just beginning to illuminate the rim.

'Here.' Sara passed him a rock. 'Help me with this wall. It'll only take a minute.'

It took them four minutes, working out in the open where anyone who had been looking up could have seen them, and where Cogan had the best view of the quarry he could have ever wanted. It was horseshoe-shaped, overlooking the plain with an east face that was not as high as he'd expected it to be. The climb had given him a false impression of the quarry's depth and, although the ground was still half-shrouded in shadow, he estimated it to be little more than sixty or seventy feet below him.

The steelwork was a surprise as well. Sara had forgotten to mention the gantry in her briefing, and Cogan hadn't thought to ask her exactly where it was.

'Will this be all right?' She pulled him down to join her behind the low rock wall she'd built.

'Yeah, should be fine.'

'Do you believe me now?' She wiped the dust from her lips. 'Do you believe everything I told you?'

He'd never disbelieved her, but his feelings

about being here were muddled. From the swamp to Savannah, to London, Ankara and finally to a quarry in Iraq. For what? Cogan wondered. Because of some extravagant idea of ridding Sara of her falcons? Or to prove something equally fanciful to himself?

'What's the matter?' she asked.

'Nothing.' He listened for a second. 'Can you hear that humming noise?'

'It's a generator. Catherine saw it once. It's in the underground service area next to the laboratory. I should've said.'

'You should've said about the gantry too.'

'I didn't know it'd still be here. I thought it would've been blown up or taken to pieces by now. I only guessed there'd be a channel like this for us to slide down. When the missile exploded I saw all the rocks crumbling away, but I didn't have a very good view from the shed.'

'Which shed?'

She glanced at him. 'Do you think Judith's there?'

'Do you remember which one?'

'Beside the hangar on the right. If you give me the binoculars I might be able to see inside the bars on the window. It's almost light enough.'

'We'll phone Bernie first. You get the co-ordinates.'

'But we don't know if Judith's here or not.'

'We'll say she is.' He unzipped the pack and removed the GPS unit and his satellite phone.

She took the GPS unit from him, but seemed reluctant to use it. 'Won't it be the middle of the night in London?'

'Bernie won't care. He'll be asleep or at home working. Go on, take the readings while I get hold of him.'

Unable to help Judith by any other means, Cogan was anxious for this last part to be over and done with — the only justification there was ever going to be for the deaths of Catherine, Jeremiah and Barzani, and the only way to clear his mind of the past so he could start thinking about tonight, tomorrow and the day after that.

Bernie was not asleep. Nor was he working. He recognized Cogan's voice and immediately started to talk.

'Hold on.' Cogan stopped him. 'I haven't called to say hello. Get a piece of paper and a pencil.'

'Are you where I think you are?'

'Yes, I am. Now listen. This is important — really important. I'm on a phone that's running on a half-charged lithium battery so I don't want to repeat anything.'

'Why did you say important twice then?

Have you got a short-term memory problem or something?'

'For Christ's sake, just listen, will you?' Cogan said. 'As soon as I hang up, the first thing you do is drive to the office, go to the top drawer of my filing cabinet and get out the stuff you sent me on oxygen-iodine lasers. Look for a sheet of paper with names and phone numbers on it. There'll be Greenwald, Reed, Dowell and Isaacs. The one you want is Isaacs — Madeline Isaacs. She's an associate administration officer with the US National Transportation Safety Board in Washington. I want you to phone her right away and say you've got an urgent message from me. If you can't get hold of her, call the Israeli Embassy in London or New York. Have you got that?'

'Yeah, I've got it. What's the message?'

'Two sets of geographic co-ordinates. One set's for an underground military base north of Ba'iji in Iraq where the Baghdad Government are developing an airborne, infrared laser. The other set identifies a point on the road that leads to the base. There's a minefield on the north side of the road — probably on the south as well. Joining the two sets of co-ordinates together gives a safe way in.'

'For who?' Bernie interrupted.

'Never mind. I haven't finished yet. Tell

Madeline Isaacs or the embassy that someone called Judith Safrai is being held at the base by the Iraqi Mukhabarat.'

'Is that where you are?' Bernie asked. 'Where you've been for the last three weeks?'

'Why?'

'Why the fuck do you think? Because of what happened to that US plane yesterday?'

'What are you talking about? What plane?'

'The one that was shot down in the Mediterranean. It's all over the papers and TV. The Americans are saying it was attacked by some kind of super-laser, so don't hand me any crap about you not knowing.'

'Jesus.' The news had caught Cogan off-guard. 'What time yesterday?' he said.

'How the hell would I know. Early, I think. It was a US Air Force 737 taking those State Department officials to Ankara. Have you forgotten I told you they were going?'

'To stop the Turkish Government from buying the oil Iraq flushes out of their pipelines?'

'Some guy called Ferris and another one call Luscombe — I think that was his name. The plane took off from Damascus and was about fifty miles off the Lebanese coast when one of the engines got knocked out, and something burned a fucking great hole in the cargo bay. The pilot radioed to say it felt like

350

they'd been hit by a surface to air missile. He was going to ditch, but he made it back to Beirut.'

Cogan's recollections of yesterday morning were particularly clear. He was remembering how he'd watched the Antonov sweep out over the plain, and how he'd avoided answering Sara when she'd asked him where he thought it was going. 'Who says it was a laser strike?' he said.

'The Americans do. They've got a million satellite photos.'

'Showing a beam?'

'Big bastard,' Bernie said. 'Long white streak running right out over Syria from the border between Jordan and Iraq. CNN have got pictures of the 737 too.'

'With burn holes?'

'Yes. Looks like Saddam's really shafted himself this time. Israel's screaming for a special meeting of the UN Security Council to reclassify airborne weapon systems, the Syrians are pissed off, and the Americans and the British are claiming it's an act of international terrorism designed to destabilize the whole of the Middle East. They're pumping it pretty hard.'

Cogan could imagine. He could also imagine Bernie over-reacting to his new-found role as an international broker in the arms race. 'Two more things,' he said. 'You keep all this to yourself, and when you talk to Madeline Isaacs, tell her that a ground team can expect helicopter surveillance at night, and that they'll need as much high-explosive as they can carry.'

'Do you want me to ring you back after I've spoken to her?'

'No. I'm going to run out of battery if I keep this switched on. I'll call you exactly twenty-four hours from now. Are you ready for the co-ordinates?'

'Yeah. Go.'

Cogan handed the receiver to Sara. 'Quickly as you can,' he said.

To save time she'd already down-loaded the numbers, using the lead tip of a bullet from the Scorpion's magazine to scratch them on a rock. She read them out to Bernie, asking him to repeat each one before she turned to Cogan.

'He wants to know if there's anything else,' she said.

'Only to be sure he's awake when we call him.'

She relayed the instruction then said goodbye and replaced the receiver. 'He asked me if I was Hazel,' she said.

'Did you say you were?'

'No.' She sprung the cartridge back into

the magazine. 'I was going to tell him my name was Shannon, but I didn't.'

In no mood for an explanation, instead of enquiring why, he summarized what Bernie had said about the laser strike, describing the attack before he went on to outline the British and American reaction to it.

'It's the way Saddam operates,' she said. 'He'll believe he's done the right thing.'

'Shooting down US diplomats is doing the right thing?'

'If you're Saddam Hussein it is. That's how he thinks. As soon as he heard that America was going to stop Turkey from buying his oil, he'd have planned to torpedo the talks. He could just as easily have planted a bomb somewhere in Ankara.'

'Maybe he should have,' Cogan said. 'His airborne laser isn't much of a secret now.'

'He won't care. A laser's not like nerve gas. It's not a weapon of mass destruction so the UN can't do anything about it even if they want to.' She stopped talking and began opening up a gap between two rocks in the wall.

'Did you see something?' Cogan became more alert.

'I thought I heard a noise. We ought to be keeping our voices down in case it's a shift change and people start coming outside.'

'Can you see anyone?'

'Not yet. You can never tell when the technicians are going to do things, though — you know, because they have to work at night or between satellite passes.'

Cogan made his own gap, using his fingers to enlarge a horizontal slot until he had a view out over the corrugated iron roof of the hangar to the plain beyond.

Now that more light was flooding into the quarry by the minute, he was able to obtain a better impression of the base. There wasn't one. Apart from sheds, the muted hum of the generator and an ostensibly derelict building where the Antonov was housed, there was nothing to see and nothing to hear. The whole place was silent and deserted, as uninteresting and as sterile as the desert which surrounded it.

'Where are the laboratories?' he asked.

Sara placed her palms down on the ledge. 'Underneath us, between the service areas and the dormitory. There are tunnels too. If we were standing at the entrance of the quarry you'd be able to see the blast doors. They're steel, but you'd never tell from a distance.'

'How do the technicians and flight crews get to the hangar if they're supposed to keep out of sight?' Cogan risked a quick look over the wall.

'I don't know. Perhaps there's a tunnel or a walkway we can't see.'

'What about chemicals for the laser and fuel for the Antonov? How do they handle those?'

She rolled onto her side. 'Why do you expect me to know? Why should I? I couldn't even find my way here — remember?'

He hadn't forgotten. It was finding a safe route back that was the problem now, he thought; a choice between a straight drive out on the road tonight to some distant bridge or intersection, or a couple of days spent waiting in the fissure while they summoned up the courage to attempt a return trip through the minefield to the valley.

'You're disappointed, aren't you?' she said.

'In what?'

'In the quarry — because it's not what you expected. And in me.'

'Let me tell you something,' Cogan said. 'Until that morning you spat at me in the swamp I didn't know what I wanted or what the hell I was doing. I was drifting, pretending to be busy, going anywhere I had the chance to go so I could keep moving. It didn't work, but I didn't give a shit whether it did or not. Then one day I wound up at a cabin having myself stitched up by some tannin-stained chippy who'd just wrecked my car for me.' He stopped what he was saying, uncertain of how to go on.

'And?' She looked at him.

'I'm not disappointed. If I hadn't met you I'd have had to spend the next five years trying to find a Shannon Lockhart.'

'That's what I meant. I'm not her. I'm me.'

'Look,' Cogan said. 'We've phoned Bernie, and we've done what we can for Judith. From here on you can be whoever you want to be.'

'Because you don't care who I am?'

'No. Not so long as I get to take home a pixie for my trouble.'

'What?'

'It's a bit like your poem.' Knowing his remark had been a mistake, but unwilling to explain, he began to scan the walls of the quarry with the binoculars, searching for the remains of other gantries or for a flicker of movement at a window of a shed.

He was refocusing on the hanger when a siren started to wail.

'Careful.' Sara put a hand on the binoculars.

Resorting to the gap in the wall, Cogan kept his head down, waiting to discover how many people would emerge from the underground facilities, hoping for an indication that might prove Judith had been brought here.

There was nothing. Nor were there any women among the fifteen or twenty staff members who had appeared. They were all men, chatting to each other as they walked over to the hangar to await the arrival of two, large articulated tankers that were crawling across the quarry floor towards it.

Accompanied by fire tenders and travelling slowly on the rough ground, the tankers parked out of sight on the south side of the building where Cogan guessed they would either begin discharging their contents into holding tanks, or perhaps transfer chemicals directly into the tanks of the Antonov itself.

Another smaller vehicle had come into view, a red pick-up with two men in it, heading not for the hangar but for the nearby shed.

Because of the pick-up's apparent destination, Cogan decided to risk the binoculars again.

'Is it who we think it is?' Sara asked the question quietly.

'Hang on.' Although the first man to get out was Khadim, Cogan wasn't yet certain that the other one was Van Reenan.

'Is she there?'

He had no need to reply. Judith was already being brought from the shed. She was dressed in dirty overalls, struggling ineffectively, arms outstretched, feet together, unable to free herself from a cross of steel tubes.

'No,' Sara breathed. 'Dear God no. They've crucified her.'

'She's only tied.' Gripping the binoculars hard enough to crush them, Cogan couldn't hold them steady. 'I can see the ropes.'

He watched Khadim clear away the sand from something on the ground, then saw Van Reenan slip the base of the steel frame into what looked like the top of a buried concrete block. Their job done, as if to anticipate the result of their handiwork, both men stood back to stare out briefly towards the mouth of the quarry before returning to their pick-up and driving away.

In the past, in other parts of the world, Cogan had been witness to things that had made his skin crawl. This was not the same. This was cruelty of a kind that the hardest terrorist would find difficult to justify. Even its purpose was unjustifiable — one last appalling and unnecessary attempt to safe-guard the existence of a weapon that since yesterday was not even the secret that Baghdad imagined it to be.

The new development had affected Sara

badly. Holding her hands over her face, she was lying absolutely still, refusing to raise her head until he reached across to touch her hair.

'They want us to see her,' she whispered. 'They've done it because of us.'

He nodded. 'Judith's the bait. They didn't have any luck with the helicopters so they're trying something else. They're hoping we'll do something stupid.'

'They can't leave her there,' she said. 'Not out in the sun.'

In different circumstances he might have been of the same opinion, but after everything that had gone before, he had not the confidence to believe that she was right.

He put down the binoculars carefully, conscious of the ledge hard and unforgiving against his chest, feeling the sun beginning to bite into his neck, tasting the dust dry and bitter in his mouth.

It was going to be a long day, he thought. But not as long as it was going to be for a young, naive, Israeli girl who, in setting out on a crusade to help her country, had found herself fighting a battle simply to stay alive.

15

On his morning drive across the Potomac in the rain Charles Greenwald had experienced a premonition. By the time he'd crossed the Arlington Bridge and turned on to Washington Drive, the rain had become much heavier, and his premonition had assumed an importance he usually reserved for matters of an entirely different nature.

He'd managed to put the notion aside while he'd found somewhere to park and made his way to the third floor of the Pentagon's east wing, but now the meeting had formally begun he knew without doubt that his intuition had been right.

Sitting beside him at the back of the room, Madeline Isaacs was either too tired to notice his unease or preoccupied with a problem of her own.

'Always before a weekend,' she whispered. 'Whatever this is about you'd think someone in the White House would have the brains to hold off until Monday, wouldn't you?'

Greenwald had long since given up expecting the White House to hold off on anything. He settled back in his seat, resigned to the inevitable, watching Hartley Porterfield use an illuminated pointer to show the flight path of the 737 and indicate where the aircraft had first encountered trouble.

'In case there are people here who don't already know,' Porterfield said, 'the attack took place over the Mediterranean at a distance of about two hundred and eighty miles from Iraq's western borders with Jordan and Syria. That means the Iraqis have a laser capability broadly similar to our own in terms of range and power, but with a much better accuracy performance. With the help of the South Africans they've evidently overcome the difficulties of steering a beam through atmospheric turbulence and varying air density. We can say, therefore, that Iraq has stolen a significant march over our own military development programme.' Porterfield pushed a button to bring up another series of pictures on the screen.

They were familiar enough to Greenwald, two black and white satellite photographs that he'd been told to release to the media showing the path of the beam itself, and six others covering the flight route of the Antonov from its base to the Iraqi border and back again. He only half-listened to what Porterfield was saying, thinking more about the consequences of what he imagined was about to be announced and wondering whether the president had any real understanding of the advice he was being offered.

'So we're facing something of a problem,' Porterfield said. 'One that the United States hasn't had before, and one that has some fairly far-reaching implications for us in the Middle East. Before I go on to explain why you've been invited here this morning, I've been asked to make certain all of us are clear on the administration's position. I know many of you resent having to hand in your cellphones and pagers at the door, but I'm sure you'll appreciate the reason once you've heard the background to what I have to say.'

Porterfield had turned up the lights — possibly, Greenwald thought, so everyone could see how remarkably important he'd become.

'Primary objectives,' Porterfield said. 'Politically and strategically fundamental to the interests of the US and, of course, to our allies too.'

'What allies?' The question came from somewhere in the centre of the room. 'Name any three.'

Porterfield ignored the remark. 'Objective one,' he said, 'demonstrate that unprovoked acts of terrorism will be met with force, not with words. If the US doesn't do something positive we're going to see more of our embassies bombed, more of our aircraft shot down and more Americans risking their lives again. We have to maintain credibility and show that America is committed to an on-going role to control weapons development in Iraq.'

'He'll never last,' Madeline Isaacs whispered. 'Some advertising agency's going to make him an offer he can't refuse.'

Greenwald was too concerned to be amused. A translation of the rhetoric had confirmed what he'd always suspected — that by agreeing to provide saturation satellite coverage of Iraq, he'd given tacit support to something which had never been supportable from the start.

'Then we have Pretoria and Baghdad,' Porterfield continued. 'A government in South Africa that's happy to sell advanced military technology to someone like Saddam Hussein, and a regime in Iraq that believes it can stop the US from putting pressure on the Turkish Government. I think we all understand that the downing of a civilian aircraft on a flight from Damascus to Ankara is a good deal more serious than the question of pipeline flushing.'

'Get to the point,' someone shouted.

On this occasion Porterfield responded.

Moving out from behind the rostrum, he inspected his watch. 'The point is this,' he said. 'I have been given the responsibility and the authority to inform you of a joint retaliatory strike by combined British and US forces on a military base south of the 36th parallel in Iraq. Before this briefing is over, a Tomahawk Land-Attack cruise missile will have been launched from a US Navy cruiser which is presently off the coast of Cyprus in the Mediterranean. British Tornado fighter-bombers will be following up the strike to assess damage and, if necessary, to complete the mission. This action is a direct reply to the attack on one of our aircraft. It is also designed to send an unequivocal message to the governments of both South Africa and Iraq.'

Madeline Isaacs was on her feet. 'I have to go,' she said. 'Let me know what happens.'

Greenwald had heard enough. He too stood up, guessing how his question was going to be received, but determined to ask it if only to prevent Porterfield from trying to justify yet another potentially disastrous White House decision.

'Mr Porterfield,' he said. 'I think we'd all like to know if this operation was pre-planned some time ago.'

'I'm not sure what it is you're asking me.'

'I'm asking you to tell us whether the US is surprised that Iraq attacked our 737. Is there perhaps a suggestion that we expected or even invited the attack?'

'Why the hell would we do that?' Porterfield's composure was slipping.

'Well, let's see, shall we?' Greenwald paused. 'Are you able to deny that the State Department has been searching for an excuse to cut short the development of a foreign weapon system that's better than anything we or the British have come up with?'

'I don't believe that deserves an answer. You know as well as I do that the State Department would never have consciously risked the lives of the crew and the passengers who were on board that aircraft.'

'So why wasn't the flight kept secret?' Greenwald was warming to his task. 'We don't usually advertise where, when and why our diplomats are going about their business. Why did we this time?'

'I'm not aware of any widespread advertising.'

'Just enough to alert the Iraqis. Is that what you're saying?'

'I'm saying no such thing.' Porterfield retreated to the rostrum. 'When your department agreed to be responsible for the satellite reconnaissance, I fail to understand why you of all people would question the need for an appropriate response.'

'I'm not questioning the need for a response,' Greenwald said. 'I'm asking you what it is we're responding to. Are we launching a cruise missile to destroy an Iraqi weapon development base because we're scared of what's going on there? Or is this an eye for an eye?'

'I've told you what it is. It's to reinforce the mandate of the UN. It's to teach Saddam Hussein another lesson and warn off the South Africans, and it's to show the rest of the world that the United States will not tolerate terrorist attacks on American citizens in any shape, in any form, in any country.'

Before Greenwald could reply he felt a tug on his sleeve.

It was Madeline. She had returned to her seat, her cheeks flushed, evidently distressed about something.

'Save your breath for damage control,' she said. 'The whole thing's a *fait accompli*. I wasn't even allowed to leave the room.'

Greenwald sat down again. 'Because there's an embargo on the information?'

'Until twenty-five past twelve. That's why they took away our phones.'

'When's the official announcement being made?'

'At the same time. They've got everyone here so we'll all have the same story before the Press starts going mad. I heard someone say the president's going to be on TV at four o'clock, but I can't believe he'll wait that long.'

The presidential address would be better made tomorrow, Greenwald thought. By then the White House spin-doctors would have a clearer idea of how to control the international fall-out and be ready to adjust the wording of the speech. They'd also know how successful the raid had been and whether the United Nations Security Council were going to condemn the action, or support it by issuing a suitably ambiguous statement that could be interpreted in a dozen different ways.

To forestall further questions, Porterfield had dimmed the lights again. 'These next slides are confidential,' he said. 'Depending on the level of public interest we may release a couple to the media, but in general they'll remain classified. The photos were taken at various times by our Lacrosse and KH-12 satellites beginning in mid-July of this year.'

Although the initial slides were unimpressive, high-altitude photos of northern Iraq showing little detail, the last five were in a class of their own. They were computer enhanced, brilliantly clear pictures of a deserted plain, of a mountain ridge and what looked as though it had once been a quarry in the foothills.

In his twenty years at the Defence Intelligence Agency, Greenwald had rarely, if ever, seen coverage of this standard. So good was the resolution that the tiniest features of buildings showed up, and it was even possible to discern shadows cast by the corrugations on their roofs.

'Despite what you might think,' Porterfield said, 'this is the Iraqi underground laser base. Now have a look at these.'

The next sequence of slides were time-lapse shots showing the quarry in various states of activity. There were twenty photographs in all, eighteen of them covering the departure and the return of the Antonov, a single close-up shot of a battered truck parked mysteriously on the plain nearly a mile out from the quarry and another photo taken at night by an infrared-imaging camera which had evidently picked up the presence of helicopters in the area.

Unlike before, this time when Porterfield turned on the lights there was a flood of questions from the floor — predictably none of them about the photos, but on the political ramifications of the US and British action.

One particularly pointed question came from Terry Reed who wanted to know why the White House had chosen to conduct the surveillance without notifying his department, and why the UN Security Council had not been and were not being consulted.

The answers were depressing. Greenwald listened to them all, knowing how carefully they must have been rehearsed and wondering why he'd ever agreed to participate in an operation that had been so obviously contrived from the beginning — an exercise that had nothing to do with sending a message to Saddam Hussein, and everything to do with the need for Britain and the US to maintain military supremacy in the field of airborne lasers. It was how things were nowadays, he thought, and how they'd continue to be until someone somewhere came to their senses.

At the conclusion of the meeting he accompanied Madeline to the door and waited while she retrieved her cellphone.

'I'll do a deal with you,' he said. 'If you don't ask me why the White House thinks we're all asleep, I'll buy you lunch somewhere that I guarantee is journalist-free.'

'Charles, I can't. There's something I have to do in a hurry.' She smiled tightly. 'I'm sorry. Another time.'

She was gone before he could say goodbye, pushing her way through the crowd until he lost sight of her. But his luncheon invitation had not been wasted. It had been overheard by Richard Dowell who'd been standing in the corridor behind him.

'I've got a better idea,' Dowell said. 'I'll pay for the drinks. You get lunch. How does that sound?'

Greenwald was ready for a drink. 'Depends if you're going to be cynical,' he said.

'Me? Never.' Dowell headed off to the elevators. 'Great photos,' he said. 'Pity the air-crew and those two guys on the 737 are being so shy.' He grinned. 'Still, we know we're on the side of the angels, don't we? What do you and I care who was or wasn't on the flight?'

'That might have been a good question to ask Porterfield.'

Dowell's grin broadened. 'My wife's taking a sociology degree. The other day I had a look through a book she'd brought home about the nineteenth-century philosopher Friedrich Nietzsche. He was a bit smarter than our friend Hartley.'

'Start quoting Nietzsche, and I'll be drinking by myself,' Greenwald said.

'Listen. Remember these six words: 'There are no facts, only interpretations'. If you want to keep your head straight in this business of ours, don't leave home without them.'

Not until Greenwald was outside, walking over to his car in the summer rain did the truth of the statement become apparent to him. For a minute he stood where he was, considering how best to apply the philosophy to what he'd heard this morning, but in the end his own cynicism got the better of him, and with the Tomahawk and the Tornados already winging their way to the target, he decided that the effort would hardly be worthwhile.

★ ★ ★

For much of the afternoon, conditions on the ledge had been intolerable. From midday onwards, what little shade there was had been provided by the skeleton of the gantry, and only in the last half-hour had Sara's wall of rocks begun to offer a degree of protection from the heat.

Sara herself had suffered throughout the day. Because of her size she'd been able to curl up to avoid the direct rays of the sun, but in doing so her body temperature had become dangerously high. She had another headache, and although Cogan had insisted that she drink their last two bottles of water, she was dehydrated and worn out from living on her nerves.

Cogan, too, was feeling the strain, drained and exhausted from maintaining his watch on Judith. At three o'clock, when she'd finally stopped moving, he'd put away the binoculars, unable to handle the pressure any longer and too sickened to continue with his vigil.

Making it worse was the indifference of the staff at the base. Either because they'd failed to recognize her plight, or because they'd been issued with instructions to ignore her, on four occasions when people had passed by the shed, no one had given her food or water or erected any form of shade. She'd been left in the sun to die, trying to support herself until her strength had ebbed away and she'd slumped against the cross to hang limply from it by her wrists.

Whether she was alive, Cogan didn't know. He knew only that if he ever encountered Khadim or Van Reenan again he wouldn't hesitate to do what he'd wanted to do for a long time now — not just since this morning when Judith had been put on display, but from the very first day he'd met Sara, the girl who, against her better judgement and because of his insistence, had come back to find this awful place.

She was lying beside him on the ledge, her eyelids red and swollen, her face streaked with three days' worth of dirt and with so much dust in her hair that it was a different colour.

'What time are we leaving?' she asked.

'Soon as it's dark — unless we have to wait because they're going to put up helicopters again.' He could see the cut on her forehead had become inflamed and that it was beginning to weep.

She glanced at him as though sensing his concern. 'What are you looking at me like that for?'

'Your cut isn't too good.'

'Oh.' She touched the wound. 'It'll be all right. I know where there's a truck-load of tetracycline.'

'We should've brought some with us.'

'What we should have brought is more water. Then I wouldn't feel so guilty about finishing what we had. I never thought it would be this bad up here.'

'It's the heat rising out of the quarry,' Cogan said. 'Another fifteen minutes and we'll be fine. Have a look at the sun.'

She peered over the wall, but quickly lowered her head.

Cogan listened for voices, hearing nothing except the generator.

'I can't look,' she said. 'Not while Judith's still out there.'

The screech of the siren made her jump. 'Change of shift,' she said. 'Maybe they're going to cut her down.'

She could not have been more wrong. Instead of the siren dying away, the wail continued. And instead of a few odd people appearing, within a matter of minutes the base was in an uproar.

From the ledge it was easy to observe what was happening. As well as people, vehicles of all kinds were emerging from the open blast doors of the tunnels — among them the tankers, half a dozen yellow-painted trucks and a number of tractor units, one of which was already speeding over to the hangar.

'It's a mission,' Sara said. 'They're getting the Antonov ready.'

Cogan didn't think so. The rush to prepare the aircraft seemed to be part of a much larger operation altogether. This was not simply a scramble to undertake a mission — this was an evacuation, a full-scale mobilization of equipment and personnel in response to some kind of emergency.

'Israelis,' Sara said. 'They know the Israelis are coming. They're going to use the laser on them.'

Certain that no ground assault team could have possibly got here this quickly, Cogan stood up, watching an evacuation that was rapidly becoming an exodus. People were hurrying now, either climbing on board trucks or sprinting across to the hangar where the Antonov was nearly clear of the doors, while beside the building, the tankers and trucks were lining up, engines running, waiting for the tractor unit to finish turning the aircraft round on the flight apron.

With the siren still wailing, the noise level was increasing by the minute, making it hard to distinguish one sound from another until Cogan heard something that made him glance out over the plain.

There was just time to shout a warning and throw himself down beside Sara before the fighter was on top of them, screaming overhead in a level flight across the quarry.

For several seconds, believing that Israel had elected to violate the US flight prohibition and sacrifice Judith, Cogan struggled to think of a safe escape route from the ledge.

But already the fighter was returning, and on this fly-past the markings on its fuselage were visible — not those of Israel but Iraq. It was an Iraqi Air Force fighter, a MiG-21 Fishbed, flying more slowly now while the pilot checked his radar and communicated with ground control.

Cogan watched it bank against the darkening sky above the hills. 'It's from the air-base,' he said. 'They're expecting real trouble here.'

Sara had started to reply when her words were drowned out by the whistling howl of the Antonov's engines coming to life.

Unshackled and clear of the tractor unit, the plane was ready to taxi, but unable to do so. Ahead of it, the runway was blocked by a tanker whose driver had panicked and set off early.

The driver of a smaller truck had made the same decision. He skirted the hangar and began to follow the tanker, presenting a further barrier to the unfortunate pilot of the Antonov.

Adding to the confusion was a lack of visibility. The sun had gone, and gradually the quarry was filling with exhaust fumes and dust being kicked up in the backwash of the propellors. There were also more vehicles milling around the hangar now, and yet another group towing equipment out of the tunnels.

Cogan had given up trying to guess what was triggering the emergency. If the base had received warning of an Israeli airborne

division parachuting into the hills somewhere, then the cavalry would be here soon
enough. But if they didn't arrive it didn't
matter. It was the emergency itself that
mattered — an opportunity for him to free
Judith while everyone else was trying to save
themselves.

Shouting to Sara above the noise, he
explained what he was going to do.

'No.' She glared at him. 'You can't. It's too
dangerous and it'll take you too long.'

'I'm going straight down — ledge to ledge.
Now listen.' He put his face close to hers.
'The minute I've gone you climb back up that
channel behind us and get away from the rim
where no one can see you. And you stay there
— right there — until it's dark. You'll only
have to keep hidden for about half an hour.
Do you understand what I'm saying?'

She nodded. 'Then what?'

'You go back the way we came, and you
wait for me at the truck.' He paused for a
moment. 'The key's in the ignition.'

'In case you don't show up?'

'Use the road,' Cogan said. 'Forget about
the valley.'

'If you think I'd leave without you, you're
crazy. I'm going with you.'

'No you're not. No one'll take a second
look at me with all that lot going on, but

they'd sure as hell notice you.' He smiled. 'I don't want you holding up the traffic.' He slipped the Scorpion under his belt. 'Promise you'll be careful.'

Instead of answering, in a repeat of the way she'd kissed him on the night of their reunion in Savannah, she brushed her lips across his mouth.

Cogan wished she hadn't done it. 'I'll see you at the truck,' he said. 'Make sure you're there.'

Below him, where the propellor wash was driving clouds of dust across the quarry floor, he could just make out the shed and the figure of the girl beside it.

A long way down, he thought, particularly if it was going to be for nothing.

To avoid wasting time, before Sara could say goodbye or wish him luck, he slithered feet-first over the ledge on his stomach and let himself go.

Although the first drop was no more than about eight feet, the uneven surface made the landing difficult and he nearly lost his balance. He took more care on the next three, checking before-hand to choose places where there were fewer rocks and where the ledges were wider and flatter.

He'd stopped counting when fading light started complicating his descent. The ledge beneath him was barely discernible and, when he looked over his shoulder, the shed was already lost in deepening shadow.

He resorted to the gantry, using the steel cross-beams as rungs, feeling them out with his feet while he hung by his arms from the one above. The technique was safer with less risk of breaking an ankle in a fall, but it was much slower.

Only after encountering the remains of a rusty ladder near the bottom was he able to progress more quickly, sliding the last few feet, gripping the side rails with lacerated hands and hitting the ground so hard that he buckled at thc knees.

He spent a second looking around him. Then he began to run.

By now the evacuation had become marginally more orderly with most of the vehicles stationary on the apron behind the Antonov. The runway, though, was still obstructed, and although the pilot had his engines at half throttle, his brakes were full on, and the aircraft had yet to move. As a result, Cogan found himself heading into a dust-storm.

He was not alone. Stragglers from the tunnels were also making their way to safety, paying no more attention to him than he did to them.

He kept going, trying to shield his eyes, leaning forwards into the whirlwind until he was forced to change direction in order to get his bearings.

Once out of the back-draught he was able to see Judith. Her head was raised, and somehow or other she'd managed to free one of her wrists.

Drawing on what strength he had left, he began to sprint.

To his right, a red pick-up was converging on him. It was being driven by Van Reenan with Khadim crouching in the back, bracing himself against the tailgate to counter the bouncing.

Still sprinting, Cogan was less than thirty feet from the shed when the pick-up halted beside it. He began yelling, Scorpion in hand, guessing what was about to happen. But he was too late.

In one callous movement, Khadim stood up, put a gun to Judith's head and squeezed the trigger.

It was the last thing he ever did. The first burst from the Scorpion caught him across his waist. The second all but cut him in half, reducing his body to a pulp of bloodstained flesh and bone.

Van Reenan was quick to react. Before Cogan could fire again, the pick-up lurched forwards, accelerating away with its wheels spinning, nearly tipping over as it went into a precariously tight turn in front of the shed.

Cogan was on his knees now, his mind more focused than it had ever been, steeling himself for the moment when the pick-up would cross his sights again. But instead of firing, he froze.

A mile out from the quarry, the MiG was approaching fast. It was flying low over the plain, following the road on a direct course for the hangar.

He couldn't hear it yet, but he could see it — see the muzzle flashes flickering from its cannons in the dusk, and suddenly he could see the outline of the missile it was chasing.

With nowhere to go except the shed, Cogan hurled himself face-down, and frantically began to crawl.

The Tomahawk missed the hangar, skimming over the roof at an altitude of fifty feet to explode in a gigantic ball of flame against the rear wall of the quarry.

In an instant, a thousand pounds of high-explosive tore away the rock-face, exposing a catacomb of fire-filled caverns and shattered tunnels.

For the pilot of the MiG the blast was fatal. Brave though he'd been, his attempt to shoot down the missile had been as futile as it had been foolhardy. Flung skywards, the fighter lasted for less than a second. Crippled and on fire with half its tail-plane gone, it cartwheeled over the rim of the quarry to crash and burn not far from where the gantry once had been.

Unlike the hangar which was badly damaged but still standing, the shed had not survived. But it had done its job. Just as the rear wall of the hangar had protected the Antonov, so had the shed protected Cogan. By collapsing on him it had injured his leg, but shielded him from the blast and from the subsequent hail of debris.

Half-deafened and with his eyes full of grit, he pushed the buckled sheets of corrugated iron aside, struggling to his feet to stare in horror and disbelief at what he saw.

A few feet away, Judith hung lifeless on her cross, her body slashed and broken by flying rocks, her one free arm dangling loosely from her shoulder. And behind him, where flames were soaring up what used to be the rear wall of the quarry, there was nothing but a mountainous pile of smoking rubble.

The horror wasn't over.

Cogan saw the Tornado early.

So did the pilot of the Antonov. On full power, he began to taxi, clearly desperate to try anything to save his aircraft and his skin.

In the distance on the runway, a red pick-up was sandwiched between a line of trucks and two slow-moving tankers. But the convoy was making steady progress, sufficiently far away to allow the aircraft to take off if circumstances had been different.

The pilot of the lead Tornado had timed his run with some precision. Like the MiG, but flying much faster, the fighter-bomber came in low over the plain, attacking the convoy and the Antonov head-on, strafing them from one end to the other with rockets and cannon fire before it peeled away to climb through the smoke cloud rising from the quarry.

The results were a catastrophe for the Antonov. Trailing sparks from one engine, its pilot dead at the controls, it gathered speed, bearing down on the group of vehicles now stationary in its path.

It never left the ground. Instead, at a speed approaching ninety miles an hour, it ploughed into a tanker, riding up over three other trucks before the inevitable occurred.

To begin with there was no explosion and the fire was small, a sixty-foot-long streak of flame that almost flickered out before it began to grow. Seconds later the streak was a column of boiling fire, spiralling higher and higher as a river of burning aviation fuel spilled out across the concrete.

And through it, as if being guided to its target, came the second Tornado.

Cogan had foreseen the danger. He was trying to run again, fearing the worst, dragging his injured leg in a vain bid to escape.

He'd moved less than twenty feet when the fighter pulled out of its dive. There was a glimpse of the Royal Air Force markings on its wings before it banked and Cogan saw the bomb begin its graceful downward flight.

Strangely unafraid, he stopped running, watching it come towards him, waiting calmly for the impact.

In the time since the cruise missile had destroyed the caverns, ruptured storage tanks had been discharging their contents into the tunnels where, among pools of evaporating gasoline deep underground, enormous quantities of chlorine and hydrogen peroxide had reacted to produce enough oxygen to fuel a thousand lasers.

The bomb blast was violent and severe, contained in part by the catacombs in which the blast had taken place. But the explosion that followed was uncontained and of unimaginable proportions.

As the ground collapsed to swallow Cogan, in a stentorian roar of fury a wall of incandescent flame burst forth.

Travelling faster than the speed of sound, the shock wave swept everything before it, scouring the quarry clean in a gale of fire and white-hot rocks.

He was able to think of Sara for one last time, remembering how soft and how warm her lips had been when she'd kissed him goodbye. Then everything became very still, very quiet and very dark.

16

Against his will, he was regaining consciousness. One by one his senses were returning. He could hear things, he could taste the vomit in his mouth and feel pain beginning to take hold in his leg again.

Taking care not to move, frightened of what he might see, he opened his eyes.

There was a light, an overpowering smell of chemicals and the sound of a voice. The voice was close. So was the light, flickering through the smoke to shine on his face and then, suddenly, into his eyes.

Hands pulled at him, lifting him to his feet while he coughed and spat out mouthfuls of dust, steadying himself against the arm of a man in a hard-hat who was saying something to him.

Aware, if only vaguely, of the need for caution, Cogan coughed again, pretending to be more shocked and bewildered than he was.

The man was carrying a flashlight and what looked like a medical kit. He was in a hurry, speaking in Arabic before he directed his flashlight at an aluminium ladder that was resting against the wall behind him.

Cogan summoned his strength, mumbling under his breath as he stumbled away and began hesitantly to climb.

It took him over a minute to reach the surface, a painful, slow ascent, using his good leg to push himself upwards into a night that was burning red beneath the sky.

To his left, a huge crevasse had opened up in the quarry floor, the remnants of the underground tunnel that had saved him from the blast, the fireball and the hail of rocks.

He stood on the edge of it, breathing in smoke and fumes, as unable to accept what had happened as he was to believe he had survived.

But reality was all around him, illuminated in an unearthly crimson glow from the caverns — a scene from hell to confirm what until now had been unthinkable.

In place of the gantry, there was a gaping rift in the east wall where the warhead of the Tomahawk had detonated. Where there had been ledges, now there was nothing but a blackened, pock-marked rock-face streaked in soot and dying flames, while of the hangar not a trace remained.

The base had gone. And with it had gone Cogan's future — everything he'd hoped for, or ever wanted. Just as he had been responsible for Judith's death, so by bringing Sara here he had killed her, a mistake too dreadful to contemplate and a truth too terrible to bear.

She'd been taken from him, but Cogan knew he couldn't leave without her — knew that he had to find her. Only by recovering her body could he begin to consider leaving. And only by finding her, by holding her in his arms again and by taking her home would he ever be able to start forgiving himself for destroying the dreams and plans she'd tried so hard to share with him.

He waited until he was certain of his sense of direction. Then he turned his back on the flames and set out for the entrance of the quarry.

Here and there, men from the rescue teams were working in groups, one still pulling survivors from the tunnel, another digging out the dead from the base of the south wall, relying on the searchlight from a hovering helicopter to illuminate the area.

Closer to him, a second helicopter was landing beside a van bearing a red crescent sign where medical staff were busy attending the injured. A few of the men glanced up, but made no effort to ask who he was or where he was going. Nor did the crew of an arriving fire-truck exhibit any interest in him. They drove past without looking, disappearing into the smoke with their lights flashing and their sirens screaming, ready to extinguish the inferno in the caverns with the few precious gallons of water they carried with them.

Cogan barely noticed. He was concentrating on his walking, experimenting to discover how best to minimize the strain on the ankle and the knee of his left leg. On flat ground the pain was endurable as long as he was careful, but once he'd reached the north flank and began to climb towards the rim, he was forced onto all fours, crawling upwards from one rock-shelf to another on what quickly turned out to be a wasted journey.

He was less than a third of the way to the top when he abandoned the struggle, realizing that the rim had subsided, falling inwards to create an impenetrable incline of jumbled boulders.

Cogan knew she was here, but he would never find her, never hold her and never be able to take her with him.

If he needed proof of how thoroughly he'd failed, of how unbelievably stupid he had been, a million tons of rock was evidence enough — a final condemnation of his recklessness and of everything else he'd done.

He started back down, his head filled with unknowns and unanswered questions. Why in

God's name hadn't he made her stay behind in the truck when he'd had the chance? Had Madeline Isaacs leaked the co-ordinates to the Americans and the British to save Israel the trouble? And, mixed up with his despair, the enigma of a poem which somehow or other seemed to have governed the way Sara had lived her life.

When she'd left him in Savannah it had been the poem she'd wanted him to have. In Erbil it had been the poem that changed her mind about going on, and on their trip to the ferry, it had been the poem that had persuaded her to keep going. And now he would never understand, never know what part of her life she'd seen mirrored in the verse that she'd refused to give him.

At the bottom of the foothills, after taking a last look back at the quarry, he began to limp along the runway in the moonlight, slowing down as he drew closer to the wreckage of the Antonov.

Like dozens of other crash sites he'd visited, there was not much to see. Apart from the Antonov's engines, a wing-tip section and the rudder which was almost intact, the aircraft was unrecognizable. The tankers and the trucks had been reduced to burned-out shells, and of Van Reenan's pick-up there was no sign whatever. Together with the other members of the convoy, the South African had perished in a fire that had been fierce enough to melt the Antonov's airframe and buckle vehicles as though they'd been plastic toys.

Cogan didn't stop. The smell was disgusting, and some of the wreckage was still smouldering. Wisps of smoke were curling upwards on the windless night, disappearing into a sky that by now was largely free of the awful glow he'd left behind him.

He carried on, using the pain in his leg to wipe out his thoughts, walking slowly and deliberately along the runway and then along the road until he was level with the escarpment and able to drag himself the last few hundred yards to the fissure.

But once inside the truck the memories of her started to flood back. No matter what he did, he could no more prevent them coming than he could handle the guilt that was threatening to overwhelm him.

She'd offered him everything, but he'd kept nothing. Because he'd torn up her letter and the poem, all he had to remember her by were two chocolate bar wrappers, a pair of her jeans and the piece of T-shirt she'd worn over her hair in the market at Erbil.

He folded the jeans to make a pillow, then lay down on the seat, burying his face in the scrap of T-shirt, drawing on his imagination, hoping the smell of her would keep the memories alive.

He should have recognized the danger. In his present state of mind, Cogan could have conjured up any fantasy he wanted.

Before he knew it she was with him again, smiling while she loosened her hair and bent over to whisper something.

He waited for her to lie down before he made sure he wasn't dreaming by searching out the mole between her breasts and touching the tiny childhood scar on the inside of her knee.

But no sooner had he recreated her than the image began to fade, displaced initially by the return of his despair and then by nightmares that were nearly as horrifying as the reality he was trying to forget.

He woke at daybreak, his lungs aching from the smoke and unable to see properly until he'd moistened his eyelids with saliva to get them open.

To prevent himself from thinking about her, he started the truck at once, reversing it out of the fissure and driving south in a straight line before he turned right onto the road and increased his speed.

He'd travelled little more than a mile when he saw vehicles coming towards him. They were troop-carriers, two of them, already stopping with men spilling out in all directions.

Secure in the knowledge that he would not be followed, he lowered the scraper blade and hauled on the wheel, swinging the truck back into the minefield, heading for the safety of the valley in the distance.

This time the Mercedes let him down. After months of overloading, this was the moment the gearbox chose to fail, disintegrating beneath the floorboards in a shower of metal fragments and hot oil.

Cogan was past caring. Praying he'd step on a mine to end everything here and now, he got out, raised his hands above his head and went to meet the approaching line of soldiers.

17

Because Bernie had left the door open, Cogan could see out of his office into the foyer. It was full of secretaries and typists, pretty girls in summer dresses and high-heeled shoes preparing to leave the building for their lunch-hour.

He watched one of them walk away. She was quite small with dark hair. And she was wearing a yellow skirt.

'For Christ's sake.' Bernie went to slam the door. 'If you don't want to finish the bloody story, why bother starting it? What the hell happened? Why didn't they blow your head off or throw you in a Baghdad jail or something?'

Cogan was reluctant to continue. Having spent the best part of an hour providing Bernie with a run down of the last three weeks, he was waiting to feel better. But he didn't feel better. The numbness was still there, and by now he was beginning to realize that telling someone wasn't going to work.

'So how did you get away?' Bernie asked.

'I didn't have to. Judith's section chief in Israel wasn't taking any risks. He knew she was inexperienced and he thought there was a chance she might get into trouble. He had people following us all the way down through Turkey into northern Iraq. Judith had hidden a locator beacon in the truck, so they knew more or less where we were from one day to the next. When I thought she was communicating with Tel Aviv, she was talking to her back-up team. They were in Erbil all the time that we were there.'

'Did they know the Iraqis had grabbed her?'

'Not until you gave Madeline Isaacs my message. They got the information over their radio, but they didn't know what the hell to do with it. All they had was a rough fix on where the truck was and the co-ordinates for the road and the quarry, so they decided they'd better try and rendezvous with us.'

'With you and Sara?'

Cogan nodded. 'They were on their way when the Tomahawk hit. Tel Aviv didn't hear about the strike until it was too late for them to do anything.'

'And they were the guys who got you out?'

'Pretty tough bunch. They hung around long enough to strap up my leg, then they threw me into one of the trucks and headed straight back to the Turkish border. We didn't stop once. Anyone who needed a leak or a crap just went over the side.'

'Better than having to walk home through a minefield,' Bernie said. 'What did they have to say about the attack?'

'Not much. I think they were too worried about roadblocks. The minute I told them there'd been an early warning at the base, they figured the Iraqis must have intercepted their radio communications. They said the cruise missile and the Tornados would have been flying too low for the Iraqis to pick them up on radar.'

'But there were no roadblocks?'

'Not that we saw. The whole thing was just one long, flat-out drive until we were out of Iraq and I got put on a plane to Italy. Four hours later I was on a flight from Rome to London. End of story.'

'You wish,' Bernie said. 'You're so screwed up, you don't know what day it is. I didn't think you could get that crazy over someone.' He tried again to read some writing on Cogan's blotter.

'If you'd seen her you'd understand. She wasn't like anyone I'd ever met. Half the time I wasn't even sure she was real.'

'Listen.' Bernie leaned across the desk. 'If you don't get yourself sorted out, you're going to fall over. It doesn't matter how things were between you, you can't bring her back.' He reached for the blotter and turned it round. ''Or never will the river run',' he said. 'What's that supposed to mean?'

'I don't know. It's a line from a poem.' Letting Bernie read it was not the only mistake Cogan had made. Earlier this morning when he'd stopped to buy a newspaper, he'd been stupid enough to collect a copy of the soft drink leaflet that Bernie was pulling out of the blotter where it had been hidden.

'Well, well.' Bernie studied the picture of the girl. 'Don't tell me,' he said. 'This is her — right?'

'No.'

'What are you doing with it then?'

'Look,' Cogan said. 'I know you're trying to help, but you're wasting your time. Talking about her or thinking about her makes it worse. If you want to do something for me, just shut up and leave me alone, will you?'

'So you can do what? So you can come in here every day and pretend you've forgotten about her? Or are you going to start your nice new job with the ministry ahead of time and hope that does it?'

'Have you got a better idea?' Cogan was tiring of the conversation.

'What about her family? Don't you think they ought to know what happened?'

'She didn't have a family. I told you. That's why she went to Iraq to start with — to look for her parents.'

'You said she had an uncle in the States.'

'What the hell would he care? It's none of your business anyway.'

Bernie shrugged. 'If you don't want to wrap things up, that's fine with me. I just think you need a way of getting her out of your head.'

'If I needed you to tell me how to get her out of my head, I'd have asked.'

'OK. Suit yourself.' Bernie dropped the leaflet onto the desk. 'You carry on collecting pretty pictures of her and writing about rivers never running. Sounds like a real good recipe. If you get around to changing your mind, let me know.'

Cogan had no intention of changing his mind. He had to find his own solution to his own problem — a means of erasing his memories that didn't involve acting on any half-baked advice from Bernie.

He spent the rest of the morning considering his future, and most of the afternoon trying to stop the line from the poem from going round inside his head like an endless tape.

At five o'clock, having failed to make any sense of the words, he made one last determined effort to think of something else before he left the office. But almost as soon as he was outside, for the second time today, he caught sight of the girl in the yellow skirt. She was getting into her car, too far away for him to see her face, but close enough to be unsettling.

Unremarkable though the incident was, for Cogan it was another reminder — this time of a hot, sticky night in Brunswick weeks ago when a street-walker had offered him the pleasure of her company — the night he'd decided to interfere in the life of a girl who'd wanted nothing more than to be left alone.

Like the encounter in Brunswick, this one was equally trivial, but was it, too, a turning point, Cogan wondered, the beginning of whatever it was he had to do to start forgetting?

To find out, on his way home he bought a bottle of bourbon, doubting that it would do much to help exorcize her ghost, but prepared to try anything at all in case it did.

By morning, the feeling of emptiness was worse, but his mind was clearer than it had been for several days and, as though the answer had always been staring him in the face, he knew now that only by allowing himself and making himself remember Sara, would he ever be able to properly let her go.

It was the smell that was most familiar, the musky odour of wet peat, slow-moving water and decaying vegetation. Cogan breathed it in, watching the scenery change as Brady guided the car around the pot-holes and tried to avoid the ruts and patches of soft mud along the roadside.

Unlike before, on this occasion the ranger had been genuinely pleased to see Cogan, grumbling at the early-morning start, but happy enough once they were on their way and he'd understood the purpose of the visit.

Cogan himself was being careful not to question his reasons for coming here, although he was finding it increasingly difficult to do so now that they were drawing closer to the clearing. What he'd believed was a good idea at the time, no longer seemed to be quite such a good idea after all, and he was already uncomfortable and on edge.

'Get those air crashes sorted out, did you?' Brady said.

'What?'

'TWA 800 and the Thunderbolt you said went down in Colorado. The crashes that guy Peter Kennedy wrote to you about.'

Cogan shook his head. 'I think he just put them in his letter to get me interested in what he had to say. There's no evidence that they were burned up by a laser.'

'There you go then,' Brady grunted. 'Serves you right. Catch the balls that some other bastard's thrown up in the air, and you can bet you're going to get your hands covered in shit. You should've torn up his letter as soon as you got it.'

'I should have done a lot of things,' Cogan said.

'Sure you should, but it doesn't mean that what happened was your fault.'

'Yes it does. If I hadn't come here Sara would still be alive.'

'What about those guys who were after her? If you hadn't showed up they could've found her.' Brady swerved to avoid an ibis that was doing its best to take off across the road. 'Blaming yourself isn't going to get you anywhere. I don't think hiking into her cabin is going to do you a hell of a lot of good either.'

Cogan had come too far to change his mind. Before he'd left London, Bernie had said much the same thing, but neither Bernie nor Brady could have any real understanding of what he was attempting to do, and even if the trip turned out to be fruitless, at least he would have tried.

On the far side of the clearing the skidder

was at rest with its engine idling, freshly painted and with new glass in the windows of the cab. There was also a new shed, built from plywood on the foundations of the old one.

Brady drove over through the mud and parked beside it, selecting a cigar from the box Cogan had brought him before he got out of the car. 'You really want to do this, do you?' he asked.

'Yeah.' Cogan stepped out into the sunshine, enjoying the humidity and the smell while he listened for chainsaws and tried to remember which of several water trails might lead in the right direction.

'That way.' Brady pointed. 'We don't need to get our feet wet. Rains aren't due for a while.' He lit his cigar and blew out a stream of smoke. 'You're lucky I know how to get there.'

'How did you find it?'

'Tip-off. About three weeks ago I got a phone call from some redneck who'd been shooting pigs illegally in the swamp. He said his dog had sniffed out what he thought were human bones lying on a bank outside some kind of shack in the woods. He wouldn't give his name, but he told me where to look.' Brady paused. 'The police are still trying to identify the body. They've only got bits and pieces to work with. Alligators aren't what you'd call picky eaters.'

'And you think I know who it was?' Cogan had seen the question coming.

'Do you want to tell me?'

'Not now. I need to go to the cabin first.'

'What are you after?'

'It's kind of personal.' He wasn't sure why he was bothering anymore. Now that other people had been poking around the cabin, as well as being less confident of finding what he'd come to find, he was beginning to doubt the wisdom of endeavouring to relive the days he'd spent there with her.

As if to prevent Cogan from having second thoughts, Brady was already on his way. 'Better watch out for roots with that leg of yours,' he said. 'And if you think you're going to sink up to your armpits in a wet patch, don't worry. You won't.'

It was easy enough for Cogan to recognize the route — the trail Sara had used when they'd been running for their lives. Although the weather was warmer than it had been then, at a slow walking pace and after being accustomed to the heat of the desert, the journey was undemanding. The creek crossing was simpler too, no longer a slippery, neck-deep wade through the water, but a few steps along a large cypress tree that had been felled to form a bridge.

When Cogan reached the dead pine, he made his announcement, explaining what he intended to do, ready to argue his case if, for some reason, there was going to be a problem.

'I know it means you've got to come back for me tomorrow,' he said. 'It's just something I need to do.'

'What the hell do I care? If you want to spend the night out here by yourself, you go right ahead.' Brady spat out the remains of his cigar and started swatting mosquitos with his hat. 'I'll tell you something, though. If you don't get eaten to death by these goddamn things, you'll get spooked for sure.'

Cogan grinned. 'No I won't,' he said. 'I've been here before. I know what it's like.'

'What about food?'

'There should be canned stuff in the cabin. Look, I'll be fine. If you're too busy to pick me up tomorrow, leave it until the next day. I'm not going anywhere.'

'OK.' Brady replaced his hat. 'Boil any water you drink and don't blame me if you end up having barbecued frogs for dinner.'

After offering advice on how best to combat the mosquitos, the ranger said goodbye and trudged away into the trees and vines, leaving Cogan to examine a small white cross that had been erected beside the cabin. It was in the wrong place, nearly ten feet away from the spot where Jeremiah had been shot, but he didn't think it mattered much.

Now that he was alone, nothing seemed to matter. Except for some pine warblers singing in the trees, and the sound of water trickling in the creek, the swamp was silent, as unspoiled and peaceful as it had always been.

He waited until he thought he was ready, then limped up the steps onto the platform and entered the cabin.

Nothing had been disturbed. Her mosquito net was still bundled up in the corner, a saucepan was still standing on the primus stove, and on the floor, her flashlight lay exactly where she had left it.

He decided to check the books first, withdrawing them in pairs from the cake tin, flicking through them without really knowing what he was expecting to come across.

There were plenty to choose from. Among biology texts from the semester she'd taken at college, there were nearly a dozen books on birds, two on plants and insects and a worn copy of James Frazer's *Golden Bough* — a book that seemed sufficiently out of place to make it worth a closer look.

He took it outside with him unopened and sat down on the platform in the sun, wondering if his instincts would be right.

The answer lay slipped in between the first two pages — a faded sheet of paper on which someone had handwritten the two verses of the poem he'd come so far to find:

When the river of your life you share,
One golden summer with your love,
Of the falcons from your past beware,
For they remain to hunt the dove.
On wings of fire into the sun,
Your falcons first must fly,
Or never will the river run,
And like the dove, your love will die.

At the bottom of the sheet, written in the same, flowing hand above a date that was too faint for him to decipher, the signature of Catherine Kennedy was unmistakable.

He read each verse several times, absorbing every line until he was certain he understood why this had always been more than just a poem. For Sara it had been a guide, a statement that with his help she'd interpreted as an instruction — words that had somehow captured the way she'd felt about her future with him and an expression of hope that she'd believed he could make come true.

But she'd put her faith in the wrong person, he thought. Her past had never been his to take away, and because he'd betrayed her trust, in the end it had been her falcons that had taken her away from him.

To memorize the poem he read it through again, then closed his eyes and embarked upon the second part of his inward journey, allowing himself to become drowsy before he started drawing on his memories in a conscious effort to remember every single thing about her that he could.

Rather as he'd thought, he'd chosen the right place to do it. Within minutes he was able to imagine her in any number of her incarnations — the headstrong skidder driver who'd turned into a yellow-skirted pixie; the girl who had been as at ease at the PUK camp as she'd been in an upmarket Savannah restaurant, and the young woman who had gradually become more and more vulnerable on an unwanted and fatal mission to find the quarry.

There were other reflections too, one moment in particular that he could remember — the time when she'd returned from her fishing trip in the canoe.

His recollection of the morning was still fresh, but his image of her was disconcertingly flawed. She was wearing the wrong clothes, and instead of getting out of the canoe, she was continuing to sit in it as though expecting him to say something.

So clear and so disturbing was the picture that Cogan felt himself break out in a sweat. He struggled to wake up, knowing the danger of repeating the mistake he'd made on his last night in the truck.

'Aren't you going to say hello?' She smiled at him.

With enormous difficulty he forced himself to think, getting to his feet while he searched for some means of proving that she could not possibly be real.

'Take off your headband,' he said.

'No. Why should I?'

'Just take it off.'

She removed it slowly, letting it drop into the creek as if to mock him.

As well as misinterpreting her response, he'd misunderstood what was happening. The stitches across her forehead were quite pronounced — stitches he could never have imagined because he'd never seen them before.

He stopped breathing, watching disbelievingly as she slipped out of the canoe and began climbing the steps towards him.

For a second he remained uncertain. Then suddenly she was in his arms, clutching him to her so hard that he could feel her heart beating.

How long they stood there, Cogan never knew. Even after her tears had stopped and he'd finally gained the confidence to let go of her, he could not bring himself to spoil the moment with questions.

'You found the poem,' she said quietly.

'It's one of the reasons I came.'

'Oh.' She smiled again. 'I thought you might have come to see me.'

'Do I have to guess why I'm not dreaming?'

She took his hands in hers. 'It's because I didn't do what you told me to do. Five minutes after you'd gone, I started back down the way we'd climbed up. I think I had some stupid idea about waiting for you at the entrance in case you needed help getting Judith to the truck. I remember seeing the missile coming, and I can sort of half-remember being caught up in a rock-slide and all the noise and the fire and the smoke. After that I'm not sure what happened to me — well, not until I got stopped on the runway.'

'Who by? Did someone pick you up?'

'They didn't exactly pick me up. They said I was wandering around shouting about having to meet someone at a truck somewhere, and that I bit one of them when they tried to help me.' She paused. 'I knew you were dead, but I wouldn't let myself believe you could be.'

'You still haven't said who found you.'

'Remember those Toyota Landcruisers that were on the ferry with us?'

Cogan had forgotten about them altogether — never once considering that she had survived, let alone been rescued by UN weapons inspectors.

'They recognized me from the ferry crossing,' she said. 'I told them I had to look for you, but they wouldn't let me because it was so dangerous.'

'What the hell were they doing at the quarry?'

'They knew about the raid. An hour after they saw the MiG take off from the air-base, they got a radio message saying that the UN Security Council wanted them to get photos of the quarry to prove it had been a military installation.' She made him sit down on the platform beside her. 'They didn't seem to care much about taking photographs — not after I told them they'd just driven down through a minefield. They were really lucky.'

'Not as lucky as you were.' Cogan couldn't stop looking at her.

'I didn't feel lucky. I was locked up in a little hotel room in Baghdad. They wouldn't fly me home until they'd found a doctor to fix my cut and checked to see if I was who I said

I was.' She shivered. 'It was awful. I couldn't stop thinking about you and about Judith and the fire, and why it was that everything had gone so horribly wrong for us.'

He reached out to touch her hair where the sunlight was falling on it. 'You should have phoned Bernie,' he said.

'I didn't know what to do. Still, it's a good job I decided to come here this morning, isn't it?' She brightened up. 'Otherwise I'd have missed you. I've been staying at my apartment in Brunswick since I got back. This is the first time I've been out to the swamp.'

Because she was very close to him, and because she was managing to keep a straight face, he almost missed the implications of what she'd said, only starting to understand when she began to giggle.

'Bernie,' he said slowly. 'And Brady. They've known all along — both of them.'

She nodded. 'I called Bernie days ago — as soon as I had the chance.' She was laughing now, enjoying his discomfort. 'We spent over an hour on the phone again last night before I went to make sure Brady wouldn't give anything away in the car this morning.'

Although Cogan's awkwardness was short-lived, he found himself at a loss for words, astonished that the secret had been kept from him so well. 'Did Bernie really tell you the whole thing?' he said.

'Of course he did. I know what happened to you after the raid. I know you went to Rome. I know you've hurt your leg and I even know what you've been writing on your office blotter. Bernie and I get on extra well over the phone.' She laid her head on his shoulder, and half-closed her eyes. 'Brady's been nice, too. So has his wife. We're supposed to be having dinner at their place on Saturday night.' Turning to face him, she kissed him gently on the mouth. 'If that's all right with you.'

It was, Cogan thought. Everything was fine. Once again the Okefenokee had cast its spell, and with the falcons gone, and with two rivers running now as one, all the golden summers in the world were theirs to share — which is what they both had wanted, and how everything should be.

We do hope that you have enjoyed reading this large print book.

Did you know that all of our titles are available for purchase?

We publish a wide range of high quality large print books including:
Romances, Mysteries, Classics
General Fiction
Non Fiction and Westerns

Special interest titles available in large print are:
The Little Oxford Dictionary
Music Book
Song Book
Hymn Book
Service Book

Also available from us courtesy of Oxford University Press:
Young Readers' Dictionary
(large print edition)
Young Readers' Thesaurus
(large print edition)

For further information or a free brochure, please contact us at:
Ulverscroft Large Print Books Ltd.,
The Green, Bradgate Road, Anstey,
Leicester, LE7 7FU, England.
Tel: (00 44) 0116 236 4325
Fax: (00 44) 0116 234 0205

NO TIME LIKE THE PRESENT

June Barraclough

Daphne Berridge, who has never married, has retired to the small Yorkshire village of Heckcliff where she grew up, intending to write the biography of an eighteenth-century woman poet. Two younger women are interested in her project: Cressida, Daphne's niece, who lives in London, and is uncertain about the direction of her life; and Judith, who keeps a shop in Heckcliff, and is a divorcee. When an old friend of Daphne falls in love with Judith, the question — as for Cressida — is marriage or independence. Then Daphne also receives a surprise proposal.

SEARCH FOR A SHADOW

Kay Christopher

On the last day of her holiday Rosemary Roberts met an intriguing American in the foyer of her London hotel. By some extraordinary coincidence, Larry Madison-Jones was due to visit the tiny Welsh village where Rosemary lived. But how much of a coincidence was Larry's erratic presence there? The moment Rosemary returned home, her life took on a subtle, though sinister edge — Larry had a secret he was not willing to share. As Rosemary was drawn deeper into a web of mysterious and suspicious occurrences, she found herself wondering if Larry really loved her — or was trying to drive her mad . . .